ILLEGAL FORMATION

GODS OF THE GRIDIRON: BOOK 4

SHANNA SWENSON

ILLEGAL FORMATION
Shanna Swenson

ILLEGAL FORMATION is an original work of fiction. Names, characters, places, organizations and incidents either are the product of the author's imagination or are used fictitiously. Any resemblance to actual persons, living or dead, events, businesses, companies, or locales is entirely coincidental.

Copyright © 2020 by Shanna Swenson

Paperback ISBN: 978-1-7329626-8-2

www.shannaswenson.com

For permission requests, write to the author at shannaswen@gmail.com

Edited by Jennifer Soucy

ebook design by: OliviaProDesign

Gods of the Gridiron logo designed by:
Books and Moods Designs

HADES- GOD OF DEATH/KING OF THE UNDERWORLD

"And I looked, and behold a pale horse: and his name that sat on him was Death, and Hell followed with him. And power was given unto them over the fourth part of the earth, to kill with sword, and with hunger, and with death, and with the beasts of the earth."
—Revelation 6:8

For my Momma,
Thank you for showing me tough love,
*I'm stronger because of **you***

FOREWORD

Hades and Persephone have a dark legacy, and I tried to follow to that theme in this book.

Quillan Layton nor Veda Ryan were inspired by real people, unlike others in this series. They came from somewhere deeper—somewhere darker—and their passions, love and hate, unfurled on their own.

WARNING: This book deals with some heavy elements that may be disturbing for some readers—READER DISCRETION IS ADVISED.

PROLOGUE
HALLOWEEN NIGHT

Quillan "Hades" Layton looked back over to the intriguingly petite figure of Medusa. Dark ribbons of hair flowed out from under a crown of plastic snakes, some hissing, some striking, others tangled into the strands that turned mahogany where the light touched it. A black mask concealed the woman's face. Alabaster skin, as fine as any piece of china he'd ever seen, stood out beneath a sleeveless, midnight-black dress, covered in various colors of ink that weaved a pattern of endless stories over slim arms and an ample chest. Plump, milky breasts spilled forth beneath the plunging neckline. A trim waist and curvy hips greeted him, but it was the bright green eyes, as piercing as emeralds, that sparkled beneath the kitchen lights that drew him in.

Quil hadn't originally been that thrilled to join the party. Although he wasn't the *only* single guy present, he was one of the few. It had been a long time since he'd had the company of a woman in his bed and even longer since he'd been on a date. His wife, Rian, had died of a cocaine overdose over a year ago. Quillan had blamed himself, blamed his career, blamed God and anyone else whom he could, but ultimately Ri had loved her drug more than him or their little angel, Quinn, which had led to her snorting far more than she ever should have and ultimately, the action had stopped her heart.

Quil had been the one to find her, cold, blue-lipped, face covered in white powder, nose and forehead bloody where her head had dropped heavily onto the glass coffee table of her hotel room in death. Remnants of that scene bounced through his head like a metal ball in a pinball machine, hitting the nerves with rapid succession.

Which is why you need to avoid this woman, his brain screamed.

She turned from speaking to Brooke Taylor and a little diamond caught the light, twinkling in her nose. Piercings, tattoos, a come-hither glance in his direction—she was trouble; trouble with a capital T. She had to be by the sheer look of her alone. Becca had introduced her as Veda, an enigmatic name for an enigma of a woman.

Quil's eyes roved her once more, his fingertips itching to explore those tattoos of hers, the lines and curves of her body. Aside from those markings, she favored her twin in practically every way. Same height, same build, same enticing lips... But the mask reminded him so much of someone he'd met before.

Much to his delight—and dismay—the woman moved closer. It wouldn't do for him to allow her the opportunity to invade his private bubble of brood, but hell, it was Halloween after all and when was the last time Quil had enjoyed himself? Quinn was home safe for the night, with the nanny he'd known since her birth, a woman he trusted with her life. And he had nowhere else to be, nothing else to do.

"You make a fine Hades, I must say," the voice was as sultry as the body and rolled into his ears like a soothing melody.

"And you, a fine Medusa." Quil gripped one of the snakes laconically, watching her eyes follow his movements. "You look so familiar to me. Have we met before tonight?"

Something about a mask had always intrigued him. Elusive, mysterious, sexual. And this woman was all three things simultaneously.

"Oh aye, we have, Quillan." He detected a slight accent. He, himself, had a slight Spanish one. His maternal grandmother was from Spain and never spoke a word of English to him. *A confusing language,* she'd told him, so she'd taught him Spanish instead. His abuela had raised him while Quil's father worked two jobs to keep a roof over their heads.

Quil's brows rose, waiting for the stranger to elaborate. When she didn't, he grinned and brought his drink up. "Just Quil works."

"Oh, you don't prefer *Hades*?" The playful smirk that pulled at the beauty's lips made his belly flutter.

"One and the same. I figured that was assumed."

Veda laughed, sexy and husky. *Damn!* "I go by several names myself."

"Oh? Pray tell what the others are." It hadn't taken her more than sixty seconds to reel him in; he was a goner.

"In certain circles I've been called *Obsidian*." A long, pink tongue snaked out of her mouth akin to the serpents in her hair, slow and calculating, until it was fully unsheathed and licking her lips provocatively, a silver barbell tongue ring showcased.

Quil's sharp intake of breath seem to please Veda and he felt his cheeks flame in both surprise and familiarity. "Holy shit," he hissed under his breath.

She was the masked dancer who'd sat on his lap at *RISE*; the one who'd brought his entire body to life with the French kiss to end all French kisses. He could still feel the dancing metal flicking across his teeth and over his tongue while his body had been engulfed in flames of scorching desire.

"You remember me, dark god?"

Remember her? How in God's holy name could he ever forget her? Pushing her off his lap to tend to Paxton's bruised ego that night had been one of the hardest things he'd ever done in his life. He'd wanted to continue to feel her tongue on his own, on his body, on his cock.

Obsidian/Medusa/Veda's smile said she knew exactly what he

was thinking, and Quil felt his body heat rise as she took a step closer. Her hand pressed lightly to his bare pec and he stifled a growl, loving her delicate touch on his hungry flesh.

Just then, Brooke and TJ squared off in a surprising conversation that promised sexual gratification and an invitation for everyone to move outdoors to watch the women dance around the bonfire Pax and Becca had made out back.

Quil's body sizzled all over as Veda took his hand in hers and began to pull him outside. She playfully invited him to watch, as he stood next to Pax; she and Becca led the women around the bonfire, swirling and swaying, imitating the flames that consumed the crackling wood inside the fire pit.

Veda's movements were smooth and sexual, like she'd been on stage, so alluring and inviting, her focus solely on Quillan. He watched with bated breath, knowing that before the night was out she was gonna be his. He couldn't wait!

VEDA FELT like she'd just won the jackpot of a lifetime. Maybe now Becca's connections had started to pay off for them both. She'd gotten to meet Brooke Taylor, Madison McFadden's sister, who was a successful model. Even better, she was pleased to make the acquaintance of gorgeous stud Quillan Layton, dressed to kill in an open leather vest, cape and black jeans, his dark hair spiked and sticking up, devilishly eye-fucking her from across the room. He'd been a magnificent addition to the Gladiators this year and Veda had found the games to be even more interesting since his instatement; he was a hell of a player. It didn't hurt that he was fine as hell either with puppy dog brown eyes, russet skin, and a hint of a sexy Spanish accent that stirred her blood in all the right ways.

Now, he was pulling her into his muscular bare arms for a slow dance and she was shivering. Could her luck really be that good?

Could she really be at an advantage to score with the heartthrob of a tight end tonight?

She couldn't help but return the wide, panty-melting smile of Quil's. Damn, he was as hot happy as he was broody. And Hades had her in his grasp as her feet moved with his and his body pressed against hers, so solid and inviting.

She knew she shouldn't even be here; she was risking her job as a cheerleader by being in the same vicinity as the players, let alone talking to them, touching them and dancing with them. If anyone saw her like this, she could be fired. But there was a small part of her that didn't care at that moment as Quil's long palm settled on the small of her back and she tingled all over.

As much as she needed the cheerleading job and as good as it was for her portfolio and PR, she hated it. She loved the recognition, the sport itself, and getting to share some of the limelight. But she hated the rigors of it, the rules. She had to cover all her tattoos, the ones that made her who she was, arrive five hours early for the games—yes, five hours—just to make sure her makeup and hair and body were perfectly groomed and manicured, all her flaws covered. And she'd gotten cussed out last week because she gained half a pound. Hell, she didn't hardly eat enough to keep a damn bird alive. She'd been working out more and knew it was muscle and not fat gain, but that hadn't mattered. Her life was a strict routine, and she was just about fed up with feeling like nothing she ever did was good enough. When she wasn't at work, helping take care of her mam, or volunteering, she was in the gym or at practice...or indulging by bingeing her favorite shows.

Her eyes wearily looked the crowd over, seeing that most people present were players and their plus ones, but someone could still sneak a photo of her. She'd just have to keep the mask on and hope no one recognized that she was a cheerleader for their team.

"For such a heavy talker, you sure don't seem like a woman of the night." Quil had realized she was shivering at his touch and seemed overly pleased with himself. She couldn't have that.

"Oh Hades, you're nothing but another snake for Medusa to tame. Don't think for one second I can't turn you to stone with one glance."

"Ooh sizzle, V. Your tongue is as sharp as your wits." The eyes that held Veda's could've frozen *her*, but she'd never let him see that.

"That's the kindest compliment I've ever been given," she smirked, getting a hearty laugh from Quil that made her sex clench.

"And to think I almost skipped this party." Quil's grip tightened around her waist and he dipped them. Veda gave a small gasp as she came back up and felt a hardness pressing into her thigh. "I love a *mujer* who can not only talk the talk but walk the walk." His penetrating gaze seemed to invade her soul and she gulped. She was being straight consumed by fire and was loving every second.

"Well, then you've met the right *mujer*, my god."

He grinned again. "Let's fill up our drinks."

She only nodded as he took her hand and pulled her back to the bar. She had a feeling that wasn't the only place he wanted to take her and her mind soared at the possibilities.

It had been a long time since Veda had been intimate. Sure, she worked at a gentleman's club but she simply teased those men, she didn't fuck them. She'd taken a small handful back to a VIP room, but she'd not done anything more than full nude dances and quick hand jobs.

Veda had been selective of her lovers after Will, her high school boyfriend, and refused to allow herself to be anyone's whore—stripper or not.

Veda didn't trust men because of what her father had done, abandoning her, her mam and sister because he'd been a coward. And since then she'd never let anyone too close.

She'd not had a real boyfriend following high school. It was—and had been for years—the three girls against the world: Veda, Becca, and their mother, Kathleen.

However, as Veda looked over at Becca—laughing, with Paxton's arms holding her in an intimate embrace—she felt it wouldn't be long before she lost her twin sister too. Damn men and their thieving ways. They took everything from women; their pride, happiness, bodies, hearts... until there was nothing left.

Veda would be damned if she allowed that to happen to her.

She was in control. She knew their motives. She knew to tread carefully or be squashed.

"Pick your poison, Medusa," Hades challenged and pulled Veda from her reverie.

"Oh, you bartend too, eh?"

"You'd be amazed at my skills, *hermosa*." Quillan's hand moved down her bare arm and the hair stood on end at his delicate touch. His fingertips hovered and stroked her gently as his eyes made her belly flip over.

Suddenly, Veda made her mind up. Quillan Layton would be hers tonight. Hers to control. Hers to use as she saw fit. Hers to corrupt. She would darken his soul, as dark as hers had become. And when the dust settled, he'd rue the day he ever flirted with the idea that he could conquer Medusa.

CHAPTER ONE

Quil laughed again as he backed the gorgeous beauty against the wall, his eyes falling over her curvy body. God, he couldn't wait to touch her, taste her, see her naked, love every inch of her porcelain skin.

They'd both had too much to drink and were buzzing, giggling like a pair of teenagers.

His head lowered and he evaluated her face, her eyes. Eyes that warned him away, but he didn't heed it. All he wanted was to run with this exhilarating feeling he'd had since first he'd laid eyes upon her—to take her, lose himself inside her...

It'd been so long since Quil had felt anything beyond anger, remorse, hate and loathing. The only other time he felt happy apart from being around his daughter was when he was playing football.

He'd come back to the game and life he'd loved this year; it had been rewarding, but something was missing. Quinn was doing so well. Her treatments were extensive but seemed to be working; their lives appeared to have found a new normal.

Quil had grown lonely over the past year and a half, though. Despite how much he'd hated Rian's horrible addiction and how it had taken control of her, he'd begun reminiscing about the good times—missing them, even though they'd been few and far between.

Now, suddenly in the arms of a woman who looked at him as if he were a giant cookie she wanted to take a bite of, he remembered how good it felt to hold and touch and desire again. Yeah, he'd had sex since Ri's death—several times—but it had meant nothing, like it would tonight. He wasn't kidding himself; a big part of him didn't want another relationship, another complication, another woman to come in and destroy him like Rian had.

He'd been weak and unaware as a young man in love. Now he was fully mindful of how women manipulated men, how conniving the lot of them were, how destructive they could be with a heart.

This woman would serve one purpose and one purpose alone. Of that, he knew they were both on the same page as her eyes and hands slid over his naked abs. He moaned, loving how her long nails tickled him there.

"Wanna find somewhere more private, Hades?" she cooed, licking her lips.

"Fuck yes I do," he answered and leaned down to taste her, recalling her skills with her tongue ring.

Just as he'd remembered, she tasted both sweet and spicy, making his entire body tingle as if his lips were touching a live wire. Veda felt it too and pulled back with a gasp.

Quil chuckled under his breath before letting his hands fall to her waist. He pulled her roughly back against him, loving and hating the torture at the same time as he kissed her again.

She was the one to moan this time; he thrust his tongue in, invading the mouth that intrigued him. Her tongue fought his back, longing to plunder his mouth as he was hers. He admired her bravado.

You might tangle with me, little rebel, but I'll be the one to own you tonight, he thought.

His hands moved up her arms slowly as his mouth feasted on hers, and she pressed herself into him seductively.

"Mmm, *dama serpiente. Me deseas,* no?" he asked breathlessly as her hands lowered to his waist.

"*Si.* I want you," she responded as his hand cupped her neck and pulled her tighter to him.

"*Ah, hablas español?*"

"*Muy poquito, señor.*"

"*Suficiente.*" When she fought his dominating hold on her, he slammed her back to the wall, getting a sharp gasp from her. "You'll see, *hermosa, con rapidez* who's in charge here."

"Oh? Is that so?" Her lips puckered in challenge.

"Indeed." His face lowered and his lips took hers again, his hand moving from her neck down her arm and to the breasts that had beckoned to him all night. He squeezed one possessively then the other, getting a grunt out of her. "I wanna see your face, Medusa."

Although the mask was sexy as hell, he wanted to look upon her, his hunger to unmask her as prominent as his desire.

He took it upon himself to peel the mask up, even as her eyes searched for anyone lurking and watching them. They were safe, he assured her, hiding in an alcove by the back staircase. His fingertips took time to stroke and ease the masquerade-style mask up.

He smiled into a beautiful, perfectly-sculpted face. Dark arched brows, intelligent and cunning, framed her emerald-green eyes, high cheekbones, and a pert little nose. He was pleased, kissing her once more to let her know that.

She basked in it, her hand cupping his jaw as she savored his lips; then her tongue plunged in again, enticing him with each velvety stroke across his own. He groaned and gripped the fabric at her waist, tightening his hold; he couldn't get her close enough as she wrapped a thigh around his and began to rub herself against his erection.

When he pulled back for a breath, they were both panting. The eyes that looked wantonly up into his own made his desire even stronger. But before he could pull her back against him, he heard a little giggle beside him.

A soaking wet Brooke Taylor had her phone up and was recording them.

"Brooke, what the *actual* fuck?" he asked, annoyed.

"Kiss her again, that was so fuckin' hot, Quil." Brooke licked her lips hungrily.

Quil's brows drew closer, but Veda grinned as if to say, "Let's give her a show." He shrugged—too drunk to care, anyway—and pulled Veda back against him, angling his head to deepen the kiss and let Brooke's phone catch his good side. He thrust his tongue in, making love to Veda's mouth as if he'd never tasted anything sweeter than her in his lifetime.

When they pulled back again, the light from Brooke's phone flashed. She was taking pictures too. Fuck! What the hell was she doing?

Just as he was about to ask her and felt anger paint his cheeks, TJ came up behind Brooke and grabbed her roughly around the waist.

"Alright, I got an Uber coming, sexy. You ready?" His hand moved to Brooke's breast and squeezed.

"I am now," Brooke smirked. "Look at this!"

Quil huffed as Brooke began to play the video back. Quillan could hear himself panting and Veda's moaning through the speaker of her phone. He didn't know whether to be turned on or frustrated by the invasion of privacy, but was completely both.

"So damn hot, right? I wanna watch it while you fuck me, *Andre the Giant Cock.*"

TJ laughed heartily. "The only thing you're gonna be watching is your big ass getting fuckin' hammered by this." He shoved his pelvis roughly up against her. "I know you like girls too, B, but tonight, you're mine. I ain't sharing you, so get the fuck over it."

TJ smacked her ass hard for good measure even as she pouted up at him. "Fine, maybe next time," Brooke winked at Veda and let TJ lead her forward and through the side door.

"Christ, sorry about that," Quil remarked as he pulled a hand through his hair.

Veda's eyes looked apprehensive for a second before she gave him a weak grin. "Bedroom?"

He pointed and motioned to the right. "There's one up there."

Veda nodded and took his hand, leading him up the staircase. He was pleased to see her desire hadn't waned by Brooke's weirdness; his own felt thick and prominent between his legs.

When they got into the room, Veda shut the door behind him and threw her mask onto the vanity, exhaling sharply. "Well, cat's out of the bag now." She looked down, her eyes grazing the carpet of the room before she looked up at Quillan.

He wasn't sure what she'd meant, but in those moments, he didn't care as he watched her begin to remove her costume. He hadn't realized just how petite Veda was until now and let the comment die as she meekly came forward.

At six foot six inches tall, Quil had always been taller than most, but Veda was tiny compared to him. If he had to guess she was maybe five foot three. She was slender, athletically built, similar to him but not as cut or bulky. He was surprised to see a diamond piercing in her belly button and steel rings in her nipples as her bra fell to the floor. Her breasts were possibly the biggest things on her, save for her plump bottom that a pair of black-lace cheekies hugged. He moaned aloud as she turned to throw her dress into a chair across from the bed.

"Mmm, leave those on and put the mask back on, *dama serpiente*," he commanded and sat on the bed to watch her. She did as he'd asked without comment.

This was the guest room he used when he'd stayed with Pax on occasion, not that he'd done so but a time or two. He didn't leave Quinn alone often, but there'd been a couple times when it was too late to drive home or he'd been too drunk.

"What about you, Hades? Aren't you gonna undress?" Veda asked as she moved forward, her creamy breasts bouncing and her pink nipples singing to him, strained by the steel surrounding them, hard and alert.

"I thought it would be more fun if you did it, sexy lady."

Veda grinned seductively and stopped in front of him, her pierced nipples centimeters from his face. He shivered at the closeness, feeling his cock jump in his pants.

"Oh, aye, I can do that. No touching though, Death."

"Death?" Quillan laughed. "You can do better than that."

"Ok, *dia an bháis*."

"Dia an bháis?" Quil frowned, trying to place the language.

"Irish," Veda answered.

That's right, this sexy little vixen was Irish... Hot!

"Now stop talking and let me get you naked."

Quil wouldn't argue as her lips hit his breastbone; her tongue began to lick the indent of his midline, down his abs, and to the trail of hair pointing to his now-raging erection. "Oh, fuck," he groaned hungrily as her fingers flirted with the button on his fly. He couldn't wait to feel those plump lips on his cock.

She tortured him with her fingertips through the rough denim, tracing the shape of him from base to tip until he was rocking into her palm. She grinned knowingly at him.

"Hmm... Impatient for a god, aren't you, Hades?"

"Don't make me punish you for your sharp tongue, Medusa," he scolded, sounding more playful than he felt. He wanted to turn her over and pound her into the mattress with a fury he'd never felt before as those green eyes held his, staring into his very soul.

"Shall I worship at your altar then?" she smirked as her eyes fell to his restrained sex. It was all he could do not to beg her to unleash the beast inside his pants and suck him into oblivion.

"That's one way you can make it up to me, snake lady."

"That's right, I have a way of charming them. Perhaps this has something to do with it." She stuck her tongue out, revealing the barbell ring through it once again, and he moaned aloud.

Veda finally unzipped him and grabbed his hard member. It was big and thick in her dainty, little hand, and he was as aroused by the look of it as by the feel. When she squeezed the base, pulled the head of him to her lips and licked—her piercing stroking up the underside of his shaft—he could have lost himself. He quaked as his hand came to her head. She immediately moved back, looking offended, and he almost balked.

"What's the matter, *Obsidian,* never seen an anaconda that size?"

She scoffed. "I just don't like being guided. This is my show, not yours."

Control. This woman wanted it all. She must not know who she was messing with.

"You want Hades, you gotta deal with the flames, *hermosa.* Pleasure comes with a price."

She evaluated his words carefully, looking down at his cock again, making him want her all the more.

Suddenly, her *cojónes* came back and she grinned. "Fine. You can feast on me then."

She popped up and launched herself at him. He laughed even as her lips slammed into his. This woman had moxie, and he admired that about her.

Quil turned them and pushed her to the bed, laying atop her as he ravished her mouth. He planted his hands on her luscious breasts, kneading and tweaking her impaled nipples, the metal cold on his fingertips. "Mmm, *bonitas cocos, mi hermosa.*"

Veda's head arched back as his head fell and he suckled her, pulling long and hard and letting his tongue and teeth fight with the hard metal of the nipple ring.

"Oh God, Quil, mmm," she gasped out and made his dick jerk in his boxers.

"*Si,* you like that, *pequeña rebelde?*"

"Shit, I don't know what you're saying, but it's hot as fuck." Veda moaned again and Quillan chuckled, assaulting her other breast as his hands lowered to her panties.

He pulled back and peeled them down her small hips, his eyes falling on yet another shimmering diamond, twinkling in the light as her legs opened before him.

"Damn, *chica*, you've got the most dazzling *papaya* I've ever seen."

It was true; his eyes fell over her smooth, pink sex to the hood of her clit, where a vertical barbell with diamonds pierced her flesh. He wondered if she tasted as enticing as she looked, not hesitating as he moved to explore her opening lips. His fingertips touched her first; she shivered and moaned as he tested the metallic barbell.

"It's fascinating. Did it hurt, Veda?"

He realized it was the first time he'd used her name. Usually he avoided that; names made it more personal, but he was truly curious about her piercing...and her.

"Yeah for a few weeks, but I've had it for years now."

"Hmmm," Quil trailed off as his mouth lowered and he kissed her delicately. Soon, his tongue was hitting the metal, over and over, and he was sucking at it, fascinated with the jewelry he'd never seen or experienced with a woman before.

His finger thrust into her, encouraging her to succumb to him, and before he even knew it, she was falling apart. He grinned as he looked back up into her red face.

"You got me all worked up, dark god. I couldn't stop myself if I tried," she defended.

"Sure, sure. Think that will be the last time I have you crying my name as you're splayed before me? Think again."

Suddenly, he was aligning his body with hers and pushing his hungry cock into the hot, silky heat he'd just prospected with his mouth and fingers.

He wasn't sure what he'd been expecting, but falling into an alternate universe wasn't it. He moaned as his sex and soul became engulfed into the hottest inferno he'd ever felt, an inferno of raging pleasure, bone-satisfying warmth, and unending ecstasy. They both gasped as he filled her to the brim and stilled there, holding himself back from the need to root like a virgin. What in God's name was happening here?

Veda's hand came to his jaw, her thumb tracing his cheekbone as her eyes sought his. "Quillan?" she murmured, her voice barely above a whisper.

But he had no answer, only the need to love her flesh with his own. He withdrew and plunged again, deeper, harder than the initial penetration, shocked when it felt even more intense than the first thrust had.

"Oh shit," he grunted as his body was assaulted by the force of something strong, something primal, something he'd not been expecting. "Veda."

"Yes, baby," a breathy whimper answered him and a moan.

He was in serious trouble here. His body and soul were captive, trapped in the feel of her heat wrapped around him, squeezing him so intimately, sweeter than anything he'd ever felt in his life before. He answered her moan with one of his own.

He continued to plunge and withdraw as her hands moved over his body, leaving a trail of scorch marks across his skin. It wasn't supposed to feel this good. It wasn't supposed to be so entrancing. He was the one in control here. He was the one who was supposed to own her. Not the other way around.

Veda's head flew back as his hand moved to caress her piercing. She screamed as her orgasm took her, her body quaking as her legs wrapped around his hips and pulled them tighter together. The motion intensified his own pleasure and yearning, making his heart gallop.

Deep, panting moans assaulted his ears as her sex milked him so close to Heaven that his eyes rolled back in his head. He was possessed. Possessed by this naughty jezebel with an agenda he didn't know, a sinful creature of the night who'd excelled at what she did for a living.

Suddenly, Quil realized that he'd been sucked right into the spell of a sorceress, a prostitute, for that's exactly what she was. Wasn't she? She worked at *RISE*, the top gentleman's club in the nation, and now she was here, and he was fucking her... No, correction, he was making love to her, he realized, his hips arching and stroking slowly.

Fuck this! he thought, pulling out and turning her over on all fours.

This was his show; he was in charge. He'd be damned if he was bested by a whore.

He drove into her and pushed her upper body down, gripping her hair in his fist as he claimed her with his sex, his member driving deep and punishingly. But the pull was too sweet, the lure of her body around him, and he couldn't contain the need to please her as his hand moved beneath her to her flat belly, her big breast. He squeezed and kneaded as he plunged and withdrew like a crazed man, needing to be one with her. He tweaked the ring in her nipple, twisting slightly, getting her to buck beneath him.

He grinned wickedly, knowing it was alternating between pain and pleasure, but he wanted to punish her for her sinful ways, this bad girl that had pulled him deeper into the Underworld.

"Oh, oh, Quil," she whimpered as he felt her womanhood tighten around him.

"Yeah, you gonna come for me again, *chica mala?* Fuckin' do it." He smacked her ass hard as he hammered into her, his own loins tightening as he heard her fall into senselessness. "Fuck yeah, baby. You're so damn hot." His hand moved up her back as she shivered and quaked, crying out in release.

She grunted and shoved back against his hips, her hands coming to his thighs. He stopped moving inside her, afraid he'd hurt her.

When he pulled out, she abruptly moved and turned, her face contorted in both rage and lust. She launched herself at him and he caught her, torn between confusion, amusement, and yearning desire. They fell, her atop him as their limbs tangled and their mouths clashed, teeth hitting as they fought for control. He felt his shaft being gripped by her small fist and being pulled back into her cavernous Heaven, the sweetest Hell he'd ever been inside.

"Oh fuck, Veda," he trailed off, his mind a muddle of nothing as she rocked her hips and rode him for all she was worth. Her hands splayed on his chest and her eyes burned lasers of green into his as he began to lose himself to her touch, her sex, the rolling of her hips.

His hands moved to cup her breasts, test their weight, then to her waist. He pulled her hips into his as her lunges became more frantic and her breathing choppy.

Before he could warn her that he was close, she was moving again. He grunted in protest as she stood, turning around then sitting again in reverse cowgirl. Her ministrations soon had the desired effect; when her soft, delicate hand began to stroke his scrotum then squeeze and pull, he was done for.

He came in a glorious, mind-blowing orgasm that pulled the very essence from his body. He poured himself inside her, gripping her like she was his lifeline.

When his body stopped spasming, he realized he was sitting up, his arms wrapped around the woman who'd just drained him of all rationale, one hand cupping her breast the other her hip. She shivered as his nose nuzzled her jawline, and he kissed her there. His fingers moved to trace the art inked across her back, a mosaic of different colorful images: flowers, Celtic crosses, hearts, animals, various intricate patterns and designs.

"So beautiful," he whispered, exploring her skin with his fingertips and all too aware of the goosebumps breaking out on her alabaster flesh as he did so.

"So are you," she replied, turning to face him and wrapping her legs around his waist.

She looked into his eyes, then studied his face as her fingertips traced the line of his cheekbones, nose, and jaw. He shivered when she touched his lips, and she grinned, pleased with herself.

They watched each other for a long time before they started kissing again, Quil's hands moving into her thick, dark hair.

"Why all the tattoos and piercings? For your job?" he asked when he pulled back, moving his fingertips down the designs on her arm.

"I could ask you the same question." Veda looked down at the tattoo on his chest, the one of his daughter's footprint as an infant and date of birth. Clearly, she didn't like his interrogation.

"It was a simple question," he retorted.

"I like to stand out..." She shrugged.

"*Pequeña rebelde.*"

"What does that mean?"

"Little rebel." He grinned.

"Boring women seldom make history."

Quil smirked. "You're unique, bad girl, I'll give you that."

"So having ink and piercings makes me bad, huh?"

"You also work in a strip club."

"Doesn't make me a slut." Her brows went up as if to dare him to say otherwise. "You don't even know me."

"Fair enough." He held his hands out in surrender.

She kissed him hard, in punishment he was sure, and when she pulled back, she smiled. "I've not yet conceded."

"Me either," Quil reassured, even as her lips fell to his again and she began to suck his tongue.

"Mmm, let me further persuade you, Hades," Veda coaxed as her hands moved down his shoulders to his pecs, then lower and lower until she gripped his growing cock in her fist.

"Mmm, your methods of persuasion are cruel, Medusa."

Veda full-out laughed, and the sound made Quillan's heart swell in his chest.

Soon, her stroking had him shivering before her mouth fell on his fevered flesh. He watched as she descended his torso ever so slowly until she was licking his shaft like a treasured lollipop, and his head was lolling back in pleasure. She used her mouth, tongue, and piercing so skillfully that before he knew it he was close to release once again.

He barely had time to enter her before he was coming again, arching hard up into her as his mind splintered in sprays of light and fire.

Veda giggled in triumph. "Looks like I have yet another snake to add to my crown."

"Yeah, yeah, you laugh now. You won't be laughing come tomorrow when you can't walk because of me, *chica mala.*"

He flipped her over and pinned her hands above her head, his mouth falling to her neck.

It was then he realized he hadn't worn a condom.

CHAPTER TWO

Veda awoke to the beautiful sight of Quillan Layton's muscular light brown back and buttocks on display atop the creamy sheets beside her. She smiled at the tribal tattoo with a dreamcatcher and feathers that covered the expanse of his right shoulder blade; she'd briefly noticed it last night. She began to trace it with her fingertips, admiring the shades of turquoise and indigo. Her fingers moved lower, over ridges of sinewy muscle that bulged in places and dipped in others. Perfect. He was six feet, six inches of masculine perfection. His bronze skin such a stark contrast to her milky white.

Her hand moved softly over his right butt cheek, plump and firm, and perfectly round, and in between, to cup his ballocks. He stirred with a deep moan as she explored the soft flesh and smiled when his brow rose at her.

"Didn't get enough last night, huh, *mamacita*?" God that Spanish accent and those caramel eyes.

Last night, she'd gotten the drop-dead gorgeous TE and being his lover had been beyond rewarding. His hands, mouth, and magnum-sized cock had felt amazing, more wonderful than any she'd had prior. But it was time to return to reality. It'd been a once in a lifetime occurrence. Now, she had to get herself back in the game and out of his bed. She was on a mission and couldn't afford any more distractions.

"Medusa can never have enough snakes, dark one." It was said with sarcasm, and he picked up on it quickly, frowning.

"Glad to know that's all it was for you, too."

The words stung her heart with bitterness and her hand withdrew from his scrotum.

His eyes roved her naked frame, unabashedly uncovered before him, in reverie for a moment, as if memorizing her before raising up on his elbow to eye her face. He studied her for a moment and reached out a hand toward her jaw, his knuckle brushing her cheekbone.

"I could have you again if I wanted and you know it," he challenged.

She couldn't hide the truth from him even if she tried. So she replied with, "Well, you have my number. I gave you my card in the club, remember?"

He averted his eyes, looking like he was leery of a future hook-up, but Veda wasn't going to let him get by that easy. The day might come when she wanted to scratch that itch again. She was always a woman apt to keeping her options open...and her legs, in Quillan Layton's case.

"Give me your phone," she insisted.

His sexy dark brows furrowed before he turned, his erection so prominent that she almost moaned aloud. When he handed her the phone from the nightstand, she put her cell into his contacts and texted herself so she'd have his number too—just in case.

She handed it back to him, more pleased than she wanted him to know. His fingertips touched hers gently as he took it, lingering before he glanced down at the phone.

Suddenly, he frowned and swore.

A notification must have popped up on the screen, for both their phones began to buzz and beep.

Veda moved and looked where Quil's Facebook page came up. Her heart literally froze in her chest as she saw that they'd been tagged in the racy pictures that Brooke had taken last night, along with the rest of the players on the team—some sixty pictures in total of the "fun times."

"*Puta madre!*" Quil swore loudly. "Did you know about this?" he looked angrily back at Veda, who gulped.

Hell no! She had no clue. She'd literally woken minutes before he had. And it had been Brooke who'd taken the pictures. But why in God's name would she post them knowing...? Shit, she didn't know Veda was a cheerleader.

"Well, there goes my day job," Veda huffed in remorse and frustration.

"What does *that* mean?"

"It means I'm no longer a Gladiators cheerleader, for one thing." She looked away and ran a hand through her wavy, mussed hair.

"Come again?" Quil sat up. "You're a fucking *cheerleader!*"

"The word you're looking for is *was*, Quillan. I *was* a cheerleader. Coach Duncan won't hesitate when he sees those pics. I'm canned. *Adios.*"

"What the hell kinda game are you playing here, lady? You're a groupie, aren't you?"

Veda laughed. No, she'd never been a groupie. She'd become a cheerleader for the spotlight, not the football players. It was good PR...and came with some perks after last night. But she shrugged and watched his eyes narrow in anger.

"I should've known better. Dammit! First the club, now this."

He jerked his gorgeously sculpted frame up and stood, hands on his narrow hips. She roved the perfect planes of his chest, rounded pectoral muscles, not a hair at all—not because he shaved it but because of his Native American roots. Her eyes moved down to his six-pack—*or was that an eight-pack?*—abs, each sinewy square rippling as his breathing accelerated, then down to the impressive manhood between his legs. Damn, he was beautiful.

Her eyes then shot back up to his face; thick, dark hair askew on his head, dark-bearded square jaw clenched, plump lips tight, dark brows drawn, brown eyes burning like liquid fire. Hades indeed.

"You used me last night, didn't you?" he asked, nostrils flaring.

"No more than you used me, Hades," Veda retorted, for it was the truest statement she'd made to him thus far.

Quil shook his head, disappointment painting his face. He then squatted down to retrieve his clothes, shoving his pants on quickly and his leather vest, his shoes, then finally he walked forward, growling as he leaned toward her.

"You wanna act like a whore, you'll be treated like one." With disgust, he withdrew his wallet and threw a hundred-dollar bill down.

QUIL TRIED to calm his anger but it was no use. He'd not been that riled up since Ri had died. The more he thought of the conniving little stripper/cheerleader Veda, the madder he got.

He hated even more that he'd been stupid enough not to bother using protection. A rookie mistake if ever there was one. But he hadn't come to the Halloween party expecting to hook-up, let alone be fucking all night long with the little stripper from *RISE* that knew how to work a tongue ring...and very well.

He should've known something was up the minute she'd told him who she was. But no, he'd been more intrigued than repulsed by her confession. Furthermore, why was he surprised to find out she was not only a practical prostitute but also a cheerleader? A woman who was that unscrupulous had a hidden agenda and something nagged at him about the whole damn thing. It hadn't just been a coincidence that she'd been at Paxton's party last night, despite that she was Becca's sister—which literally blew his mind. How could someone who was the complete polar opposite of Rebecca be her freakin' twin?

He was in an exceptionally foul mood all day, especially at practice where he treated his QB with disrespect, which only served to make him even angrier. He was mad at the world and he knew it was all because he'd had the best sex last night he'd had in years—with a glorified slut. He was also livid that he hadn't used a condom on a woman of that reputation and character. Shouldn't she have demanded he use one with the kind of job she had? He'd been sure to ask about getting tested when he arrived at the complex that morning, getting a brow raise from his trainer but no comment.

When he got home and saw his baby girl, life seemed right again. That bright, beaming smile of hers filled his heart with the happiness he needed to see him through the night.

"Daddy!" she'd cried when he came through the door around six fifteen.

Quinn ran to him and he scooped her up, burying his nose in her fresh floral-scented brown locks.

"Mmm, *mi reinita*, I missed you, love."

"I missed you too, Daddy. Did you have fun at your party last night?"

He had. Too much fun and that was the problem too. "I did. Did you have fun with Tia?"

"Yes, but I didn't get to make a pumpkin." She pouted and those big lips puckered. He kissed them because he couldn't resist.

"Oh, *mi corazón*, did you not do what your *tia* asked you?"

"Well..." she began and he grinned, hugging her back to him, her little body squeezing his tightly.

He thanked God every day for his child. He'd lost his wife, but his daughter was happy, and despite her medical condition, she was doing well—even if the color of her skin always appeared sallow. It worried him greatly. Her mother had had the same condition but nowhere near as bad. However, it'd ultimately led to her early demise, notwithstanding the cocaine addiction she had that thinned her blood further and stopped her heart.

Quinn had been diagnosed at six months old with Cooley's

anemia or thalassemia major—the most severe form of beta thalassemia; she not only had severe anemia but also a lack of oxygen in many parts of her body due to poor hemoglobin levels. Both Quil and his wife had been carriers and hadn't known it. Rian had to take iron, but Quil had never had any issues. Neither of them had suspected a thing until their newborn continued to stay sick with infections, always fussy, and never wanted to nurse. Their nanny, Quinn's great aunt—Juanita, or Tia Nita as she was known— had called it early on, stating that something wasn't right. Quil believed her because Quinn had always had a yellow tint to her skin, akin to the color of Quil's uncle who'd suffered from jaundice due to alcoholism and cirrhosis.

Her prognosis had been grim; regular blood transfusions would be required along with many other treatments. Her longevity would be only about thirty years. The news had been disheartening, to say the least, and Quil had thrown himself into football to keep his depression at bay. His wife, on the other hand, had found a substance that gave her wings to fly away from their problems. It wasn't long before Quillan knew she had a serious problem, but he couldn't keep her in rehab long enough for it to matter.

By the time Quinn was four, he'd kicked Ri out of the house at least a dozen times and paid for her fifteenth stint in rehab. He'd wanted a divorce but knew the pain of it would only worsen matters; he'd still loved his wife dearly, even if she'd turned her back on them. He empathized with her pain, even if he didn't understand how her obsession with drugs superseded all else. He'd never done drugs, save for smoking a little pot when he was in high school; but it was only fun, a substance he could definitely live without.

Quillan had postponed getting a divorce at first because Quinn didn't need more stress. With Juanita around to care for his child, Quil knew that Rian would never be alone with Quinn. And when she *was* around, she was withdrawing from her beloved cocaine and keeping to herself; or she hung out in her usual places, getting high, away from Quinn all together.

Quinn had never really bonded with her mother anyway; Rian never fed her, hardly ever held her, and was never around by the time their daughter was a year old. Quinn was a daddy's girl; Quillan thanked God for that divine intervention. With her mother always gone, whether it be in rehab or closed up in a room coming down off a high, Tia took the place of her mother. Quinn never even asked about Rian anymore, which was just as well; the memories were too painful in the first place.

Despite Rian's failures, Quil still painted her in a good light for Quinn. Ri was dead, after all, and he would never speak ill of the dead. Everyone had their cross to bear; the least he could do was preserve Rian's memory for her daughter, even if it meant skirting around her shortcomings and making her seem a better person than she was. For all her bad decisions, she did love Quinn even if, in the end, she'd loved herself more.

Quillan let his daughter go on about why she'd misbehaved, internally amused as she wove the over-dramatized tales she was known for.

They had a hearty dinner of grilled mahi and pineapple salsa with jasmine rice and veggies, Quinn enjoying every bite. Despite that she wasn't healthy, she loved eating foods that were good for her, much to Quil's delight. She could be fairly picky, as any child could, but for the most part she didn't complain too much.

They spoke about their day, him, Quinn and Tia, the middle-aged woman who'd been their lifesaver for as long as Quinn had been alive, and Quil's mood lightened some.

When he tucked his daughter into bed that night, she grinned up at him and pulled his shirt down for "one more kiss." He got all teary-eyed as he looked her beautiful little face over. She looked so much like her mother, who, prior to her addiction, had been a model —beautiful, with big eyes and plump lips.

"What's the matter, Daddy?"

"Your beauty takes my breath away, *mi corazón*."

"That's not all." She was getting wiser in her old age. "What else?"

They could read each other well, it was both a blessing and a curse. "I met someone last night."

"A lady?"

"She was no lady," Quil said under his breath. "She hurt my feelings, baby, that's all. I'll be ok. Time heals all wounds, right, *reinita*?"

"*Princesa*, not *reinita* yet, Daddy."

"But you are, my little angel, you are my little *queen*. The queen of my heart." He pulled her little hand to his breast, dramatically, getting a giggle out of her and making his frown transform into a big smile. "Do you know how much I love you?"

Quinn opened her arms wide. "This much?"

"*Infinitamente, mi alma.*"

This was their usual every evening, for him to confess his infinite love to his sweet little angel. He would cherish every day he had with her, until their Creator decided to call her home; he prayed she would outlive him by decades upon decades.

"Now get some sleep." He kissed her forehead and turned to exit.

"Daddy?"

"Yes, Quinn?"

She always had just one more question or comment for him. Perhaps she was simply her father's child and enjoyed having the last word. He grinned, awaiting what it would be tonight.

"I'm sorry she hurt your feelings."

He gave her a soft laugh. "There's nothing for you to be sorry for, *chiquita*. Daddy will get over it, I promise."

Quinn's lips pulled to one side, thoughtfully, but she said no more as he bade her a goodnight and pulled her door closed.

Time *would* heal all wounds, but there was a nagging in his gut telling him that he hadn't seen the last of Medusa, and something told him he would rue the day he ever met her.

ALL SAINTS DAY was a terrible day for Veda. After she'd left Paxton's, pissing pretty much everyone in the house off thanks to her sour mood, she'd come home and cried in her mother's arms.

Her mother, Kathleen, had always been able to read her girls well. The minute Veda had sat her purse down in the overstuffed chair she favored, her mam had said, "What happened, *mo chroí?*"

She hadn't been able to give her full details. Despite their closeness, their strict Catholic upbringing prevented Veda from expelling TMI to her demure mother. So she'd just told her mam she'd made an ass out of herself, which wasn't far from the truth. She'd slept with a man who now hated her, lost her job, and got the entire football team *and* Becca mad at her for sounding like a slag—a gold-digging slag.

And she was no closer to her long sought-after modeling career, despite that Becca was living among the elite. But she *had* met Brooke Taylor at least.

Her mam held her and soothed her, making her some chamomile tea with a shot of whiskey, honey, and lime—her mam's own special concoction—and sent her off to bed to sleep it off. Her mam looked like she could use the rest too. Veda did as her mam said but found herself tossing and turning, remembering every detail of her and Quil's delicious love-making...and how angry he'd been when she'd made him believe she'd been out to get him.

Yeah, he won't be calling me... ever!

The minute she'd left Pax's and gotten into her car, her model Thunderbird she'd had since high school, she'd gotten a call from her coach giving her the bad news of her termination. As if she hadn't known *that* was coming. She was canned, and Quil wouldn't even get talked to about his bad behavior, not even a slap on the wrist. It would all be swept under the proverbial table with his PR team, and the picture would be eradicated from Facebook as quickly as it went up. Funny how women were treated differently than men. She'd known the rules before she'd started. Yet, deep down, she was grateful she'd even gotten to be a part in such a lifestyle, if only for a short amount of time. She hadn't even put up a fuss, and Coach must have heard the acceptance in her tone.

"I truly am sorry, Veda, but you knew the rules and you've deliberately overstepped more than once now. We let the first incident go with a warning. I can't let this one."

"I understand," Veda answered truthfully, not arguing. Hell, it wasn't like it would have mattered at that point.

Coach gave a sigh. She'd not really discussed with him at length what she wanted, but he must have known it wasn't just to be a cheerleader. "Keep at it. You have spunk. It will pay off one day. I'll still give you a stellar reference wherever you go, know that."

He had been a hard-ass from the minute she'd stepped on the field. He had a job to do, but he'd seen how hard she worked and how important it had been...well, in the beginning before Becca had worried her sick to death.

Now, V recalled the conversation in the kitchen, her foul actions, and all because Quil had been rude to her in response to her bating. She remembered the look on her sweet sister's face when she'd acted like an absolute cunt.

"VEDA! Do you know who you were speaking to?" Becca's voice was both hurt and angry.

"Just another rich bitch from what I can gather," Veda smarted, scrambling eggs into a bowl and avoiding her sister's eyes.

"That 'rich bitch' is our CEO," Pax growled.

"My bad." She knew she needed to calm her jets, but she was fired up by Quil's treatment of her, even if she'd deserved it. And these women were all spoiled brats in her eyes, not knowing what it was like to have to scrape the bottom of the barrel to get what they needed—rich bitches indeed.

"Well... I'm sure it's not a big deal that she was here, so long as no photos leak out of her without her mask or anything," Travis spoke up. Oh, he didn't know yet. Check your phone, handsome, she wanted to say. They already have!

"Oops," Veda *smirked under her breath. She simply couldn't stop her sarcasm from getting a rise out of them.*

The QB, big Brett, huffed and crossed his arms over his chest. He stepped forward toward Veda. Her eyes shot up to his. "Are you just trying to get fired?" he asked.

"At least getting fired is better than quitting. I'll get unemployment benefits."

Brett's green eyes burned with rage and he scoffed, shaking his head. He turned on his heel and left.

Becca looked horrified, and Veda felt bad for how she was acting, even if she was in a horrible mood.

Travis spoke first, breaking the silence. "Wow... got a thermos, Pax? I think I'll take my coffee to go." Then he up and left, too.

Pax frowned, his brows knitting together on his forehead. "I know what you're trying to pull and guess what? It isn't gonna fly. Do you really hate me that much?"

"Hate is a strong word, Paxton." Yes, I hate you, you chummy bastard.

"Veda, what—?"

Pax interrupted Becca, stepping in front of her even as he took her outstretched hand in his and squeezed it tight. "You don't get to tell me how to live my life."

"I don't give two shits about your life. I just want mine back and ever since this happened." Veda turned and pulled Paxton's hand from Becca's. "I haven't had a moment's peace."

"Jealous much, are ya, lass?" Pax mimicked their Irish roots, and it pissed Veda off when people did that shit. She growled and slapped him across the face, getting a gasp from her sister.

"Veda! Stop it!" Becca pleaded.

"Keep it up and I'll fuckin' marry her just to piss you the fuck off." Paxton's blue eyes narrowed.

"Stop!" Becca shouted to the top of her lungs. Both heads turned to face her then, surprised by her bravado. "I am not a bargaining chip, I am not a

toy, and I am not going to sit here and allow either of ye to treat me like I'm not standing right fecking here. To hell with ye both."

When Becca left, leaving just Pax and Veda, he threw his hands to his face and swore loudly.

"You fuckin' happy now?" he asked, taking a step forward.

"And fiancé of the year goes to..." Veda gave a sinister laugh. Looks like she was getting her wish. Too bad she didn't feel any better.

"What the hell have I ever done to you?"

"You mean besides be born?"

Pax tilted his head inquisitively and crossed his arms over his chest. "I haven't figured you out yet, Veda, but I'm onto you. You really can't be happy for your twin sister? Is it jealousy? Wow, that's low...even for you."

Veda loudly banged the fork against the bowl then threw it into the concoction of eggs and milk. "Don't act like you know a damn thing about us. Either of us! You get to live in a mansion, drive numerous high-end cars around, and don't have to worry about things like paying bills, going to the grocery store, or finding enough change to pay for a damn Happy Meal at McDonalds, so fuck you, Paxton Guthrie and curse the day you ever laid eyes on my sister."

SHE'D LEFT that room so quickly, seething in anger as she moved to retrieve her keys and her purse from the mudroom. She hadn't been able to get out of the door quickly enough. Fuck them all. The rich sons-of-bitches. They couldn't even begin to comprehend the life Becca, Veda, and Kathleen had. Praying for a miracle against cancer, to keep a roof over their heads, food on their tables, while assholes like Paxton Guthrie lived in a house that costs millions and owned clothes that would keep the Ryans up for years to come.

Following the call from her coach, Veda had stayed angry, reliving all of it. When she'd gotten home, the dam broke and she collapsed in her mother's arms in grief and anguish.

She'd royally fucked up. Now she was no better off than she had been. And now she owed her sister an apology, more than one if she were being so bold. But even if she tried to call, Becca wouldn't answer. Veda knew her sister well and she knew it would be a couple days before Bec would wanna talk to her. Becca had always needed time to get over something; she held grudges. Not unlike Veda. And Veda had built a heavy grudge up against the Gladiators football team.

As happy as V should be that Becca and Pax were mad at one another, she wasn't. Becca's misery fueled her own, and she didn't sleep much that night or the next.

She watched the Monday night game, drooling over Quil more than usual as she remembered his hands moving over her naked body, his deep, sexy moans in her ears, his big, thick member filling her so fully. She masturbated that night thinking about him, then cursed herself for being such a desperate idiot. She was pathetic.

After Veda's anger and sorrow had run their course, reason came crashing in hard. She finally called her sister on Wednesday, not getting an answer as she suspected she wouldn't. She didn't volunteer Tuesday, using the excuse to her mom that she was job-hunting, which wasn't a lie. She applied at the local Hooters and Tilted Kilt.

They weren't her first choice, but those types of jobs helped get her the attention she needed—or, at least, that's what she told herself. She enjoyed having men look at her, and that night at *RISE* she was eager to have their eyes loving her flesh, even if they couldn't love the rest of her.

Veda realized that was the problem as she swung her body around the pole with the ease and grace of a fish swimming. She was seeking "love" in the wrong outlets. The love she had from her mother and sister was, apparently, no longer enough; but she was wary of men and their ways, finding any excuse why she couldn't let someone else into the fold.

They'd been content with just the three of them for so long, forsaking all others to keep their close-knit family together once Pa had left them. It had been easy to avoid a steady relationship following what Will did to her... and even now, focusing only on taking care of their mother and making enough money to keep them afloat. But now that Becca had ventured out, the allure of companionship didn't seem so implausible.

There was the other problem, though: true love didn't exist. Not in the sense that Becca thought. Not in the real world. Love hadn't been enough to keep their father in their mother's bed when her lymphoma took her health, not enough to keep his vows to her when he'd abandoned her. Men were visual creatures after all, sexual fiends that desired flesh above all else.

Veda was seeing proof of it sprouting before her very eyes as she moved from the pole to crawl across the stage, her breasts popping easily out of the lace as the thin straps of her gown fell down her shoulders.

She watched the man's eyes move from her licking lips to her perky tits, like she'd just set a feast before a starving vagabond. The look only intensified as she stopped, sat back on her heels, and spread her legs, revealing a cut-out in the lace between them and the diamond embellishments there.

"Oh, fuck yeah," the bastard groaned and his hand fell to his Gucci-suited crotch.

Veda squeezed her breast, moaning back at him even as her mind went somewhere else. Back to Quillan.

She popped up, teasing the man who looked like she'd just taken his puppy away as she turned around and bent over, giving him a shot of her practically bare ass.

Whistles answered her before she stood and moved back to her pole. If they wanted a private show, they had to pay. *RISE* wasn't a typical strip club, which Veda respected. The women danced, not necessarily stripped if they weren't comfortable with it. And bouncers were always around and took care of the girls, protective as fathers to the founding members when they were on stage.

No one was allowed to touch them, unless they took their hands and placed them on them. No one could take advantage. It was a safe haven for women. It was a dance hall; a stage for broken ballerinas to fulfill their dreams. And if they got the notion to take it further, there were bedrooms where they got to do as they wished.

Veda hadn't used one of them. And wasn't sure if or when she would. She didn't want to be someone's whore. Stripping was enough…for now. It paid the bills until she was forced to do more. She wouldn't, but the call of money was getting stronger and stronger as of late; she knew some of these men would pay a big chunk of change to fuck her.

They loved her tattoos and piercings and always hinted as to how they would love to taste them, especially her hood piercing. It got them all horny as hell.

She'd gotten herself off on stage one night in front of a well-paying customer who'd been awed by it, earning an extra $500 for fingering herself, letting the perv watch, and grumble his kinky wishes for her as he rubbed one out beneath his table.

Madam Roxie didn't like for them to do things like that out on the public floor, stuff like that was usually reserved for the private rooms—where they could charge whatever they wanted—but it had been a slow Tuesday night and no one else was around, so Veda took advantage of the situation when it was presented before her.

Perhaps soon, she would do it again. It had made her feel odd though, leaving a bad taste in her mouth, like she'd cheated him or herself… After all, he'd had a ring on his finger.

She got back to dancing; the reason she'd been eager to work at *RISE* in the first place. Where she could perform, lose herself to the rhythm of the music and escape.

And she did, letting all the troubles and trials melt away as the lights bounced off her sweaty skin.

For now, she was fine, all was fine, and nothing else mattered.

CHAPTER THREE

B y the following Monday, Veda had texted Becca—for the umpteenth time—and gotten a text back. She'd only called about half a dozen times, leaving messages every single time.

Veda: You can't still be mad at me...are you?

Becca: Yes!

Veda: Fine, be mad. I'm not apologizing anymore.

Becca: Fine then don't.

Ugh, she was so stubborn.

Veda: I'm coming to the hospital to volunteer tomorrow.

Becca: Fine!

Veda: Stop saying that damn word, Bec. I'm your sister, I love you. And for the record, I'm still mad at YOU.

Becca: Just because you love me doesn't mean you know what's best for me.

Convenient how she completely ignored the last part!

Veda: I never said I did.

After ten more minutes, she finally got a response.

Becca: I love you too. I'll see you tomorrow.

QUILLAN PACED BACK and forth in the atrium of the hospital, just outside the waiting area of the infusion center. He felt ill at ease, unable to stop thinking about Veda. This obsession of his was starting to become unhealthy, he knew, but he hadn't been able to get the sexy, little inked and embellished snake lady out of his mind. Her touch, taste, and feel haunted him at night.

He'd found her profile on Instagram a few nights ago and was now browsing her stories. Her latest post was a sexy short video of her in a bikini doing a saucy little dance finishing with her tongue sticking out, looking like she wanted to do naughty things to the viewer. He could remember the feel of that tongue—in his mouth, on his belly, on his cock. He knew he would be watching this video again tonight…before he went to bed.

"Quil!" Quillan heard Paxton's voice as he turned. He locked his phone quickly and shoved it into his back pocket. He approached Pax with a grin.

"Pax, *qué pasó*, man? What are you doing here?"

"I could ask you the same question, brother." Pax laughed and pumped his hand.

"Oh, just waiting on Quinn to get her transfusions; they take a while." Quil didn't like talking about Quinn's condition—not that he was ashamed of it, but it was often misunderstood.

"She doing ok?" Pax asked, concerned.

"Yeah, she's ok, she…" he trailed off, not sure how to explain his concern. He brushed it off. "What about you? What are you doing here?"

"Becca's mom is getting chemo, and we volunteer while we wait. It passes the time."

"Oh, well that's good. I should probably start doing that. It will distract me." And Lord knew, he needed a distraction from day-dreaming about Veda Ryan.

"Yeah, you should!" Pax stated but frowned as he turned, seeing the woman Quil was just thinking about, as if he'd conjured her.

Veda was swiftly coming toward them, dressed in a collared blue shirt with the hospital logo and khaki slacks, Quinn in tow. Quinn was her usual self, talking a mile a minute, her little hand holding Veda's, making Quil's heart melt even as it jumped up into his throat.

"And then Daddy said I jumped *so* high I could've touched the sky." Quinn giggled.

Veda gave a sultry laugh in response, and Quil's body became engulfed in licking flames of burning desire. He wanted to hear that same sound while he loved her body as he had on Halloween night, wanted to trace his tongue across the Celtic crosses, hibiscus flowers, and skeleton heads that called to him from her forearm.

Veda stopped dead in her tracks when she saw him, her jaw falling in shock. Her dark waves framed her surprised face; her beautiful, full lips opened and she stared up at him as if he'd just emerged from the Underworld.

"Veda?" Quil felt as if he were dreaming. Was she really there? "Wh—?"

"Quillan?" Her green eyes danced. She was happy to see him! But he'd insulted her last he'd remembered…

"Daddy!"

He stood in awe of the woman of his fantasies. She was really there! And was now giving him a sly smile. Perhaps she'd forgiven him for his harsh words, even if at the time he'd been intentionally cruel.

"Daddy!" Quinn practically shouted, her voice echoing in the high-ceiling atrium, getting Quil's attention…finally.

"Yes, *reinita*?" Quil looked down at his sweet angel and gave her a smile.

"I want to have lunch with Veda."

Quillan's mouth opened slightly in surprise and his eyes went to Veda's, whose locked with his again. A brow went up. She was down. And he was too.

"That's fine, Quinn. Whatever you want, *mi amor*."

"Pax, would you like to join us?" Quil asked suddenly, not wanting to seem rude. Pax's hesitation was answer enough, but then Becca came to the rescue.

"Quil, what a surprise?" Her broad smile gave nothing away.

"Becca," Pax mumbled, "uh, Quil and Veda were going to lunch with the little princess here and wondered if we'd like to join them."

Quinn looked up at Becca frowning, confused. "Whoa. Daddy! They look alike."

"She's my twin sister. Her name is Rebecca," Veda answered Quinn with the patience of Job.

"Hi! I'm Quinn." Quil's daughter gave Becca a grin.

"Hi, Quinn." Becca waved back and answered Pax, "Sure, we can go to lunch. We're all caught up."

"Great! I'm starved," Veda answered, her eyes moving back to Quil's. His body heat rose as he followed her. He knew she'd not been speaking of food if her popping hips in front of him were any indication. Had it only been a little over a week since they'd been together? It felt like an eternity.

He couldn't keep his eyes off her alluring bottom as it bounced and fought the urge to squeeze it in his palms and test the firmness he recalled there.

What had he been thinking when he agreed to have lunch with her? Now, he was going to be tortured as she ate and he imagined that mouth on him. He was an idiot!

"So, how's your day been so far, sister?" Becca asked from behind Quillan. It was a leading question, if ever there was one.

"It's been fun, right, Quinn?" she shook Quinn's little arm, getting another giggle from his little angel.

"So much fun!"

"How'd you two meet?" Quil asked, attempting to assess the situation he'd gotten sucked into thanks to his daughter.

They passed a few families, one little bald kid's mouth dropping as he saw giant Quillan Layton, TE for the Atlanta Gladiators, and

Quil gave the kid a wave and a sly smile. They passed by the gift shop before Quil got an answer.

"Veda was in the infusion center passing out coloring books, and I asked her about her tattoos," Quinn answered, sounding far older than her age of six. "Daddy, did you know that the Celts are the ones who invented Halloween?"

Well, that wasn't *exactly* how it happened, but he wouldn't correct her. "I did."

"We learned that in class recently, you know?"

"What the heck are they teaching these kids in school now?" Pax scoffed behind Quil, getting a laugh out of them all.

Knowing his daughter, she'd probably been the one to start that conversation, with her curious mind and all.

"Then I was telling Veda about *your* tattoos, Daddy."

Oh baby, that woman knows all about them, he thought.

"Becca, do you have tattoos?" Quinn asked and turned her head to look behind her father.

"No, ma'am, I don't. Not a single one."

"Me neither. Pax?"

By then, they'd all stopped in the line for the cafeteria, which stretched out the door a little. It was lunch time after all.

"I got a couple," Pax answered and raised his shirt, revealing the tribal one across his bicep.

"I like those. They look Native American, like great-grand Paw Paw Blackhorn—don't they, Daddy?"

"They do indeed. What do you wanna eat, sweet pea?"

Quil noticed the large crowd milling around, stopping to gaze at both him and Paxton.

"Strawberries!" Quinn squealed as she saw an apron-clad lady filling the bucket of them on the salad bar buffet.

"You gotta eat more than strawberries, *reinita*. How about some mac and cheese?"

Quinn wrinkled her nose and shook her head dramatically. "No."

"How about pizza?" he asked, trying again.

43

"Nope, that's yucky!"

"Yucky?" Pax asked and tickled at Quinn's belly. "What kinda kid doesn't like pizza?"

Quinn giggled and attempted to tickle back at Paxton, getting a smile from Becca.

"This kid," Quil answered. "She likes healthy foods." He shrugged when Veda turned, a surprised look on her face.

"Wow! That's crazy."

"Yup. Thai, Mediterranean, Mexican and sushi."

"Sushi! I want sushi, Daddy."

"Of course you do, Quinn, but we're in a hospital cafeteria. I doubt very seriously they have sushi."

"They do and it's rather good, actually. Made fresh daily," Veda answered with a smirk.

"Well, you're in luck then, kiddo." Quil ran a hand through his daughter's thick brown curls.

"Daddy, can I sit by Veda?"

"Sure. If she's ok with that."

Quinn looked up at Veda, and the intensity there almost knocked Quillan off his feet.

Had his daughter ever even looked at her mother with that same fascination? It had been so long, he couldn't even remember. It made his chest hurt to think she'd never had the connection most children got with their mothers; she was missing out. Quil owed it to her to get her a mother, one she could love and admire, before her time on earth was through.

But Veda wasn't mother material. He knew that, but it didn't stop the ache in his chest that came with that knowledge.

He shook it off as they moved to order and pay for their food.

Quil carried a tray over to the salad bar and loaded Quinn's plate with her requests, including strawberries and various pieces of sushi. He hated the stuff and opted for a piece of grilled chicken and a salad with raspberry vinaigrette.

Quinn ran over to the table Pax and Becca had selected, jumping up at Veda as she set her tray down. In turn, Veda picked Quinn up and hugged her with equal fervor. Again, the onslaught on Quillan's heart threatened to suffocate him. What the hell was happening here?

He cleared his throat as he took the seat opposite his daughter, Veda cutting her strawberries as Quinn placed a piece of sushi in her mouth.

"Chew chew, Quinn, not too fast. No one is taking it away from you," Quillan scolded.

Veda giggled at a blushing Quinn who immediately slowed in the midst of her heroine.

"One would think I starve the kid to death by the time she eats."

Paxton laughed beside him. "Ah, it's their metabolisms. That's a good thing. Means she's growing."

Quinn smiled big beneath her too-yellow skin, making Quillan's heart flutter in uncertainty. "See Daddy, I told you."

Quill gulped his fears down even as Veda caught his eyes, cautiously. Did she know about Quinn's thalassemia? What all had Quinn told her?

Becca began commenting on the food and Pax flirted with her, scooping up a hearty helping of mac and cheese for her to try and she laughed, getting grins from Quil, Veda, and Quinn. Whatever was going on between them, it was nice to see their strong connection. Quillan had noticed positive changes in his teammate since Pax had announced his engagement and thought Rebecca was good for him. It was very clear, though, that Veda was either jealous or simply didn't like Pax; the eyes she gave him were full of scorn.

Quil tried not to let that affect the flow of their meal, enjoying the company and seeing Quinn interact with everyone. Socializing was good for her, but he knew the minute they got home, she was gonna crash. She always did after her treatments.

Veda took her to get some frozen yogurt, and her kindness toward his daughter made Quil's heart happy. What had happened between them on Halloween, the mean words he'd said the following morning, hadn't forced her to take her vengeance out on his daughter; realizing this, he knew he owed her an apology.

He watched Veda eating ice cream, laughing with Quinn, and his desire for her overcame him. That sexy pink tongue licked at the cone and when her eyes caught his, he had to stifle the groan at his lips as his hardening cock bulged in his jeans. *Fuck!* She was so gorgeous. All he could think about was getting her beneath him and making her his all over again. He wanted her and he had to have her, and when she slurped the chocolate ice cream and licked the corner of her mouth, she knew it, for the raised brow told him she did.

They were all walking out to the parking lot not long after that. Quinn had perched herself on Veda's shoulder, her eyes succumbing to sleep. Quil felt his heart lurch seeing his daughter so comfortable in Veda's care. As they came to stop in front of his truck, they waved to Becca and Pax who had gone to retrieve Kathleen, Becca and Veda's mom, from her treatment.

"I can take her," Quil began to lift Quinn to his shoulder, taking her easily from Veda's arms. "She gets heavy when she goes all limp like that," he stated softly and stepped back as Veda opened the passenger door he'd unlocked.

Quil sat his daughter down in the seat, rested her head against his jacket laying there, and buckled her in, smiling down at her peaceful form.

"She's an angel," Veda answered as she brushed her hand across Quinn's forehead, moving the sweaty hair off her cheek. Quil's heart did another queer jerk; he worried he might need to go see a cardiologist after today.

He studied Veda as she pulled back, blushing and fiddling with her hands, a stark contrast to the feisty rebel he was used to.

"Well, I uh... I guess I gotta go get ready for work." It was well after 3 PM, Quil noted as he looked at his watch.

"Yeah, I should head home and get her to bed," Quil answered, simply to have a response. "Look, I—"

"Please don't." Veda looked up. "You don't need to apologize."

"Are you sure about that? Because I'm not."

"It was great, Quillan, honestly it was, but…"

"It was, wasn't it? Great." He couldn't stop his hand from reaching for hers, shivering when it interlaced within his own. So small and petite, like the rest of her—tiny compared to him.

Her eyes were so open, so vulnerable that it took his breath. She was a bad girl, a rebel, a hell-raiser—and Quil was a single dad who'd lived through the curse of his wife's addiction; now here he was with one of his own. He suddenly felt bad for getting so angry with Rian over hers. Even if his mind was screaming at him to be sensible.

He knew that he couldn't do this again. He couldn't go down this road. Couldn't let himself get involved with a woman like Veda. She would only pull him down with her; he'd been at rock bottom before, he wouldn't do it again, to himself…or to Quinn.

Veda sensed his hesitations and gave him a sad smile. "You take care of her, Quil."

He returned her smile even as he felt his heart tearing. "I will. She's my everything."

"As she should be. It was good seeing you again."

"You too." It was true. Seeing her made him happy, and he couldn't remember the last time he'd felt so light. He nodded because he wasn't sure what to say.

He waited for her to step back before closing the passenger door and moving to the driver's side, then he called back to Veda, "Hey, thanks for being so good to my daughter, V."

Veda turned, her eyes glimmering cynically. "Children don't always have to pay for the sins of their fathers, now do they, Quillan?"

Quil frowned even as Veda planted her hands on her hips and puckered her lips at him. In a flash, she was moving inside, leaving him to ponder just what the hell she'd meant by that statement.

CHAPTER FOUR

It had been a week since he'd seen her, a week since his heart had been floating in his chest at the sight of her with his child, holding his sweet angel in her arms and turning his life upside down.

So, following practice on Monday, he'd gone back to the one place he'd never expected to again—*RISE*.

"Mr. Layton, right this way."

Quillan was escorted to a private room with plush red walls by a masked hostess where a gold-wigged and black masked Amazon-type goddess greeted him.

"Why, Quillan Layton? To what do I owe the pleasure?"

Damn! She was built like a brick shit house, solid, firm—muscle and legs that went on for days. Curves. A wet dream come to life. "Uh…" Quil began as she motioned for him to sit down in the chair next to her. "I, uh." Why was he here again? Oh yes! "I've come to see Madam Obsidian."

"Obsidian, huh? Well, lucky for you, she just started her shift. I'll go retrieve her for you, handsome."

Those damn masks, there was something about them that added to the seduction.

His nerves were frayed as he watched the firm ass of the tall madam disappear behind a door within the curtain at the back of the room. He took in deep breaths as he tried to remind himself what an idiot he was for coming to the club again. But he had to see her.

He needed to do something aside from jerk himself off to a video of her. It was becoming unhealthy. He needed to feel flesh and blood against him and Veda was the one he wanted... despite the anger that immediately filled him when she entered the room, dark purple and black mask and wig gleaming in the sparse lighting. How many men had she brought to this room to seduce? How many men had been inside her body? He was engulfed in a possessive rage as the thought destroyed his resolve and he shot up off the chair, toppling it to the ground as he stepped forward.

Veda was clad in a ridiculous excuse for a garment, sheer plum lace that exposed her pierced nipples, belly button, and hood piercing. He growled, the need to punish her strong within him.

"Quillan?" her surprised whisper jarred the animal within him, and he stifled a roar in answer.

"How many, Veda?" He needed to know, *had* to know!

If she was frowning, he couldn't tell. "How many what?" she asked, sounding so innocent that he laughed incredulously.

"You know exactly what! Stop being coy with me, or I'm gonna hurt you and enjoy every fuckin' second of it!"

Quil was like a crazed lion, feeling something primitive inside bubbling beneath the surface.

"If you think for one second you're gonna come to my place of work and treat me—"

"Treat you like what? A whore? Well, isn't that what you are, *señorita*?" he mocked. "Correct me if I'm wrong, and I'll gladly apologize. You play Mother Theresa at the hospital one minute, then you come here and get your rocks off, mocking the God you pray to by playing a harlot the next. Who the hell are you, Veda Ryan?"

"Don't you dare use my real name in here, you *bastard!*" Veda quickly stepped forward, pointing a finger in his face as she separated the distance between them. His skin began to itch with the need to spar with her; spar, then fuck her sexy body without mercy. "I'll be damned if you think you can come here and intimidate me. I'm not my sweet sister. Don't fuckin' threaten *me*, asshole!"

"Oh, you're so big and bad! All hundred and twenty pounds of you, tiny. I can break you. Maybe that's exactly what a wild little filly like you needs!"

With that, he grabbed her even as she fought him. He pulled her hands over her head, laughing as he slammed her against the soft, plush wall.

"Hmm, not so tough now are ya, *pequeña rebelde?*" Quil ran a knuckle from her cheekbone to her chin, his nose brushing hers as his body caged hers in, his stiffening cock pressing into her pubic bone. He moaned aloud.

"Fuck you," she whimpered, more from the blow of defeat than his dominance.

"That's exactly what I plan to do, *chica mala*, against this wall, on the floor, in that chair, on that bed...until I've fucked you right out of my system. But first, you're gonna give me a number and you're going to tell me the truth because if you don't, I'll fucking ruin you. And I don't just mean your bedazzled little *chimichanga, puta.*"

"*Fuck* you, Quillan. I don't owe you a damn thing. I'm not afraid of you. Call me all the names you like. Think that hurts my feelings? Think again!" She spit in his face and said something in Irish Gaelic that he didn't understand but knew it was probably another "Fuck you," if he had to guess.

He wiped it off with his arm with a growl then picked her up, his chest holding her captive as his hands moved to his pants to unbutton himself. He jerked his slacks and boxers down and ripped the sorry excuse of a lace teddy from her chest, exposing her naked torso.

His head fell to the mound of her breast and sucked her nipple into his mouth, punishing it with a rough tongue, biting at the piercing and getting a whimper from Veda.

"Mmm, you like that, don't you, you bad girl?" he chuckled as he pulled back and his fingers went at her lace-covered clit, assaulting it with the same fervor. She gasped even as her wrists fought at the palm that held them. "Uh uh, not until you tell me how many." She grunted, but didn't answer. "Have it your way. I'll get it out of you one way or another." He raised her higher, his mouth kissing down her belly to the sparkling sex he uncovered with the hook of his index finger through the thin lace. He unleashed the fury he'd been holding back, letting his tongue thrash her relentlessly, angry with himself for being so drawn to a woman of such character as Veda. He thrust his fingers inside her for good measure. When her moans echoed through his ears, pleasure reverberated within as her walls clenched.

She began to writhe and whimper, whether she was aching for more or fighting him he wasn't sure but he insisted again. "Tell me, Veda. I deserve to know who I'm getting involved with. How many men have you fucked here at *RISE*?"

"Fuck you," she groaned as his scruffy chin tickled her hood piercing.

"Oh, I intend to fuck you so hard you're beggin' me to stop. But first, a number."

"I won't, and you can't make me." She bucked against his face even as he sucked the jewel into his mouth and bit down, his fingers diving deeper. Her resolve faltered as she moaned deeply.

"You *will* and I can." He was crazed, horny, angry and needy, needy for her sex. He had to have it. He couldn't go on living without it.

He pulled back and let her body fall slightly down the wall, his cock hovering just beneath her womanhood, the heat and dampness driving him insane with lust. Anger pulsed as prominent as desire in that moment. He peeled the mask down her face and jerked the wig from her hair, getting a yelp out of her as he fisted her dark waves and pulled back slightly. He noted the tears that fell down her cheeks and hated himself for it, but he had to know if she was really using him. Did he mean anything to her beyond this incredible sexual electricity that sparked between them like lightening during a raging storm?

"Number."

"Go to Hell, *Hades!*" she shouted.

"Wrong answer."

And with that, he thrust hard and deep inside her.

"Jesus Christ, how does it feel *so* fucking good every time?" Quil whined as he thrust hard, punishing himself or her, Veda wasn't sure.

"Because I'm a *whore*. It's supposed to, right? That's my profession," she smarted and got a hair pull in return, making her sex tighten around him.

He moaned and looked into her face. "I don't know. You tell me. I need that number, Veda. You *will* tell me."

Veda didn't know why she was being so obtuse. Why did it matter if she wasn't what he thought she was; would it change anything? *No*, she told herself. So why didn't she tell him? Because she was stubborn AF and that was the allure between them. She was forbidden. Which was why he was here, wasn't it? He wanted the taboo, what was off-limits; it made her irresistible to him, which was why he'd come to take her again.

"Oh God, Quil..." she moaned as pleasure unraveled inside her. "Fuck, yes. Fuck me, baby," she encouraged because her list of sins wasn't long enough yet. Damn, she was a glutton for punishment.

"Mmm, yeah. You love it, don't you, *chica mala*? You love being fucked by my big cock. Watch it go inside you. It's so fuckin' hot."

He lightened his grip on her hair so she could watch where their bodies were connecting. It *was* hot, and she felt her climax building.

Quil's mouth moved to her nipple and suckled her as his thumb moved back to her clit. He continued to hammer her against the wall, faster and harder, bringing her closer to oblivion in his arms.

"Quil," she whimpered as her walls squeezed him, the need to fight him as strong as the need to succumb.

"Shit V, mmm." He cupped her face then leaned in to kiss her, sucking her tongue into his mouth. "Come for me, sexy lady." He pulled back only long enough to speak before sucking again.

"Mmm," Veda answered back, and as her mind began to protest, her body betrayed her, splitting at the seams into a volcanic-like eruption that soaked them both as his cock hit a sensitive spot deep within and his thumb struck her jeweled clit over and over. "Ah, ah, ah," she groaned as spasms shook her to the very core.

"Oh baby." He looked down at the mess she'd made. "That's a first, huh?" He noted the shock on her face. "Me too, but damn, that was sexy as fuck." The sinister grin on his face said as much.

He pulled out and stepped back, releasing her wrists even as he moved her to the bed, letting her upper body fall forward as he turned her around and thrust in from behind, getting a gasp from them both.

"I've been patient, Veda. Now give me that fucking number, or you're gonna wish you had." His thrust was punishing as he arched high, the head of his cock hitting the hilt of her and she whimpered. His hand moved back into her hair, fisting again as he pulled hard. "The fucking number, now!" he shouted, his tone changing.

"It's insulting to want a whore so much, isn't it, Quillan?" she sassed, knowing she was pushing the line. "I bet it bruises that big ego of yours, doesn't it?"

He shoved her head down to the bed and pressed harder on top of her.

"If you break me in half, you won't be able to fuck me anymore, *ese*," She gritted and shoved her ass against his thighs. He immediately moved back, withdrawing from her. The look of fear on his face was a surprise; he'd not actually believed himself capable of hurting her.

Veda popped up and turned around, shoving her chest hard into his. "You think that just because I'm a stripper with tattoos and piercings that I'm automatically a whore. Shows what the fuck you know." Anger thrummed through her veins, and she saw red.

She made to move, but he scooped her up and threw her onto her back.

"Just where the fuck do you think you're going?" he growled and moved his big body atop hers. "When I'm done with you, you'll fucking know it."

His thrust this time was painful, which was just as well. Nothing hurt more than him thinking himself above her—and he had, since Halloween... but it was all her fault. She'd led him to believe she was nothing but trash, so she'd allowed him to treat her as such. She had no one to blame but herself.

Tears ran unbidden down her face as he drove deep and hard inside her, punishing them both for their wickedness, for their lust for one another. Sin had never felt so good or stung so deep as her body surrendered to his once more. As they came together, Quillan's pleasure cry was loud and deep—a mighty roar. He spilled himself inside her and continued to plunge and withdraw. Veda felt her spirit recede to some dark corner to lick her wounds.

She wasn't aware of her sobs until she felt Quillan cradling her, pulling her hard to his chest, his face resting into the space between her neck and shoulder. He stroked her hair as he pulled her up onto his lap, astraddle of his crossed legs. When Veda finally stopped crying, she looked into his eyes. Beautiful caramel brown irises stared hard into hers, dark brows furrowed on a light brown face, a face so handsome it hurt her heart.

"The number you wanted is one, Quil. One man. You. Here and now."

Quillan looked surprised, and that surprise was enough to kill her. He really *did* think so little of her.

"Now are we done here?" her tone was dismissive as her heart broke in two. "Or you wanna fuck again? Because if so, that'll cost you more money." She begged her backbone to hold up just another minute longer until she could take the last shred of confidence she had left and run out of the door.

Quillan assessed her face solemnly for a moment before he gave a simple nod and gulped hard. So he had no smart-ass comment to make back? *Figures*, Veda thought.

She moved off his lap then, holding her chin up as she achingly slowly made her way to the door, searing pain scorching her vagina from his roughness, only to stop as Quillan called, "Ved—I mean, Obsidian."

She turned, her eyes falling to his outstretched hand, his bare thighs hard and muscled, his impressive length dangling between them.

"Here," he said, a stack of hundreds in his hand.

As much as she wanted to tell him to shove the money up his arrogant ass and die a fiery death, she had as much pride as he did… and by God, she needed the money, so for the second time in two weeks, she took his cash. For the second time, she'd made herself Quillan Layton's whore.

"You can talk to me, Veda," Madam Roxie called to Veda as she pulled her knees up in the shower and let the water rain down on her.

She gasped, realizing she'd been crying for far too long. She stood and turned the water off, squeezing her hair out. She took the towel extended to her and stepped out.

Roxie, for she didn't know her real name, was the club owner; a beautiful, tall, voluptuous brunette with a sultry voice.

Veda dried herself off, wrapping the towel around her before stepping into the locker room.

"If he hurt you, that won't be tolerated here. You know that."

Veda gave her a weak smile and shook her head. "He didn't beat me."

"*Beat* you or not, he was rough, I can see the bruises on your wrists."

Sure as shit there were red and blue marks where Quil had held her hands up above her head. But the thrill that ran through her wasn't fear but raw lust. How could it be that she wanted him all over again? After how he'd talked to her and how he'd treated her? Was she a victim of some weird mental condition? Some strange fetish? She was a sadist!

"I like it rough, apparently," Veda snorted, annoyed with herself.

"You aren't the only one," Roxie's brow went up.

That's right, they didn't call her room "Roxie's room of pain" for no reason.

Veda laughed. "Thanks. I appreciate it, but I just wanna go home."

Hell, after all, Quillan had given her close to a thousand dollars. Who carried that kinda money around Atlanta? Oh yeah, professional football players—*duh*!

"Get some rest. I'll see you tomorrow."

With that, Veda thanked her, dressed, and headed home.

What she hadn't counted on was seeing her sister when she got there and the fight that followed. Her cynicism was at an all-time high and between what had happened with Quil, Becca and Pax, and worrying about everything else, Veda's patience and nerves were shot.

But then Becca told her something she hadn't ever thought was possible. There might be a way out of all this mess. A way to save them from eviction. A way to get ahead of the curve. A way to get money that would sustain them for not just tomorrow, next week, or next month but for years. And Madison McFadden held their golden ticket.

CHAPTER FIVE

V eda cleared her throat as she got off the elevator at Gladiators Headquarters, feeling sick to her stomach. Why was she doing this again? Oh yeah, because it was three million dollars and because it was what was best for her mother and sister. Or at least that's what she told herself as she approached the door labeled "Madison McFadden, CEO and VP." *Man, it must be nice to have a title like that,* Veda thought as she mustered through the last of her hesitations and knocked on the heavy oak door that the security guard had ushered her to.

A giggle and the sound of something heavy falling from the desk greeted her, along with, "Just a minute."

More than a minute passed before Brett McFadden, red faced and hair disheveled, opened the door, looking as annoyed as embarrassed. A brow went up as he looked from the security guard to Veda.

"Becca! Um, hi... uh, Mad?" He turned to look at his wife who approached, her face just as red as her husband's. It didn't take a rocket scientist to figure out what these two had been doing prior to being interrupted.

Veda couldn't help but smile, amused.

"Hi Rebecca, to what do we owe the pleasure?" Madi looked just as surprised to see "Becca" there.

Veda had taken it upon herself to imitate her sister, dressing in a long-sleeved sweater dress, glasses, and a bun. It wasn't the first time and probably wouldn't be the last. Becca had never had the guts to impersonate Veda, but it was always fun and sneaky and she'd gotten away with it. Plus, with money like this on the line, Veda couldn't possibly pass up this opportunity. Becca was too chicken to do it, so it had been left to her twin to intervene.

"Hi Madi, I um, I wanted to speak with you about something." Veda tried her best to soften her voice and sound more like Becca.

Madi seemed to take the hint—and believe her to be Becca—and nodded to her husband, who gave Veda a grin before kissing his wife's cheek and exiting her office.

Veda looked down bashfully, something her sister would do when interrupting an intimate moment between another couple, and Madi gave a little giggle.

"Bad timing, Becca, but I'll forgive you. I can see you're nervous about being here. What's on your mind?"

Veda took in a deep breath, acting as if she were torn, something her sister would be on the topic at hand. She wrung her hands so as to appear "nervous" as Madi had sensed. *Good, this is working.*

"Well, I've been considering the proposal you put forth a few weeks ago, and I think I wanna take you up on your offer."

Madi stilled in moving back to her desk, her hand going to her small baby bump. "Oh really? So... you changed your mind?" A perfectly-shaped brow lifted and Madi's eyes zeroed in on her. Veda felt like she was being squeezed. "You don't seem the type to accept a bribe, Rebecca. After all, you acted offended by the offer originally."

"Desperate times call for desperate measures, Mrs. McFadden." Veda looked up, widening her eyes as if pleading for understanding, instead of frowning like she wanted to do.

Did Madison McFadden, practically raised with a silver spoon shoved down her throat, have any idea the guts it had taken for Veda to come here and beg for help? Could she even fathom the debt and struggles the Ryans had incurred over the years? Did she have any clue as to how desperate a person had to get in order to demean themselves with a bribe? No, she'd never been in Veda, Becca, or Kathleen's shoes. How could she possibly understand!

"I'm sorry to hear that." It was a humble statement, given with a humble look as the woman took Veda's hand in her own. "Please forgive my forwardness, but are things not going well with Paxton?"

Veda nodded. "They are... I'm just..." she trailed off, not sure how to word it without sounding presumptuous. "I'm just worried about the future. I need security, and we both know how immature Paxton is. When this is over..." Veda's gut tightened at the thoughts of her sister's pain when Pax finally tired of Becca. For he would, eventually. He was a famous football player; what could Becca possibly offer him that another woman couldn't? There would always be other women fighting for his attention, and Becca was likely to lose.

It wasn't that Veda didn't love her sister and put her on a pedestal. She was beautiful, both inside and out, but Becca was too soft for this hard world. The football world, the world of fame, the spotlight. A world that Veda longed to be a part of—for some reason —but Becca never had... she wasn't prepared for all that came with it.

"I understand," Madi said and withdrew her hand from Becca's. She moved to the window, looking out at the practice field below. "You have your mother to think of."

Veda nodded. "I do, and I just can't take the chance that he'll..."

"He's a good person, a giving person, but he's got a lot of growing up to do." When Veda didn't respond, Madi continued, "But you're not a threat to me or him, are you, Rebecca?"

Madi turned and evaluated her, her blue-green eyes narrowed. "So there really isn't any 'deal' to make is there? After all, you can leave at any time."

It was true. Becca had come close to leaving him once already, and why hadn't she? But they needed the money.

"I'll do whatever I have to do."

Madi's arms came across her chest then and she tilted her blonde head. "If you leave now, it might cause more of a problem than if you'd just ended things when I made the original offer. Thanksgiving will be here soon, then Christmas and New Year's. You plan to leave *now*? The whole reason I made the offer in the first place was so you would leave in the very beginning. Now, it would just be a bad idea, causing undue negativity." Madi mulled this over as she sat down in her executive leather chair behind a large and expensive-looking mahogany desk. She shook her head. "No. I can't afford for the press to pry right now. They might unearth the truth—that you both lied to begin with. Can you wait?"

Veda's brows furrowed. She shrugged. "What do you have in mind?"

"Well, if you'll stay with Paxton at least until after the holidays, then you two can break up before the Super Bowl. That'll give us about a month in between to let the dust settle. By then we'll be Super Bowl bound and it shouldn't shed any negative light on our team. And even if it does, it won't be enough to matter...or at least, I don't think so." Madi rubbed her chin in thought. "So, here's the deal. You stay with him at least until January 2nd, then you'll go your separate ways and not tell the media anything aside from that it was a mutual decision. You won't bad mouth the team or him in any way, shape, or form, or you'll live to regret it, you got me?"

Veda simply nodded, trying to seem as genuine as Rebecca would in this situation; deep down, she wanted to tell Madi to go to hell, but of course she wouldn't.

"If you even think of betraying my trust, I'll ruin you. This goes for your sister and mother too."

Veda internally growled but cleared her throat and nodded again. "I have no reason to do so. I just want my life back." It was the truth; getting their lives back had been her sole purpose in coming here.

"Alright, as soon as you uphold your part of the deal, I'll send you the money."

"And how do I know you'll do that?"

"It's called trust. I'm sure you've heard of it."

Veda warred with that. But for this to work, they had to trust each other. For all Madi knew, she could simply walk out of the office that instant and go to the press, leaking their secrets for all the world to know. It would destroy Paxton and stain the team's good name; but Veda didn't want that for her sister either. She really simply just wanted Becca to come out of the whole incident intact—even if her virginity wasn't any longer.

"Ok." Veda sighed in finality. "It's a deal."

"Good. I'm glad we could work things out." Madi gave a soft smile then tilted her head again, thoughtfully. "How are things at the museum? I assume that incident with your stalker has settled down now, thanks to Paxton and Josh?"

What the hell was Madi talking about? *What* stalker? Becca had another stalker?

And when Veda gaped up into Madi's smirking face, she knew she'd been caught.

"Right... she didn't tell you about that—did she, *Veda?*"

"Madi, what—?"

"Don't! Don't you dare! You think I'm a fool?"

"No, of course not. I—"

"Don't worry, I'm not gonna say a word." Madi's hand went up. "Your secret is safe with me, and I do understand. I have a little sister too, you know?"

Veda pulled in a deep breath and sighed heavily.

"It took me a little while to figure it out. You two look and sound so much alike... but it was your mannerisms that were off. Your body language."

"So I guess we don't have a deal then, huh?" Veda grumbled.

"Oh, we have a deal alright. And when that deal is done, I'm washing my hands of the both of you."

We'll just see about that, won't we? Veda thought and turned on her heel to leave.

She was hyperventilating by the time she got back in the elevator and almost plunged headlong into Brooke Taylor on the way out.

"Becca! Jeez, are you alright?"

Dammit! Was she really crying again? What the hell was her problem lately?

"Oh yes, fine. I'm sorry, Brooke."

"Hey, wait up. I was gonna ask you about your sister."

"My—my sister?"

"Yeah, remember, you'd mentioned that she was interested in modeling? I got a gig I wanted to run by her. You got her number?"

Veda looked Brooke's face over for a second, unsure if she should give Brooke her number. Why did she feel like there was more to it than that? What would she be required to do? Wasn't Brooke bisexual and shown interest in Veda at the Halloween party a couple weeks ago?

"Uh yeah, you wanna give me your phone?"

Fuck it! Whatever it took to break into modeling and out of stripping at *RISE*, she'd do it. *Anything* was better than selling her soul on stage every night while secretly pining for Quillan Layton to come ravish her again. Right?

QUILLAN LOOKED at Becca the day after Thanksgiving with a big smile on his face. God, she looked so much like Veda; twins and all…

"How's your sister?" he couldn't help but ask when Pax walked away to talk to Jerry, the owner of their team.

"Veda? She's good."

"Is she, uh, she still working at *RISE*?"

Becca's brows went up in surprise at his question, and he could've cursed himself to Hell and back. *Dammit!* Veda hadn't discussed their meeting there or what had happened. Then again, why would she? It was more violent than any sexual encounter he'd ever had. He'd been the aggressor, he'd been rough and, God help him, he'd fucking loved it!

Becca blushed and looked down as she answered with, "Uh, yeah... for now. But I think she's planning to quit soon."

Quil was shocked at the way his heart dropped at that revelation. "Oh? What's she doing in the meantime?" He scolded himself for needing info about Veda even as he looked over at Quinn in Travis's arms at the bountiful buffet table and smiled at his angelic daughter. He had to stop this thing with Veda before it ever began. She was bad news and he was vulnerable...apparently.

"She's actually been modeling with Brooke."

Quil literally took a step back. Modeling, huh? That was surprising. He didn't know she was interested in that. "Oh cool. Well good. I wish her the best of luck."

Becca's eyes lingered on him for a moment longer, as if she wanted to say more on the matter but didn't. She gave him a weak smile and turned as Pax rounded the corner with a couple drinks.

"Here you go, Amphitrite. One whiskey sour for my little lass." Pax handed her the highball glass and toasted to Quil's soda.

"Happy Thanksgiving, buddy."

"Happy Thanksgiving, Pax." Quil nodded to his LB and his fiancée, the one who looked far too much like the woman he'd not been able to get off his mind since Halloween night.

Travis brought Quinn over, who giggled as she was set down. Linc's twins ran over then, each one taking a hand of Quinn's, who looked up at Quil then with an innocent face, and they ran off squealing. Quil chuckled, again thinking of Veda. Dammit, when was he gonna stop this charade? It wasn't healthy. She wasn't the right woman for him, and he knew it. She would only bring him and Quinn heartbreak, and they'd both been through enough with Rian's addiction and death. He wouldn't put his daughter through that shit ever again.

But Veda didn't do drugs. Despite her weird sense of style, her disreputable jobs, and irresponsibility, it was obvious from her health that she didn't abuse her body that way. Well, at least nothing as potent as heroin or cocaine from what he could tell. He'd looked for tracks on her arms and feet the last time they'd been together, even though he couldn't see much in the darkness of the club.

Plus, she took care of her sick mother; one wouldn't be able to do that if they were high or coming down, he knew.

He looked back over at Pax and Becca; despite that their relationship had been impromptu, they seemed happy with one another. Pax seemed different and in a good way; his head wasn't as far up his ass.

"Doing ok, Quil?" Madi asked as she patted his bicep.

"I am, thanks for asking. And you?"

"I'm just trying to get through this first trimester. Please tell me it gets easier," Madi grumbled and looked green around the gills.

Quil couldn't help but grin at the blonde beauty, the queen of the gods herself. Even fighting her morning sickness, pregnancy became her. "Rian, my wife, didn't handle the first trimester well either. But it did get better for her after the first third of the pregnancy." Quil could recall how much she'd glowed; it was the most beautiful she'd been following their wedding, before her health declined and she got so skinny she was a practical skeleton.

"Oh good, I'm glad to hear it."

"I know you've probably heard this before, but it's totally worth it."

Madi grinned as she watched Quinn chasing after the boys. They were so sweet with her. It made Quil want another baby, he realized painfully. But in order to have another baby, he'd need a stable relationship; the risk of that was more than he was willing to take.

"You guys ready to eat?" Brett asked as his arm wrapped around his wife's waist and she settled against him. His eyes saw nothing but hers, and Quil envied their love even as he knew he'd never feel that way again, ever. Nothing softened the tough Zeus like being in the presence of his queen; the peace oozed from them and made Quil's brooding all the more poignant.

Val and Linc each grabbed a twin and pulled them over to the kitchen island as Quil's hands rested on his daughter's shoulders. She looked back at him and he grinned. As much as he adored his child, and knew that nothing would ever make him as happy as being a father, he wondered if his heart could be opened again. He knew it would take a woman like Madi, Sky, Val, or Becca in order to do so as he heard Skyla giggle over at Travis. Her smile was so playful, Quil longed to know the secret behind it.

What was his deal today?

The holidays; that had to be it. He was simply more keenly aware of his solitude this time of year. But deep down he knew it was more and that Veda Ryan had stirred feelings within him he hadn't felt in a long time.

After a delicious meal and memorable dinner of traditional Thanksgiving foods, everyone sat around with a helping of dessert, coffee, and after-dinner drinks. Some talked, some watched the Bears v. Vikings game, some were outside playing cornhole and laughing. Quil headed toward TJ and Brooke who talked with Berkeley White.

"Dude no, that is *not* how it works," Berk shoved TJ as Brooke leaned against him with a smirk.

"How what works?" Quil asked.

Berk turned as red as the Jell-O mold Travis was feeding to his nephew, Lennox.

"A threesome," TJ answered for him, and Quil's brows shot up to his forehead.

"A threesome?" Quil couldn't help but scoff. "What the hell does TJ need to know about a threesome?"

"A lot, apparently," Brooke giggled and took another sip of her martini.

"You're the one who needs to know, not even participating. Hell, that's not a threesome at all then. That's you fuckin' while someone else watches and masturbates," he told Brooke and TJ, who laughed loudly.

Jesus, the conversations they all had sometimes. It was ludicrous.

"Lord help, I think I chose to walk up at the wrong time." Quil shook his head.

"Wait! Answer honestly, Hades, if you were gonna participate in a threesome between yourself and two chicks, wouldn't you be hammering the ass of one while the other sits on your face or somethin'?"

Quil tried to keep his composure. What the hell kinda question was that? "I dunno, Berk. I've never participated in one."

"Maybe we should make it a foursome then, what'd ya say, baby?" The look TJ gave Brooke said lots, and Quil looked down, amused.

"Quil, you've really never had a threesome?" Brooke looked over at Quil then, stunned, her lips puckered.

He shook his head. "No *señorita*, I haven't. Can't say as I would, either."

"And why the hell not?" TJ frowned at him as if he were nuts.

"Only got one dick, buddy, and my attention span is low." He elbowed Berkeley, who laughed heartily at him.

"I bet it'd be fun to watch you fuck 'er though." Brooke licked her plump lips and eyed Quil deceptively.

He smirked, "Who?"

"Veda."

At the name, Quil stilled. What the hell was Brooke talking about?

Before she could answer him, Berk took over. "Yeah, apparently Brooke bribed this hot ex-stripper into a threesome, but told her she didn't have to participate if she wasn't comfortable with it. So they've been watching her touch herself while fucking. Isn't that jacked up?"

Brooke's brow rose in defiance, and Quil's stomach fell to the floor.

He didn't know whether to hurl, swear, or laugh. Holy fucking shit! Brooke was as ruthless as fuckin' Veda was, but to think she'd stoop so low as to ask that of Veda. Anger won out and he scowled over at Brooke. "Just when I think you can't surprise me anymore, you go and do so. You're *all* fifty shades of fucked up, aren't you, Taylor?"

Brooke giggled, unperturbed. "You have no idea, Quillan."

"Sick. That's what you are, *puta loco.*"

"Don't knock it 'til you try it, Hades," Brooke grabbed his arm as he moved to escape. The air felt stifling, despite that they were outside.

"Don't touch me," Quil growled, angry with her for tricking Veda into a modeling career with such an unorthodox proposal. "I'd hate to think I'd have to resort to blackmailing someone into fucking around with me in order to trick them into doing something they always wanted to do… You knew she wasn't a lesbian, why push it?"

"Just another fallen angel to pull to Hell with me." Brooke's eyes were hollow as they held his.

"You're twisted, but even I didn't know how low you were. Now I do. What beast destroyed you so badly that you'd demean yourself to such corruption, Brooke?" his tone had softened as the hurt of what she'd done to Veda took hold. Veda, who'd suffered her own lot in life—he was sure. For her to go from being his call girl only to become Brooke Taylor's now… It was wrong, and Quil hated injustice, even if Veda wasn't the greatest person in the world herself.

"We all have a price, Quillan. Even you." Brooke's voice dropped. "And anytime you're up for the challenge, I'd love to see you with her, right in front of my eyes… until then, I'll have my puppet on her string."

With that Brooke cackled and walked away, leaving Quillan to choke down his rage at the thoughts of Veda being so helpless, even if he'd not treated her any better than a mere puppet himself the last time he'd taken her.

CHAPTER SIX

Veda gulped in deep breaths as she awoke in a sweat, the nightmare coming back to her sharply. Only it wasn't a nightmare, it was a memory.

"FATHER..."

"You must! This is your *sin to absolve. With all that's happened with yer Mam and sister, how could ye be so selfish? Oh wait, I know, because you're the* evil twin." *It hadn't been the first time her father had said it, and it wouldn't be the last. His anger was all encompassing now though as he slammed his fist down onto the steering wheel.*

He was furious with her, not just because of the fact that she'd had premarital sex and gotten pregnant, but because she'd caught him red-handed having an affair. Of which he'd blamed her for that, too. Her evilness was leaching out into the world, he'd said, and had corrupted him too, which accounted for the position she'd found him in a week ago. Now this was recompense for his imagined slights—an eye for an eye, so to speak.

"Ye've made yer bed, now yer to lay in it, ye hear? Go, take care of it.

We have enough to deal with. We don't need a bastard babe of yourn to have to worry about now, too."

Veda couldn't believe this was happening, couldn't believe her father would betray her like this. She was just a girl. A girl who'd fallen in love with a boy. A boy who'd impregnated her with his child and abandoned her. A boy who'd washed his hands of her when she'd told him, as her father was now doing too.

Take care of it! Like it was a paper cup to be thrown into the receptacle: unwanted, shameful, distasteful, unbearable. Veda not only felt soiled, she felt unworthy, contaminated. Her father had made her grovel as he'd driven to the clinic, grovel for the unborn baby inside her, the life that would never be because he was unable to make ends meet as it was; conventional to wayward thinkers and intolerable of her 'immortal sins', as he'd called them —sins that weren't so different from his own.

"Ye put your family in a dire predicament, Veda Angeline, and God will punish ye greatly. Mark me. Ye'd best pray for your soul and that of this child, for you're damning him to Hell even now."

She hated her father at that moment as she'd sobbed and grabbed his lapels, pleading with him to not force her to do this. That she'd never tell Becca or Mam about anything, but she was in fact a minor; her health and her child's in his hands, not her own, and there was nothing more she could do.

He literally shoved her into the clinic, filled out all the necessary paper-work, and watched as the nurses began assisting her to the door that sealed her fate. He'd lied and told them this baby was going to kill his daughter and it had to go.

"Father, please?" she begged once more, reaching for him.

His deep green eyes burned hard into hers, his face sterner than she'd ever seen it.

"I can no longer stand by and watch you destroy my family," he whispered into her ear, making it appear as if he were hugging her. "You're a rotten egg, and your curse has touched us all. One bad apple ruins the bunch and you, Veda, have been a bad apple since the day ye were born. I wash my hands of ye."

. . .

VEDA COULD STILL HEAR the plea come from the depths of her soul, the sounds of her father's footfalls as he'd exited, leaving her alone to kill the unborn fetus growing in her womb.

Tears streamed down her face even now as hate, guilt, rage, and regret filled her. He'd abandoned her, his child, while she had her own aborted at 16 weeks' gestation that fateful December day almost ten years ago. The memory never failed to rip her heart out, depress her, and make her sick as it was now. She pulled her knees into her chest and breathed deeply.

She tried to tell herself that she'd been too young, she'd had no choice, that it was what had been best, that she couldn't have kept it —monetarily, religiously, or socially. But the stigma of what she'd done had never left her—and never would as long as she lived.

She was able to keep her stomach contents down and pulled herself from bed, noting the clock only read 9 PM. She knew that this nightmare always plagued her when she was stressed, when something bad had happened, or when her emotions were high, and those three things were happening simultaneously. It didn't help that she'd had no one to share the burden with—her mother and Becca had never known the truth.

Following the abortion, she'd called her best friend, Anna, and stayed with her that weekend. She acted surprised when she came home to find that her father was missing. She even volunteered to help search, when deep down she'd known he'd hightailed it out of there, assuming his daughter would spill all the untold secrets; after all, she was the spawn of Satan, or some equally as corrupt being, in his eyes.

So Veda had made it a point to become the "bad girl" he'd always accused her of being; she'd been careless with her decisions, body, and careers. If Niall Ryan believed her to be a wicked bean sí— banshee—of old, then Veda was going to own it. After all, she'd never lived up to her father's expectations. Looking back, she realized he was nothing but a superstitious and paranoid zealot who'd made ridiculous accusations about her from the time her life began. He'd had some silly notion that her and Becca's twinly powers were of the Devil, and that Veda was Rebecca's fetch—doppelgänger— bringing the church in many times to bless their house of evil.

Becca had only remembered the praises their father had given her and his love. She'd never been aware of how deranged he actually was, and Veda had never enlightened her. It had been her own cross to bear in the end, no need to have her sister's childhood ruined by something no one could change now.

But it had always caused an invisible rift between them, a wedge Veda had never been able to mend. Becca knew Veda had been keeping something dark from her; she'd pleaded with her to expel her secrets many times over the last decade, but Veda simply couldn't hurt her sister to clear her own conscience. She loved her far too much to burden her with her disreputable past.

Veda pulled herself from her bed and moved into the kitchen to grab a drink of water.

She was wide awake now and decided to sit down to her laptop and watch Disney +. She'd barely got the browser up when the door opened and her sister came in, red-faced and dejected looking. "I told you so," just didn't seem to do the cause justice, so Veda raised a brow and waited for her twin to speak first.

"How *could* you?" Becca asked and threw her bag down dramatically into the empty recliner next to her.

"One day you'll thank me for getting you out of this mess," Veda smarted.

"I don't *need* you to rescue me, Veda."

"Obviously you do!" Veda couldn't help the snort at the back of her throat.

"I didn't tell you to go to Madison. I was going to—"

"*No*, you weren't. You would've chickened out like you do everything else. We need that money and now this BS is over and done with." Veda crossed her arms over her chest in finality.

"You could've given me a heads up. You made me look like a fool."

"Oh, you got to be the bad guy for a change? So sorry, little nun. Doesn't feel so good, does it? But someone has to do the dirty deeds around here." Veda shrugged, feeling unsympathetic.

"Not every man is evil, Vey."

Tears glistened in her twin's eyes and the lack of sympathy Veda didn't have came flooding in. "I just brought you to reality before he had a chance to break your heart in two, like he would've if you'd a'let him."

"I can stand up for myself."

"No, you can't! You're soft, just like Mammy."

It might hurt, but it was true. They were three strong and independent women, but when it came to men, making tough decisions, or letting someone down, Becca and Mam turned to mush. Someone had to hold down the fort, and it always fell on Veda to do it.

"I want you to stay out of my business from now on. I mean it." Becca pointed her finger at her sister. The audacity!

"Oh, did you grow a set of balls, little sis? Well grand, since you don't *need* me anymore, I'll be in my room!" Anger overtook Veda then and she stalked off, slamming her door with force.

This is the thanks I get? After all the shit I've done for her! Veda had practically sold her soul to keep her family safe; but instead of being grateful, Becca was misplacing her anger and pain at Veda. It didn't take the sting away, even if she knew Bec would eventually apologize and they would be right as rain again soon enough. They never could stay mad at each other for very long, after all.

But there was a storm building, Veda could feel it; she feared this deluge was turning into a super cell, growing with force as it threatened all they held dear. There were too many secrets, too much unrest between the two of them, and soon, a heart-wrenching climax would come.

Veda prayed they were prepared for the force and the aftermath of what their deceptions had come to. Veda had a lot to answer for. As her mam used to say, *"Your chickens have come home to roost, lass."*

QUILLAN SIGHED DEEPLY as he suited up that night, his heart heavy for his teammate Travis and the loss of his unborn child. Quil couldn't even comprehend how difficult that must be; the chronic illness of his own child was never far from his mind. Travis and Sky were so happy, and Trav had been looking forward to having a baby with her. He'd just told them all so recently, too.

Quil's mood didn't improve as the night progressed and his team continued to receive the beating of their season through the first half of the game. Each yard felt practically unobtainable as they got their butts handed to them.

Brett, their stoic QB, was grimmer than ever as he slammed Paxton against his locker after he smarted off; kid was gonna get his ass kicked if he didn't pull his head out of it. He was cool and easy-going, but damn, he was so self-serving sometimes. *Oh, to be so clueless*, Quil thought.

Pax looked like he'd been slapped as Brett enlightened him about the spontaneous miscarriage following Skyla's car accident.

"Quil, let's go show these Chiefs that the Gods of the Gridiron aren't backing down without a fight," Brett remarked after he let Paxton go and turned. "Let's go win this game—for Ares."

"For Ares!" Quil nodded and gave Zeus a fist bump.

Quil followed Brett out of the tunnel and back onto the field, along with the rest of the team. They were more pumped, more aware of the stigma of the loss, more knowledgeable of what this win would mean—despite that Travis's talent and contagious attitude were greatly needed at that moment.

But the air had changed, and every one of his teammates looked ready to be the gods of their namesakes.

Quil took the field with his offense. They'd chosen to defer at the coin toss, so they got the ball first in the second half.

At kickoff, their special teams had received the football and ran it to the thirty-five; good field position considering the shitty start to their game.

Quil's head was solidly in the play as Brett went into a shotgun formation first thing, motioning for his receivers to go wide. Quil took off running downfield, getting open, and waving his arm for Zeus to throw him a thunderbolt.

The pass that came at him was perfectly thrown and the aim true as it hit him between the numbers. Hades tucked the ball into the crook of his arm and headed into the red zone, chariot ablaze. He practically hurdled a defender as he leapt into the end zone, aiming for the pylon.

He was aware of the roaring crowd chanting the namesake of the god he'd been deemed and saw the ref with both arms raised, signaling a TD.

Quillan jumped up and into the arms of their center, Robicheaux, who laughed heartily and slammed a big palm down onto his helmet. Quil laughed and began a victory dance, the adrenaline coursing through him like rivulets in a whirlpool.

It was a strong start to the third quarter. The extra point was kicked and the opposing offense took the field. The Gladiators defense stopped the run with a turn-over on their fourth down.

Quil was back on the field before he'd had time to catch his breath, but it didn't matter because he was pumped up and ready to score again.

He played defense as Zeus handed the ball off to RB Bennett Jackson, blocking a defender from smashing into him as he ran up the middle, spun, and shifted left for a fifteen-yard run.

In three plays, they were back in the red zone again, and Brett ran the ball in himself for another TD.

They were back on the board, and it didn't appear they'd be going down without a close comeback when the offense fumbled and Linc grabbed the ball up for an interception.

By their tenth offensive play in the third quarter, Quil was tiring but his resolve was clear. If they lost this game, it wasn't gonna be because they didn't want it bad enough. Quil and Brett were on the same page, play for play, move for move and yard for yard. They were seamless as they progressed forward, moving the ball slowly back toward the goal line.

It was fourth and inches when Brett smirked and read the blitz coming. He turned his upper body toward the sidelines and gave the ref the "Timeout" signal.

"Let's switch up one of our underutilized plays, full-back dive. Quil, you're gettin' the ball." Brett said as he huddled them together before the thirty second timeout was done.

They put their hands in for a "G.O.G" then separated and moved to their respective positions.

Quil filled the full back position as Brett took the snap and handed it off to him. Hades, with his head down and shoulder pads square, ran it up the middle, pushing back the defensive line. The sound of pad-clad bodies colliding and helmets clashing echoed in his ears. He could hear the deafening cheering of the crowd as he gained the necessary yards for the first down.

But he wasn't done; no, he had his eyes on the prize and he was free to run across the goal line for yet another six points.

The lights were bright, the chanting of his namesake making him raise his arms in victory. He felt like the god of everything but death and the Underworld as he was recognized for his quick moves. It was a surreal feeling as his team ran to him and clapped his helmet, back, and shoulders. They ran over to a camera and began their practiced team victory pose.

Soon, the defense was taking the field and Quil was breathless as he and Brett moved to the bench to remove their helmets and re-hydrate.

"Damn! The tables have turned, man. All we need is one more touchdown and we'll win this thing."

"We can do this, Zeus."

Zeus smirked and nodded. "We can, Hades. Thanks to you."

"Me? There's no I in team, Cap."

"Yeah, yeah, but with Trav out, we're all feeding off of you right now."

"Nah, you Brett, you're the leader. I'm just following you."

And Quil realized he would follow the mighty Zeus, for he had befriended the man and respected the hell out of him. He'd follow him right into the playoffs and beyond.

VEDA RECALLED her words to Becca a few nights ago, still feeling the same shame, anger, and resentment at her situation mount as she moved through the doors of the hospital.

"HE THINKS I'm a bad news slut."

"Were those his words?" Becca wore an expression of surprise; no, of course those hadn't been his words, they'd been Veda's.

"I know that's what he thinks of me," she huffed with a sharp tone, knowing it was true.

"Wait, what aren't you saying?"

"I saw him, at RISE week before last."

"Oh." Becca blushed.

"I'll be quitting soon by the way, as soon as I can get a steady thing going with modeling."

"I'm glad to hear that." Veda knew how much Bec hated that she was a stripper...as much as her mam would if she knew.

"I got a few promising gigs from Brooke," Veda answered and lowered her eyes. She wouldn't mention what she'd been conned into doing in order to get them.

"Oh, good. I'm so glad."

Veda gave her a withered smile. "She said I have a lot of potential." Among other things, *Veda thought.*

"See, our lives don't suck as bad as you thought, lassie."

"Don't say that," Veda felt herself shudder; Bec had no idea how bad things sucked for them at the moment.

"What is it, Vey? Please tell me. You know you can talk to me about anything."

"I know, and I'm so grateful you're my sister. But I feel so ashamed." The shame of all the things that had happened recently was enough to suck her down into the very pit of despair.

"Why? There's nothing for you to be ashamed about."

"But there is... Becca, Quil and I didn't use protection at the Halloween party." Veda exhaled, steeling her nerves in order to regurgitate her ultimate mortification. "I didn't even think about it at the time. I mean, we were in the moment and it was so unexpected... I just took a test, and Becca, it's positive."

Becca looked at her with intense apprehension. "Vey, what—?"

"And I can't keep it, God knows I should, but I can't have a child born out of wedlock, Mam has enough to worry about... but it's eating me up inside." V began to sob, thinking about having to have another abortion and what it was going to do to her mental state, but they were just too broke, struggling to make it as it was.

"Wait! Veda, what are you saying?" Becca's voice echoed in her ears.

Veda felt Becca squeeze her hand and the look in her twin's eyes pierced her soul. "Becca, I'm pregnant."

SHE COULDN'T BELIEVE IT. Pregnant. Again. What the hell had she been thinking not using protection? She'd been a fool. Quillan had been a fool.

And now he would think she was even more of a bad news slut— a bad news slut who'd tricked him into knocking her up. She could just hear him now; broody asshole that he was cussing her out for being so careless.

"Veda!" came a sweet little voice V recognized, and her stomach dropped as she saw Quinn running toward her.

Oh, God, where's her father? Veda thought and looked around frantically.

"Quinn. Hey honey," Veda stated with a grunt as Quinn squeezed her tightly before pulling back to beam into her face.

"I missed you! I'm so glad you're here."

"I missed you too, sweetie. Uh, where's your dad?"

"He's at practice. I have Brandy with me today."

Quinn pointed to Brandy, a short blonde with the bluest eyes Veda had ever seen and a smile that was genuine. Veda waved and smiled back at the woman now approaching them.

"I'm gonna go with Veda now, thanks Brandy." When Brandy went to protest, Quinn added, "It's ok, she knows my dad. She's a volunteer here, too."

Veda snorted a stifled laugh before standing from her crouch in front of Quinn to show Brandy the lanyard with her badge around her neck. Brandy nodded and moved away.

The fact that Veda knew Quinn's dad and knew him *well*—well, his body anyway—caused the pit in Veda's stomach to return. She was also pregnant with Quinn's brother or sister, and that concept blew her mind. *Well, actually, no, you won't be for long. You're gonna abort it, aren't you?* The angel on her shoulder reminded her, and she almost whimpered aloud.

"Where've you been?" Quinn asked, her little brows drawing.

"Oh, just here and there. Looking for work and taking care of Mam."

"Who's Mam?"

"My mother. Wanna meet her?" Veda checked her watch. She was going to have to head over and grab her.

Quinn nodded vigorously as she took Veda's hand, and they began to head out the doors of one hospital and into the courtyard of the other.

Quinn jabbered away, a mile a minute talking about all things that fascinated a six-year-old with a heart bigger than the anxiety clenching Veda's heart. She found herself lighter in the little girl's presence, her precociousness ebbing away at Veda's thoughts for the time being.

"So, your mommy is sick?" she asked, and Veda nodded. "Mine was, too. I didn't see her much."

"I'm sorry," Veda frowned. She didn't know a lot about Quil's deceased wife and hadn't been of a mind—or position—to discuss her when they'd been together.

"Yeah, maybe I'll get a new mom; I would like that."

This kid deserved a great mom. A great mom who adored her in every way because she was one of the most lovable kids Veda had ever been around.

She gave her a smile even as her own mother walked out into the front atrium of the hospital to meet them.

"Well, well, who have we here?" Kathleen asked and smiled down at Quinn.

Quinn introduced herself and greeted Veda's mam with delight. "Hi, Mam. I'm Quinn."

Kathleen gave a laugh and said, "It's good to meet ye, Quinn. You can call me Grand Mam, if you'd like."

Veda gulped at that title. She wanted to confess her secrets to her mother and tell her she was indeed going to be a grand mammy. But she'd never break her mother or Quinn's hearts like that. For now, she kept it all inside, wishing things could be different, that she didn't have to destroy yet another life before it began. But there wasn't any other choice. She wouldn't hurt her mother or this sweet child of Quillan Layton's any more than they'd already been hurt.

She resigned herself to the task at hand and asked, "You guys hungry?"

"Starved," both her mam and Quinn answered simultaneously, giggling at one another, and they all set off for lunch.

CHAPTER SEVEN

"Veda, you *don't* have to do this," Becca insisted, taking her twin's hand. The last couple days, things had been as good as they used to be between the two of them—back when they were kids and didn't have a care in the world aside from daydreaming about Brad Pitt, shooting for the stars, and falling in love with love. What a joke! There was no such thing as true love; it was a myth.

Despite that Pax had apologized to Becca, confessed his love, and promised to care for her, Veda wasn't convinced that what they had was "true love". She was happy for her sister, she was convinced Pax felt *something* for Becca. Hell, he had to. Why else would he "slum it"?

But that didn't mean it was everlasting love.

Maybe Veda was just cynical and bitter. Maybe she was wrong. Maybe she was numb to love. All because she'd decided to—once more—destroy a life growing inside her. It hadn't been an easy decision. Not any easier than walking into the clinic the last time had been, but here she was.

She looked over at the clock above the door of the solemn-as-hell waiting area, feeling like a traitor to women everywhere. She kept telling herself she was making the right decision, that it was what was best under the circumstances, that it was all going to be ok. Another bold-faced lie. She was *never* going to be ok after this. She'd done it once before as a minor, a mere child herself, unable to change the mind of her father's stern authority.

But Veda was a responsible adult now, and she would live to regret this decision for the rest of her life because it wasn't really and truly what she wanted. But her mother didn't need any more worries in her life; an unplanned baby keeping her awake at night while she had chemicals pumped into her body and tried to fight lymphoma wouldn't help their situation. And financially, Veda couldn't afford any more bills. Babies were expensive, and she couldn't even hold down a stable job. Being a stripper/model wasn't exactly the role model she imagined for a child of hers, not that she'd ever imagined getting pregnant out of wedlock or having to make the dreadful decision she had to again either.

She felt her stomach take and gulped down the bile burning the back of her throat.

Becca had been so sweet and understanding when Veda had made the suggestion of abortion. "No, it's ok, we can do this. A baby is a wonderful surprise."

A wonderful surprise! That was putting it mildly. *An unexpected, expensive, and unwanted surprise!* Veda had wanted to shout. And fathered by a man who practically hated its mother. And wouldn't want it either. What kind of child wanted to be born into a world with a father like hers had been? What kind of person would that make her?

"Veda, you need to think about this. We can figure it out. We'll make it work!" Becca had pleaded when Veda insisted she had to terminate the pregnancy.

"We can't afford it!" Veda had shouted in anger. How could Becca even suggest that? It wasn't an option.

"But Pax—"

"No, don't you dare! Leave your former-fake-now-real fiancé out of this. It's not his place, and I *refuse* to take his charity." Veda's eyes had narrowed, burning into her sister's, daring her to argue.

Becca had lowered her head then, the last of her resolve taken from her sails. She sat quietly fiddling with her hands before she said, "Veda, abortion is—"

"I know," Veda had finished for her. It was murder, against their religion, and highly controversial. So was using condoms, but Veda did that anyway too; along with getting tattoos, having premarital relations, and stripping for money. What was one more sin in the line of sins she'd already committed?

Veda had begun to sob then, her hands shaking with the overwhelming need to expel her long-bottled secrets; they'd all come flooding out in a ramble of gasps.

She'd told her twin sister everything. From the minute she'd realized she was pregnant at sixteen, to seeing their dad's affair up close and personal, and him accidentally hearing the conversation she'd had with her boyfriend, Will, when he'd told her he didn't want their baby. Veda told Becca how she'd begged and pleaded for her father not to take her to the clinic, not to make her kill her baby, how he'd always felt about her... *Everything*.

When she'd finished and her tears had been spent, she'd looked up into eyes so understanding that it had taken her breath.

"Oh Veda," Becca had gasped on a sob and pulled Veda to her shaking frame. "I'm so sorry. I had no idea. I knew that the breakup with Will was hard, but now I know why you got so depressed after. I thought it was just the combination of Sarah dying and Mam getting sick and..."

"It was all those things and so much more, Bec."

"I'm so sorry," Becca had said again.

"You always loved Pa so much and saw only the good in him. I couldn't take that last shred of light away from you, not when I was plunged into such darkness by what he did. I couldn't force you into it with me."

They'd held each other for a long time after that, just comforting one another; for a lost child, a lost father, a lost sister—loss, the pungent sting of it.

Now, here they sat. Veda facing another abortion she didn't want but not understanding how she possibly had any other choice. They'd given Madison's money back to her. It hadn't been right to keep it, and Pax had already paid the hospital bills for their mother. Veda wouldn't—couldn't—ask any more from him, even if he had millions to give. This was her screw-up and she would face the consequences of her own actions, no matter that her heart burned with regret, loathing, and torment or that her stomach was threatening to evacuate its scarce contents into the nearest trash can.

Becca went back with Veda when her name was called, holding tightly to her hand as the room spun upon entering it.

Veda didn't even have time to grab the exam table or hear the nurse's instructions as she began to fall, losing consciousness.

Her last shred of awareness was hearing Becca call her name, saying, "I'm here, Veda. I'm right here."

"I love you so much, pookey," Will said as he stroked her cheek, his body still jerking as he came down from his climax.

"I love you," she murmured and kissed his lips, adoring every inch of his tall, lanky frame atop hers.

She hadn't told him about the baby yet, but she knew it wouldn't matter. He would love her no matter what. He'd said he did, and he'd always meant what he said.

They'd been together for two years, having sex for just the last three months, losing their virginities together that junior prom night.

It was midsummer now and the cab of his Nissan Altima was humid. Veda smiled at the fog covering the windows and the smell of their love thick in the air.

She giggled as he began to kiss her breasts and belly and gripped his jet-black hair as his tongue licked her belly button.

Suddenly, the visions changed, and she was sobbing on the phone with him.

"I'm sorry. I—"

"Sorry doesn't cut it, Veda! My parents are gonna freak. What about my tennis scholarship? Am I just supposed to throw all that away because you got yourself knocked up?"

She didn't correct him—he'd been the one to knock her up, not the other way around!

"Please? I don't know what—"

"I know. How about get rid of it? I mean, how do I even know that it's mine?"

Her heart literally froze in her chest. He hadn't really said that, had he? How could he ever think it was anyone else's; she'd never been with anyone but Will.

She stayed quiet at that moment, afraid to speak for her soul was imploding into itself. After several moments she said, "Will, the baby is yours."

Will sighed heavily and huffed out, "You know what? It's your problem, Veda, not mine. So you deal with it."

The sound of the line going dead beeped into her ear, echoing through space and time to the moment she'd been forced to go through with killing the first child she'd gotten pregnant with. She was aware of lights blinding her eyes as she laid back on the exam table, feet up in stirrups, her naked body covered by a gown. Her legs quaked as she was touched by a gloved hand that ran down her inner thigh, the invasive gesture making her stomach clench even as her heart hardened.

"Shh, it's alright. You'll feel some pressure now, ok, Veda?"

Pressure was an understatement; pain was all she felt. Pain and lots of it.

It ripped through her center, into her womb, up her belly, into her chest... Her heart felt like it was literally being torn in two.

She screamed.

And screamed.

And screamed.

. . .

VEDA WAS aware that she was still screaming as she awoke from the visions, aware that she was flat on her back, on an exam table. Just as she'd been ten years ago.

She shot up as fast as lightning, her hand falling between her legs. Momentary relief shot through her to feel her jeans covering her crotch.

The nurse's hands came up in surrender. Veda noticed her sister was standing beside her, tears falling down her face, tears like the ones soaking Veda's own cheeks.

"It's alright," The scrub clad woman said.

"Did I go through with it? Is the baby gone?" Panic threatened her throat as her hand fell to her belly.

"No ma'am, we haven't even gotten started."

"Oh, thank God!" Veda's head fell back, and she squeezed her eyes shut in silent prayer.

"You passed out. The doctor wants to—"

"Oh, no. I'm fine. Thank you very much. But that won't be necessary." The nurse frowned at Veda even as she turned to her sister. "Let's go, Becca."

She was all too aware of the palpable relief on Becca's face as she got slowly off the table, and they walked out the exam room door.

QUILLAN SMIRKED at Paxton as Pax's lips drew in and he eyed him in the shower room mirror for the third time. How long did it take someone to brush his teeth? And what was going on with Paxton today?

"Alright, *gringo*, you're starting to creep me out. I thought you and Becca were a serious thing now. Are you having second thoughts? Because if you tell me you're into me, I might just punch you today."

Pax's shoulders fell and he pulled a deep breath in, spitting and rinsing before slamming his toothbrush back into a little baggie and turning toward Quil.

"If you knew something but you weren't supposed to tell it, but you knew it could save a life, would you?" Paxton's blond brows furrowed and he planted his hands on his towel-covered hips.

Quil's brow shot up and he smirked again. "What is this, high school all over again?"

"Seriously, Quil!" Paxton's frown deepened and he gulped.

"I mean," Quil shrugged, then crossed his arms over his chest. "It's life and death so that makes it important."

"Exactly!" Pax nodded.

"Let me guess, it's between your girl and her sister?"

It didn't take a rocket scientist to figure that out, especially when Pax looked away for a second.

"Come into the sauna with me," Pax grated and moved off, looking dejected.

Quil started to make a smart-assed retort back but held his tongue, not used to seeing the smiling Pax so out of sorts. He followed wordlessly.

When Pax closed the door to the empty sauna, he crossed his arms over his chest and propped himself against the wall. "Alright, Pax, what did Becca do? What's so heavy that it's weighing you down so, *amigo?*"

"I overheard her and Veda talking about going to a clinic. An *abortion* clinic," Pax explained, his cheeks flaming red. "I know it's none of my business, and I should stay out of it and all but…" He trailed off and turned away, shaking his head.

Quillan patted his friend's bare shoulder, feeling sympathetic for his plight. After all, Becca could have at least talked to him about being pregnant and given him a choice. "Look, I know that you're pro-life and all, merman, but—"

"Pro-*life?*" Pax turned and gave Quil a frown. "It's not just that I'm pro-life, dude. I mean, I *am* pro-life and—Dammit, never mind all that. If it were *my* kid, I'd wanna know!" He shouted and grumbled again. "I mean, Hell—here's Travis, who just lost his unborn baby in a car accident, and Veda is willingly disposing of *yours*." Pax turned then and stared hard into Quil's eyes.

Quil literally felt the wind get knocked out of his sails, his stomach sank and he bent double, holding his middle. He was gonna be sick. What had Paxton just said? *His*? It was Veda who was pregnant, and the baby was *his*?

He had a quick flashback of Halloween night, of the sexy seductress Medusa. Not wearing a condom. Fast forward to just weeks ago when he'd taken her at the club. Again, no condom. Dammit! Her words had haunted him these last few weeks, embedding in his brain at night, keeping him from a restful sleep. *One. One man. You*! Of course she was pregnant. And of course he was the father! Damn fate and its conniving plans. Or had she intentionally done this? As a means to get his attention...his money?

"Fuck," Quil squatted down then fell forward on all fours, aware of only the ringing in his ears. Halloween night had been just over six weeks ago. It was possible. It was very, very possible.

But this wasn't happening. He couldn't be a father again. He couldn't be losing another child to something out of his control. It might already be too late. He had to go. He had to stop her from taking the choice away from him. Dammit, this was his baby too and he had a say in the matter, just as she did.

"Quil, man, I'm sorry. It's been eating me. I had to say something, I—"

Quil felt Pax's hand hit his back just as he popped up off the ground. "Where does she live?" he growled.

Pax gulped and nodded for him to follow him out of the sauna.

VEDA HEARD the deep voice before she saw the face and immediately froze as she turned with the bag full of groceries, her heart jumping up into her throat.

"Let me get that bag for you, *señora*."

Veda heard her mother giggle and the sound of the paper bag rustle as it was taken from her mom's hands. "Oh, thank you so kindly, lad."

Quillan Layton stood on the sidewalk, looking as gorgeous as ever in a ball cap, leather jacket, and tight jeans. He had a crimson red polo shirt beneath the jacket and donned matching sneakers, both with Gladiators logos on them.

"Q—Quil," Veda croaked out as she approached with her own bag. "What are you doin' here?"

"Oh, I was in the neighborhood and thought I'd stop by."

Bullshit! Veda thought and immediately felt a shiver of fear pass through her as his eyes narrowed for a brief instant before he grinned down at her mother.

"Quil, as in Quillan Layton?"

"That's me," Quil answered with a nod of his dark head.

"Well, you're even more handsome in person than on the telly."

"*Gracias*, Mrs. Ryan."

"Call me Kathy." Veda's mom blushed, getting an eye roll from Veda.

Quil gave them a beaming smile that made Veda's sex tingle before she huffed and moved toward the apartment lobby door, pulling it open dramatically as she struggled with the bags in her hands. Quil came up behind her and held the door, letting her mam in before following them into the elevator.

"You are *not* coming to our apartment...stalker," Veda smarted.

"Veda Angeline, you aren't to be rude to Mr. Layton for being a gentleman. I'll no stand for it."

Veda glanced incredulously at her mother. Despite his kind gesture, he *was* a stranger to her; and for all her mother knew, he meant them harm. But Veda just rolled her eyes again and furrowed her brows at Quil, who looked smug even as he had to hunch slightly, due to his massive height of six foot six inches, through the door as they exited to their floor.

Her mom opened the front door, and Veda went in after she did, sighing in relief as she set the bags of groceries down. Veda ignored Quillan as she began pulling their items from the bags and putting them away, wondering why on earth he was there, in their home.

Then realization dawned on her. *Oh shit!*

She hadn't realized she'd gasped until her mother elbowed her, asking if she were alright. Veda just gulped and nodded, unable to speak, for she felt her world caving in suddenly as she looked up to Quil, whose eyes narrowed darkly. *He knows.*

"Mam!" Veda stammered and grabbed her mother's shoulder. "Uh, I need to talk to Quillan. Can you uh, finish up and start dinner?"

"Oh, of course, love. Take your time." She grinned up at Quil and winked even as Veda pulled in a deep breath and moved toward the door, feeling like she was about to hyperventilate.

QUILLAN EYED VEDA as she wrung her hands out in front of her, watching her shiver as the cold December wind blew her dark hair from her face. They stood outside on the expansive back balcony of the apartment complex, one of the commons areas, overlooking the parking deck. He felt she didn't get rattled often and was seeing a side of her no one else ever got to.

"So I guess you, uh... Somehow, you know."

"Some*how*? Your twin—who just so happens to be dating my very pro-life teammate— goes to an abortion clinic with a 'mystery girl' that looks a great deal like her; the media is on this like stink on shit, Veda. They're questioning Pax right now as we speak, wondering why and who his fiancée was accompanied by."

"*Fuck* my life! So that's why Becca hasn't answered my texts."

"Yeah, she's knee-deep in a shit-storm at the moment."

He was sure V felt bad. She'd apparently left the clinic and come home while Becca had gone to work, now Becca was having to disarm a virtual bomb.

"It won't take them long to figure out it wasn't Rebecca who had an abortion."

Veda's eyes looked in panic up at him. "Quil, I—"

"You didn't go through with it, did you?" He gulped. God, what if he was too late?

Veda's eyes fell, but she shook her head, and he sighed heavily in relief.

"Ok, good. I was hoping I wasn't too late."

Veda's head snapped up and she looked at him as if he'd lost his mind. "Why?"

"You honestly think I would want you to murder my child? And what the hell were you thinking? Not even talking to me about it before making that kind of decision!" Quil growled and backed Veda into the nearest column on the path they'd been walking on. "And don't give me that 'It's my body, it's my decision' crap either. It was my seed, and I implanted it into you so there *is* that!"

Veda's mouth gaped open, her tongue ring visible in the setting sun. Quillan suddenly remembered all the wonderful things she'd done to him with that erotic piece of metal. His body hummed with excitement, wanting it again which only worsened his mood. He growled. "Now this is what's going to happen—"

"Wait just one feckin' minute here, big shot. If you think for one second you're going to come here and bully me into—"

"I think you need to remember who the hell you're talking to, *dama serpiente*." His jaw clenched. "I have the money and the resources to rip that baby out of your arms the minute he comes out of the birth canal—and don't think I won't, if you give me any reason to. For all I know, you set this whole thing up."

Veda scoffed and shoved at his chest, not budging him an inch. "You bastard, you wouldn't dare!"

Quillan squared off with her, bringing his nose to hers even as he stepped closer, caging her in. "No, I wouldn't. A baby needs his mother. But I am getting joint custody because he's mine, and I *will* see him when I want to."

"How do you know he's yours?" Veda smarted and crossed her arms over her chest.

"Oh, I plan to get a paternity test—middle of next week, in fact—to verify that he is. After all, his mother has been both a stripper and a cheerleader, so I'd be a fool not to, wouldn't I?"

That comment got a sharp smack to his cheek which barely moved his head, but he growled again anyway, simply because he was irritated all to hell and back.

"Do that again and I'll make your life a living hell."

"You already have, in more ways than one." She spat at his feet and swore in Irish.

"Oh, I haven't even begun, little girl," Quil smirked, getting another frown from Veda.

"What do you mean?"

"Well, since you're pregnant with my child now, some things are gonna change. We've been dating since Halloween, thanks to your sister, by the way."

Veda shook her head, dumbfounded.

Quil continued, "I'm gonna break your apartment contract; the movers are coming next week."

"What?" Veda's shrill voice shrieked. "Why would you—?"

"You're moving in with me."

"What about my mother?"

"She's going to stay with Pax and Becca, and of course she can visit whenever she likes."

"I don't even *know* you."

"Well, I guess you should've thought about that before you slept with me, huh, *chica mala?*"

Veda growled and raised her chin. "You're an asshole."

"No, an asshole would tell you to go fuck yourself. I'm supporting the mother of my child, as any good father would. You should be grateful."

"You just wanna save your reputation; this is all for show."

"Think what you want, see if I care," Quil smarted again and turned to leave.

"And what if I tell *you* to go fuck yourself? I don't want your damned charity, big shot."

"That's just too bad. I'm running this show now, V. And if you want to stay in your baby's life, you'll do as I tell you...at least until after he's born."

Veda's arms crossed over her sweater clad frame and her plump lips quivered. "Why are you doing this, Quillan?"

"Because I care, Veda. I won't have the mother of my child shamed and her name smeared across the headlines like it's likely to be, come morning. My daughter and I have been the victims of defamation and ridicule before. Never again. Now start packing your stuff... oh, and as of right now you no longer work for Brooke Taylor or *RISE*. You're welcome, by the way."

With that, Quillan leaned down and kissed Veda's cheek softly. "I'll be in touch, *lover*."

He was all too aware of how his body sizzled with hot energy. His lips tingled from the touch of her skin as he left her to consider his words.

VEDA LEANED into the door as she closed it shut, shutting out the worst mistake she'd ever made in her life...sleeping with Quillan Layton. Her axis had shifted and she was off kilter, thrown into a new orbit, unsure which way was up and which way was down. She was going to be sick, she knew; her stomach pitched at the thought of him controlling her life from there on out.

You should've had the abortion, the devil on her shoulder said, but she knew she wouldn't have been able to do it this go 'round. She'd barely been able to live with herself when she'd done it the first time. Only alive because her mother and sister had needed her—her strength, of which she hadn't been sure she'd had any left at that point in time. But she still did. She could do this, she could play this little game of Quil's, be the pawn in his twisted plan.

Her mother's voice pulled her from her inner reverie.

"What did you do to that man, Veda?" Her mother's emerald eyes pierced through her like a shard of glass through a Jell-O mold.

She should lie, should make something up, but her mother was and always had been able to see right through her. Instead, she attempted to distract. "Why do I always have to be the bad guy in everything?"

"I didn't see you going to him, but the other way around, which leads me to believe he has unfinished business with you."

Unfinished business, indeed. "I'm pregnant with his child."

There. She'd said it. Pulled the scab right off and let it bleed out.

Her mother gaped at her, unsure what to say to that.

"Oh, and pack your shit because since your daughter got knocked up by a pro football player, you'll be getting an upgraded crib. You'll be staying with Becca at Paxton's for now."

"No. I'm not."

Veda frowned as she looked back at her mother, shocked at the backbone hidden beneath her five-foot nothing frame. "Mam, I—"

"Where do you think you get your tough exterior from, Veda? Your father didn't have your guts, you know that verra well, don't you?"

Veda gulped hard and shivered.

"You never have told me exactly what happened that day. Perhaps it's time to get it off your chest." Her mother motioned for her to sit down on the couch as she moved from the foyer into the living room.

Kathleen sat and her look grew stern as she pointed to the seat beside her.

Veda reluctantly sat too and sighed, feeling years of pent-up emotion fill her core.

"I got pregnant with Will's baby," Veda whispered as her mom's soft hand settled on her forearm. "I was so scared, Mam. Ashamed. Remorseful. I wanted to do the right thing, but when I told Will he..." Veda trailed off, feeling the hate pour into her gut, souring her already sour stomach. "He didn't want it."

"Oh baby," her mother cooed and moved her hand up to Veda's cheek, stroking her there lightly.

"Pa overheard our conversation and decided to punish me because I'd caught him red-handed having an affair. Next thing I knew, he was pulling into an abortion clinic and forcing me in." Veda closed her eyes against the flood of memories that overfilled her chest, spilling forth in the form of giant, crocodile tears. "It was horrible. So painful, so mortifying. I wanted to die along with the baby. I'm the reason he left us, Mam."

"Oh, my darling, no. You aren't the reason. I should've told you a long time ago, but I always thought you'd be the one to come to me first. I knew, baby. He told me."

Veda gasped and blinked through the tears into her mother's beautiful, scarcely wrinkled face. "What?"

"He told me what a bad girl you'd been. What you'd done. How you'd always been a scourge of our family and how he'd destroyed the demon in your womb."

Jesus Christ! He'd said those things?

"That's when I told him to leave and ne'er return."

Veda felt her jaw drop to the floor. Her mother. Her mother had been... "Mam?"

"How could I live with a man who did something so vile to my child? A man who thought you were evil. You and your sisters are the most precious gifts I've ever received. You've blessed my life with so much love and goodness. It was your father who was the scourge after we lost Sarah. I think her death truly destroyed him, and he was trying to find any scapegoat he could. But I couldn't let his foolishness cause me to lose another one of me daughters, so I made him go. I knew he'd cheated on me. I'm no fool, Veda."

"Oh, Mam," Veda murmured and fell into her mother's lap, crying into her cozy wool sweater. Kathleen stroked her daughter's hair, all the while cooing to her and reassuring her.

Veda wasn't aware of how long she cried or how long her mind and heart drifted to a safe place before she pulled herself upright and blushed into her mother's understanding face.

"I came close to doing it again. Becca and I went to an abortion clinic, but I couldn't go through with it."

"Oh my love, why did you—?"

"I was only thinking of our financial burden and how much I've screwed up already. I didn't want anything else to corrupt."

"Veda, look at me." Veda did as her mother instructed. "There is nothing about you that's corrupt and never has been."

That was debatable, especially now that Quil was taking the lead and forcing her to come live with him. She told her mother all of this, all that Quillan had told her, his plans for her.

Her mom smiled. "It doesn't sound quite so bad, honestly, does it? An ungodly handsome, rich man has invited you to come live with him so he can support you and his baby..."

"Mom, I'll be more like a captive. I don't even really know the guy, truthfully."

"Well, now's your chance to get to know him. He's the father of your child, after all."

Veda rolled her eyes. Her mam watched too much reality television. She needed to lay off of *The Bachelor*. "And what about you?"

"I'm staying here."

"What? By yourself? Out of the question."

"I'm a grown woman. I don't need you to tell me what to do, ye ken?"

Lord help. She was starting to see the strength her mother had been speaking of.

"Besides, I might not be alone." When Veda's brow perked up, her mam grinned like the cat that ate the canary. "I've been seeing someone of my own. You recall Walt from downstairs?"

"The tall, old guy who gives you the eye in the elevator?"

"One and the same."

"Mam, you slag." Veda teased and bumped her hip into her mom's.

"Ach, takes one to know one."

CHAPTER EIGHT

The next two days passed slowly, much to Veda's dismay. By Wednesday, Becca and Pax had stopped answering the media's nagging questions about the mystery girl who was with Becca that day at the clinic and speculating on the situation. But the news coverage hadn't stopped talking about it. The team was once again in the spotlight for more than just the incredible talent there within.

Veda knew it was just a matter of time before they figured it out; she was going to have to step in. Becca had told her that she was "handling" it, but Veda was the "older" sibling and didn't like allowing her sister to take the fall for her mistakes. It was so un-Veda like.

So she simply kept to herself that week, sulking while waiting for the seven-week mark to hit so that she and Quil could have a prenatal paternity test done. She already knew he was the father; there'd been no one else, as much as she'd made him think otherwise.

She took her mam for an infusion on Thursday. After, they did some online last-minute Christmas shopping, baking and watching

Hallmark Christmas movies until Veda felt a ripple come out of nowhere and pull at her heartstrings.

Life was going to be different now that she'd decided to keep the baby. It was the first time in her life she felt so out of sorts and unsure of what to do. She'd been living her whole life on the edge, uncaring of what happened so long as her family was safe. She'd been working toward the ultimate goal of becoming a model, building a portfolio where and when she could, but now it seemed as if that were all in vain.

Quil came to the apartment on Thursday around lunchtime and took Veda out to a big, dark green Land Rover.

"Fancy," she smirked as he opened the door for her and helped her into the passenger seat.

He didn't reply, but she could tell he wanted to just by his facial expressions as he settled into the driver's seat and cranked the vehicle.

His serious face grew tighter as he looked over at her once she'd buckled her seatbelt, wondering why they weren't moving.

"I want you to be as real with me as you've ever been before, Veda. No bullshit, just honest answers. Can you do that?"

Veda felt her cheeks heat in anger before she huffed out and nodded tersely.

Quillan looked away for a brief moment before his caramel brown eyes whipped back to hers.

"Am I the father of this baby?"

Without blinking, Veda gave another terse nod. "It can't be anyone else's. Like I told you in the club—"

"There's been *no one*... before me?"

"Not in a good six months, Quil," Veda smirked, thinking of the last douchebag she'd been with. "Taking care of Mam and working various jobs to make ends meet didn't leave much time for dating."

"You met men at the club all the time. Surely you—"

"How many *times* do I have to repeat myself?" she grated out and slammed her hand down on the dashboard. "I thought that was why you were here! To take me to get a paternity test since you obviously don't trust what I tell you."

"How am I supposed to trust you when all you've done is skirt around the truth?"

She realized it was true. She'd never lied to him per se; she'd just not been forthcoming with information. He hadn't been exactly a Chatty Cathy himself, so he was one to talk.

Veda just looked down and wrung her hands. "Look Quil, I know we got off on the wrong foot in the beginning..."

"No, we didn't. We clicked Halloween night. We both wanted the same thing. No strings attached. Hot sex. And that's exactly what we got, wasn't it?" he smirked and ran a hand through his thick, jet black hair. The sun caught it, making it look silver in the beaming rays of sunlight.

She recalled their night of "hot sex" and the even hotter sex weeks after, at the club. Quil was a fierce lover, a gorgeous man with an incredible body. A body she wouldn't mind to see and touch and fuck again. She gulped as his eyes lowered down her chest, making her think he was envisioning the same.

"I'm sorry," Veda stated, feeling like it needed to be said.

"For what?" he asked, his features softening so that it took her breath.

"For making you think the morning after that I was just some random groupie out to get you. For not talking to you about the baby before going to the clinic. For *all* this." She rested her hand on her lower belly.

"Veda, why in God's name would you apologize for that? A baby is a gift." His perfectly-sculpted black brows drew. Did he really feel that way? *Honestly?* "Besides, I'm the one who got you pregnant, not the other way around. I was the jackass who didn't use protection either night we had sex."

Veda started to say it was as much her place to remember that as it was his, but his hand covering hers stilled her speech.

"I guess it's no excuse, but I *was* a bit distracted." He gave her a slow grin. A grin she'd not seen but a few times and her heart began to hammer in her chest.

She was taken back ten years into the past and the harsh words that Will had said reverberated through her whole body, making her lips quiver as they embedded deep into her heart. She hadn't realized she was crying until she felt a big palm settle softly on her cheek, a thumb gently sweeping the tear that fell beneath her eye.

She couldn't have held her words or emotions back if she tried, needing to vent in that moment more than she ever had in her entire life. Her mother and sister had only recently found out the truth. Had her pregnancy loosened her tongue and resolve to nothing? For here she was, suddenly telling her deepest regret to the dark and handsome stranger who'd fathered her child before she ever knew what happened.

"I was forced into an abortion at sixteen… by my father. The boy who impregnated me didn't want it, of course. He had too much at stake, and some foreign young jezebel who'd 'trapped' him hadn't been part of his plan. He even had the audacity to ask me if it was his when he damn well knew no other man had ever touched me." Veda paused with a hiccup, her chest burning with anger and pain. "I didn't always look and act like—well, like I do now." She trailed off, feeling self-conscious and inadequate in those moments. Once more she was the poor, second-class female burdened with a rich man's unwanted spawn.

When she finally got the guts to look up into the face of the man whose index finger was bringing her chin up, she immediately felt calmer, warmer, less stressed. His smile widened, showcasing his perfectly straight, pearly whites. God, she'd been blessed to have such a beautiful man be the father of her child. She returned it before his face grew serious again and he said, "V, I know you'll be surprised to hear me say that I'm excited about this *bebé*. Honestly."

Oh, that's right, it was easy to be excited when one had millions and not a care in the world, save for catching a damn football, Veda thought to herself.

She simply looked down to keep from smarting off.

Quillan continued, "And I don't wanna risk having a prenatal paternity test and hurting the baby or causing a miscarriage."

Veda knew she was gaping as shock took over her.

"I mean, I know the likelihood of miscarriage is fairly low, but it's still a possibility. With you having had an abortion in the past, that might make you even higher risk. I won't push you to have the test done. We can always wait until after the baby's born and then do it, if you're ok with that."

This man was mental. She'd chosen a beautiful but stupid man to father her child.

Before she could respond, he went on. "Since we're having a baby together, we need to trust each other... and also get to know one another."

That made sense.

"And we'll of course be getting married."

Veda scoffed. The *hell* he said!

"It's non-negotiable." He pulled his hand from her cheek and held it up in a "Don't even think about arguing with me" gesture. "This child *is* and will be mine in every legal sense of the word from the very beginning. We'll draft a prenup and all, but it will be more advantageous for the child if he's *not* born outside of wedlock."

Veda rolled her eyes but understood why Quil would want that. She nodded after crossing her arms over her chest. "I do have a favor to ask though."

"And what's that?"

"I want to clear Becca and Pax's names as soon as possible."

"And how do you plan on doing that?" The corner of Quil's mouth drew up in a crooked grin, making Veda's thighs clench in longing.

"I'm gonna go to the media and tell them the truth."

"What? Are you out of your ever-loving mind?" Quil stammered.

"Not the *whole* truth...obviously. But our version of it. Becca and Pax don't deserve to take the fall for what I did." Her eyes pierced through to his soul and he looked away, huffing. "But I need your help in order to call a press conference and—"

"Fine," he grumbled and dropped his hand down to the gear shift.

Veda relaxed back into her seat and inhaled the scent of pine, cologne, and leather that emanated from the Rover's interior.

"Where are we going?" she asked.

She got another crooked grin in return. "To eat lunch, I'm starved."

She looked him over. He wore clean, white, polyester, league-grade shorts that hit mid-thigh, a fitted Under Armour crimson red tank that showcased his impressively defined arms and matching sneakers. He'd clearly been at practice, showered, and headed to her house.

She shivered in her cream angora wool sweater and olive-green leggings tucked into a pair of brown leather riding boots, but not from the cold. He glanced her way and flicked the seat warmer on. She thanked him and he held her gaze for a moment before turning up one road and down another, obviously knowing where he intended to take her to dine.

She looked up at the sign of the French bistro on the corner she'd not been in but had wondered about frequently as she'd headed into *RISE*, seeing as it was across the street from it. Eating out was a luxury she and Becca hadn't gotten often in the last few years.

He pulled beneath a canopy and allowed the valet to assist her out before taking her elbow and ushering her inside. Her eyes moved around the large expanse of the beautifully decorated open restaurant, the perfectly placed bar, the kitchen in the background, and the alcove they were headed into before she realized the server was closing the door behind them. They had the entire room to themselves? Holy moly! Service with a smile, indeed.

"I wanted privacy, so..." Quil trailed off, redness tinting his stubbled, russet cheeks.

She didn't reply as she browsed the menu and he followed suit.

She had no idea what to order. Everything sounded delicious... and was outrageously overpriced, of course.

Salad, stick with salad and soup, she told herself.

"What's good here?" Veda asked.

"I don't know. I've never eaten here...*señorita.*"

Veda's eyes flitted to his and she gulped as a jolt of electricity spiked through her center. Damn him and his sexy Spanish words. He didn't use them all the time, but when he did... *drool!* Her tongue flicked across her lips, and she pulled her lip into her mouth to keep from speaking, giving herself away.

He looked back to the menu, a faint smile flashing across his face before disappearing. That smug bastard!

Veda tried to calm her nerves and focus, but being in a room alone with him, having him an arm's reach away, began to quickly unnerve her. She was aware of his smell, the way his big shoulders filled out the crimson hoodie he'd jerked over his head before they'd entered the restaurant, and that his thigh was mere inches from hers.

When the waiter came back into the room with fresh Aqua Panna and bread, they ordered. Veda stuck to an endive salad with a Dijon vinaigrette and French onion soup—when in Rome—and Quil ordered a quiche Florentine and oysters Rockefeller.

They ended up splitting the oysters and ordering another half dozen as Quil laughed at her slurping.

"Sorry." She found herself giggling. "This is the most incredible thing I've eaten in a long time."

"*Oui,*" he smirked and grabbed another half shell up to slurp down.

"So, uh, what's Quinn gonna think about all this?" Veda couldn't help but ask as she realized how much time she was going to be spending with Quil and his daughter soon.

Quil's easy face had tensed again, his square jaw ticking as he looked down at his plate.

"She—uh, we'll just tell her that you're to be her other nanny."

"Nanny?" Veda asked incredulously.

"Yeah, it would explain why you're to be there as much and often as you will be. She doesn't need to know all the details. Then when the baby's born, you can do as you please. We'll get a divorce and you can..." he trailed off.

Whether they divorced or not, it made no never mind. He was stuck with her now. He and Quinn were. Like it or not. Unless...

"Quil, it's not too late to—"

"Don't you *dare* finish that statement," he growled and threw his napkin down as he stood abruptly, getting a gasp out of Veda.

He paced the floor for a moment, running his hands through his hair before they settled on his hips and he turned to face her.

"I don't believe in abortion, ok? It's nothing political, anti-liberal, or religious even... it goes far deeper than that for me. It's your body and I respect that." He held his hands up in surrender, seeing her glare before placing them back to his hips. "I mean, I guess if you really don't want the baby then I understand, but please... please..." He sighed heavily and sat down again.

His palms covered his face as he placed his elbows on the table-top. He got quiet, deathly silent, and Veda feared he would speak no more. Finally, his deep voice filled the hollow of his hands and she had to strain her ears to understand him.

"My wife didn't even know her own daughter, Veda. She was a cocaine addict by the time our baby girl was barely a year old. She used drugs to hide her pain after we found out that Quinn..." A big gulp echoed into Quil's cupped palms. Veda's heart stopped, seeing this strong, unshakable god shaken so. "Quinn has a very rare and very dangerous form of anemia. It's more than just anemia. Her blood doesn't form properly, which makes her life harder." Quil pulled his hands down quickly, unshed tears shining in his eyes. "She'll be lucky to live into her late twenties at this rate. I see her weakness every day. I see her struggle, and I fear the worst. Every. Fucking. Day, Veda." Quillan sighed and looked to her limp hand on the table. "Then my wife died of an overdose. Of her own hand. No matter how many times I tried to help her or the amount of money I shoved into a rehab center to attempt to cure her. It didn't matter. She loved the drugs more than her family, and I still hate her for that." He growled and slammed his fist down on the table.

"Now the woman I haven't been able to stop thinking about since the night I met her in a club back in October has come to me and told me I'm to be a father again. I have another chance at love, at a life I must fulfill, and I feel hope again. So please? Please let me have this opportunity, this chance to fix my wrongs? If you don't want him, then I'll adopt him. But let him be born, let him live. Give me my child, Veda, please?"

Tears poured from her eyes in rivulets, like steady rain on a window pane. How could she say no, how could she take the choice away from him? She couldn't, she realized, as he reached for her hand and she allowed him to pull her toward him. She fell, practically weak-kneed, into his lap, wrapping her arms around his neck as his eyes roved her face.

"Please, Veda?" he begged on a whisper, but by then Veda felt he was asking for more than her permission not to end a life before it began. He was asking for permission to—what?

She didn't have a chance to overanalyze it before he was pulling her against him and his lips were falling to hers, sipping slowly at first, coaxing submission from her shocked system. His tongue slid easily into her mouth once she'd kissed him back, and she felt the invasive warmth flood her entire being with liquid fire. Quillan was desire, and she was immediately consumed by him. A deep, hungry whimper escaped her throat and he gripped her thigh, pulling her astride him as her chest hit his hard. His growl answered her moan as his palm slid up her back and into her hair, fisting it and pulling as his mouth began to punish hers for making it wait so long for sustenance.

His hands were needy, his mouth starving as his lips and tongue and teeth assaulted hers in a brutal dance of power and submission, give and take, anger and happiness, punishment and reward. Veda found her resolve slipping further and further from her grasp as his mouth fucked hers into surrender. Her hands moved over his hard, muscled torso as her hips writhed against his, seeking the restrained, steely member that throbbed at the apex of her thighs.

"Oh God, Quil, yes," she grunted as he arched the solid outline of it against her.

"Mmm, Veda, I want you so much, my little rebel. I wanna hurt you and love you and *fuck* you mindless." His teeth bit into her throat, and she felt slickness coat her panties, the ache within her demanding to be answered.

She groaned out in a mixture of pain and pleasure, the need for both overwhelming her.

"You sick fuck," she murmured as her palm gripped his neck and she aligned her mouth back to his, bruising his lips with her own.

He gave an evil laugh in answer and pulled back for a breath after a moment. "I *am* Hades, you know?"

God of the Underworld indeed. He had her under his spell. That handsome devil.

His hands moved to cup her breasts and a hiss whistled through her teeth as the sensitive tips burned for both relief and more simultaneously.

"Oh, oh God, Quillan," she whimpered as one hand gripped her ass through her leggings, the other at her scalp, his tongue licking her quivering neck. She slid herself along his rock-hard cock, dry-humping his crotch like her life depended on it, her sex as hungry for his as her belly was for food. Nothing existed in that moment but release, sweet and complete.

"You gonna come for me, *dama serpiente?*" he encouraged.

Fuck yes, I am, my sexy god, she thought even as her eyes sought his and his big hand moved into her desire-coated thongs.

"Mmm, God, I wanna fuck this succulent little *papaya* until I'm drenched in your juices again." His fingers explored the 'papaya' he'd just spoken of with a curiosity and expertise that pushed her further to the edge.

His words only succeeded in getting her there as he thrust two thick, long fingers into her just as she succumbed to the flames of their self-imposed hell.

She was coming down from her orgasm just as the door opened and the waiter came in with their food. She threw herself at Quill's frame, hiding her face into his broad shoulder, hearing the dishes as the server set their plates down. She didn't budge until she heard the door close behind him and felt Quil's rumble of laughter reverberating from his chest to hers.

She smiled into his handsome face as his hand withdrew from her leggings and moved to her waist.

"That was close," she sighed.

He only nodded and motioned to her food. "Hungry?"

She licked her lips and nodded in answer. *But not for food*, she wanted to say.

"Eat now, beautiful. *Mi dama serpiente* needs fuel for my baby. She can tame her snake later." He patted her bottom then kissed her lips with such promise she was fumbling, her body swirling into a hot pit of lust all over again.

She moaned even as she pulled back, for she didn't want to appear overeager.

Maybe being forced to get married wasn't going to be as bad as she thought. After all, she was to be married to Quillan "Hades" Layton, the dark and sexy God of the Gridiron.

How bad could that really be?

"WHAT?" Madi screeched at Quillan as he told her what he was planning on doing tomorrow.

"You heard me."

Madison McFadden pointed her finger at him. "What the hell is the matter with you and Paxton? These two women have—"

"Madi, a marriage will get the press off everyone's back. The Gladiators will be back in good light again."

Madi just stared at him as if he'd grown horns, then realization suddenly dawned on her. "Holy shit! It was Veda. She had an *abortion?*" Madi gulped down hard and looked away. When her eyes returned back to Quil's, she had her answer. "Jesus, Quillan."

"I know. Once we get married, I'm calling a press conference right afterward and we're gonna sort the whole mess out."

"You don't have to do that."

"Veda wants to. She insists."

Madi's brows went up in surprise then she smirked. "She's just trying to save her sister's reputation."

"Perhaps, but even *you* should be able to understand that," he quipped smartly.

"Even still, I appreciate your sacrifice."

"Sacrifice?" Why was it a sacrifice to do the right thing?

Madi gave him a wilted look and turned in her chair to look out over the practice field. "This year has been interesting, to say the least." It indeed had, beginning with the death of Hunter, Madi's former husband, in mid-February. From there, she'd been married to her childhood sweetheart—and father of her unborn child—in early September. Paxton had gone on his date with Becca in October, and Quil'd hooked up with Veda on Halloween. It was now a week prior to Christmas.

"Well," Madi sighed and turned back to look at him. "I thank you for informing me of your plan, Quil, and I'm grateful for your commitment to the team. Enjoy the rest of your evening. I'll see you tomorrow."

Quillan gave Madi a nod and rose.

"Oh, and I guess, congrats are in order as well. Although, I have a feeling you've got your work cut out for you. Veda is one tough cookie."

Tough cookie was putting it mildly, but Quil knew that Veda was like a Chips Ahoy, all soft in the middle. Misunderstood, that's what Veda was. Misunderstood, like him.

He rode home that night, pondering his quandary once more.

He'd not told Quinn what was really happening. He didn't figure Veda would want to stay married long after the baby got there, so he felt it prudent not to get his daughter's hopes up. She'd mentioned having a mother for far too long now for him to just break her heart the way it would if he told her she had one, only to lose her months later. For now, she would just know that Veda was going to be her other nanny, someone to help Juanita. Perhaps when Quinn got older he could explain it all, but she was just six and weak enough. She didn't need any more worries in her young life.

He admired the sun setting beyond the trees and over the pastures as he rode from the complex to his subdivision, just a mere ten minutes away. He, Pax, and Travis all lived in the same resort-like community. Quil hadn't realized he had them for neighbors until he'd already begun signing the closing documents but was grateful to have his teammates close, seeing as they felt as much like family as coworkers.

He watched the sun burst into colors of auburn, magenta, and lavender as he pulled through the gate, waved to the security guard in the booth, and headed over the bridge. He smiled at the ducks swimming in a V toward the mirrored sun along the large lake that bordered the houses in the subdivision. He'd bought in a beautiful area and was grateful for the grandeur of a well-developed community with large trees, long driveways, and large lots with generous front and back yards. Each property consisted of at least five acres and had an excellent lakeside view. It was also nice not to be a stone's throw from his neighbors and not be able to see every house from the main road.

Quillan's home was a large three-story grey brick and stone Cape Cod style home with a big porch. Quinn had fallen in love with the large pool and giant oak tree in the back that had been perfect for the little *reinita's* treehouse. Her pleasure had cemented his decision when she'd seen the big playroom upstairs with a custom slide. He'd simply been glad for the price and closeness to the complex, the good schools, and proximity to the hospital.

Quil was pleased to see Veda shutting her car door as he pulled into the circular driveway, glad she was finally there.

He'd hired movers to help bring her stuff to his house, mostly clothes since her mom was staying in the apartment for now. He and Veda had been seen out in public all week, making sure to laugh, touch, and kiss to the press's wonder. They were making their press release tomorrow after their small chapel wedding, although things had quieted down some following Becca and Paxton's statements; thanks to the firing and arrest of the head coach for the Washington Wolves after he'd been caught in a hotel room with a minor, and the death of actress Betty Hamilton at 92 years old.

Quil waved as he pulled into the garage and motioned for her to wait for him to enter, of which he assumed she would do anyway, redness tinting her cheeks as she pulled the duffle bag to her shoulder.

"I'll grab that," Quil stated once he'd parked and jumped out, approaching Veda.

She looked lovely tonight in a red sweater dress, her hair pulled back in a barrette showcasing the necklace-like tattoo that ran along her collarbone with intricate vines.

"Thank you." She gave him a bright smile, her nose ring sparkling in the lights of the garage as he led her in past his vehicle.

He opened the side door, the house alarm giving a chime as they entered.

"Daddy!" he heard Quinn squeal and the sound of her little foot-falls hitting the hardwoods filled his soul to bursting with over-whelming happiness.

Quinn stopped when she saw Veda, her eyes moving from her father to his lover.

The smile that lit her sweet face made his heart flutter.

"Veda? Veda!" Quinn squealed even louder and ran at Veda, her arms open wide.

Quillan gulped as Veda folded his daughter in her arms and Quinn's little curly head rested on Veda's inked shoulder.

"Oh Veda, I missed you. Daddy said you were coming. I was so excited!"

Veda cuddled his child, and Quil felt a jerk in his chest as he thought about how tough this would be once Veda moved on with her life; but this was the right thing to do, he kept telling himself.

"I know, me too, sweetie."

"You're gonna stay here, with us?"

"I am," Veda assured her and set her down, taking hold of her hand.

"Oh, goodie, goodie. I wanna show you my room and my tree-house and my new dolly and…my…my playroom."

Veda laughed at her enthusiasm, a soft, sexy laugh.

"Hold up there, *mi niña*. Let's have dinner first, then you can show V your stuff, alright? Let Veda get settled in, then we'll give her a tour, ok?"

"Ok, Daddy. Can I take her up to her room?"

Veda turned and gave him a gorgeous smile, stilling his breath.

"Daddy!"

"What?" Quillan glanced back down at his little doll, who'd crossed her arms over her chest. "Uh, I'll take her up, you go wash up and tell Juanita we need one more plate set at the table."

That got her attention as she squealed again and moved off in the direction of the kitchen.

"Wow," Veda looked around at the tan walls covered in photographs, the high coffered ceilings, and the large living room that lay beyond the foyer they stood in. "Your house is huge."

Quil just shrugged and nodded to the staircase. She went up first and he followed, trying hard to not focus his eyes on the plump bottom in front of him. He couldn't help it though and the sight of such splendor forced him to remember the feel of his palms on her firm flesh, his grip on her as he slammed her down onto his manhood again and again.

Tomorrow night, he told himself, *she'll be yours to do with as you please.*

Veda stopped on the landing and looked around at the closed doors. "So many rooms," she stated in surprise.

"Oh, yeah... uh, this way." He motioned to the third one ahead of them. "The first door is the guest room, second is a bathroom, third is yours."

"I assume the last three are yours and Quinn's?" Veda pointed, even as she followed him to her door.

"That one with the French doors is my office. That's Quinn's there beside it, and the corner one is mine."

"Ah yes, the master's suite." Her brows bobbed and his sex jerked hard in his pants. Man, how he wanted her to call him *master*.

He cleared his throat and gave her a swift nod as he opened the door to her room.

"Here you are, Nanny Veda. Your quarters."

Quil stepped in after her and set her duffle bag down on the bed, watching as her mouth fell open in awe at the large bedroom with a bay window overlooking the lake. She took in the four-poster iron bed covered in a safari style comforter, large sitting area, and elegantly tiled bathroom. She covered her blunder with a smirk. "I prefer the term governess, thank you."

Quil's brow went up. "Oh, you're a teacher now too, huh?"

"Sure, why not? I know all there is to know about streaming entertainment."

Quillan actually laughed. For all her sarcasm, the woman had a great sense of humor. "So long as you don't teach her how to dance, I don't have any issues."

Veda's smile faded and her eyes flitted back up to his. He should apologize because he hadn't meant to offend her, but the cold, hard exterior she'd first had when he'd met her at *RISE* surfaced.

"As you know, I don't dance anymore."

He didn't respond; his words not enough to make her understand she didn't have to explain herself to him.

They stood silently for a moment before Quil looked around the room and opened his arms wide. "Well, make yourself at home.

Dinner will be served soon. Feel free to freshen up and come on down. I'll let Quinn show you your new home."

He moved past her then turned before he exited, wanting her to know. "For the record, I *love* the way you dance."

With that, he shut the door and headed down to talk to Juanita about the new living arrangement.

VEDA LOOKED AROUND THE ROOM, her room, and felt like she was on an episode of some reality TV series. This wasn't real, this wasn't really happening, was it? She now knew how her sister had felt when she'd moved in with Paxton and yet, Veda had made her feel like an ass. If anyone was the ass here, it was Veda.

She pulled out her phone and texted her mom and sis in their group text.

Vey: I made it. This place is HUGE! Love you two.

Bec: Oh, good. Glad you made it ok. Paxton is grilling us fish for dinner. Call me before you go to bed. Love you guys too.

Mam: Take pics! Love you both. I'm with Walt. It's BINGO night at the Y.

Her mother was having the time of her life, it seemed, with her new beau, and Veda couldn't help but smile. Compared to a year ago, life had been good for all of them... at least until Veda had gone and gotten herself knocked up.

She hadn't told Becca what she planned to do and wouldn't. This was Veda's mess and she had to fix it once and for all, clearing Becca's name for good.

Veda began unpacking her bag, placing clothes in the dresser drawers. Her clothes and shoes were already filling the closet she opened and she smiled, glad for Quillan's thoughtfulness. His generosity was really helping her; she was both stunned and grateful to be in his care, although she wouldn't tell him that if the world were on fire.

He'd made her feel beholden to him and she hated that feeling, so she planned to do her part, state her truth to the media, and help Quil take care of Quinn as recompense. But it didn't help the fact that he'd slept with the off-limits cheerleader that night at Paxton's and was now playing her knight in shining armor. Perhaps he felt bad, or he was just old-school. Perhaps he was honest and didn't want more bad publicity, especially before the season was over. Perhaps he'd merely wanted another wife and mother for his daughter, who already knew and loved Veda. Perhaps Quillan was a crazy, psycho serial killer, who—

No, stop that! She'd been watching too much Netflix as of late and refused to feed her overstimulated imagination with any more nonsense. Besides, if he was a serial killer he could have already killed her by now... right?

Veda moved to the luxurious white and coral bathroom with three times the drawers she'd ever need in a lifetime and splashed some water on her face from the pedestal sink, feeling flushed as she thought of marrying Quillan tomorrow. Tomorrow, she would be Veda Angeline Layton and she wasn't sure how she felt about that. Sure, Quil was gorgeous—a worthy prize any woman would love to call her own—but he was also demanding, grumpy, and didn't love her. Did he honestly expect that they would consummate the marriage?

The thought of being his lover again was incredibly enticing but also intimidating when she remembered the first two times. He'd been dominating, more so than she'd ever experienced, and she didn't know if she liked it or not. It felt naughty, it felt forbidden, it felt...*fucking amazing!*

She was kidding herself to say she hadn't thoroughly enjoyed being in Quillan's intimate embrace, feeling his hands own her body, her sex devouring his like it'd never had a meal so filling...and she hadn't, not ever.

Besides, the damage was done now that she was pregnant with

his baby; she might as well take advantage of all the perks of being married to such a hottie.

Her palm settled on her lower belly. She was so glad she'd decided to keep this child. Quil seemed just as eager, although it worried her what would happen in the future. For now, she would simply allow him to help her, help pay her medical bills, help support her, and help ensure a future for the life they'd created that fated Samhain night.

She took in a deep breath and checked her appearance in the mirror once more.

Heading out the door and down the stairs, Veda was drawn by Quinn's sweet giggle. She moved through the foyer and into the open, yellow-walled kitchen to see Quil lifting his daughter as she stirred the contents of a pot.

This room was by far the coziest of the home thus far and had clearly been decorated by a woman. It had white cabinets with decorative brushed nickel knobs, stainless steel appliances, and grey and white granite countertops. It was accented with colors and décor that mixed both Quil's Native American and Spanish cultures. The walls were adorned with paintings of landscapes, sunset plains, and pictures of Quil and Quinn. A china cabinet sat in the corner with a bowl of lemons. It was stock full of ancient-looking trinkets, cookbooks, and lovely green plants.

Veda smiled as she closed in on the trio—Quil, Quinn, and a lovely middle-aged silver-haired Latina woman with a plump middle, white apron, and beautiful accent.

She spoke to Quil in Spanish and motioned for him to sit Quinn down, who squealed as she saw Veda in her periphery.

"*There* you are. I was wondering if you'd gotten lost."

"I came close. This place is like a labyrinth."

Quinn giggled, her brown eyes squinting as she covered her mouth. "That's a funny word. What's a lab—lab rinse?"

Veda couldn't help but laugh herself. "A labyrinth. It's a maze." *See Quil, a governess already!*

"I'll show you. Come with me, we'll—"

"After dinner, little priss. I already told you, my *reinita*."

"But Daddy…"

"No buts, Quinny."

Quinn's little lips pursed and she turned fiercely, arms crossed across her middle. God, she looked so much like her father at that moment.

Veda held her breath, wanting to intervene but not wanting to get Quinn in any more trouble.

The Latina woman spoke to Quinn then, and she perked up before setting off toward the table set within view of the bay window; another lakeside view.

"Oh, forgive my manners. Veda this is Juanita, my third and fourth set of hands, lifesaver, and second mother to Quinn. Juanita, meet Veda Ryan."

Juanita gave Veda a tight smile and the once over, quickly returning to the pot on the stove. She said something in Spanish to Quil, whose brow rose and he smirked something back. Clearly, Juanita wasn't as pleased to have Veda there as Quinn and Quillan were.

No surprise there. Veda was used to people not liking her. What was one more enemy in the bountiful line of them?

Quil gave her a regretful grin and motioned her to the dinner table, set for three.

When Veda frowned in confusion, Quil answered, "Juanita doesn't stay for supper. She'll be back tomorrow morning to get Quinn. She's got school, then dance, and she's staying the night at Juanita's with her granddaughter, Aislynn."

"Oh?" So, they would have the house to themselves tomorrow night—their wedding night? How convenient.

"Yeah, she's been begging to stay with her for some time now; they go to school together."

Veda just gave Quil a soft smile and took Quinn's hand as she pulled her toward the table. "You're sitting across from me, Veda."

Veda nodded and allowed Quinn to help her into the seat. The little brown-haired doll placed a white linen napkin across her lap and moved to push her chair in toward the table—with Veda's assistance, of course. Veda smiled as Quinn's brown locks bobbed around to the other side of the table and she sat in her spot grinning over at her; all the innocent precociousness of a child. Veda suddenly had a vision of another child, a child who favored Quinn a great deal, and the name "Tessa" echoed through her head.

By the time Quil joined them and a tray of steaming bowls was set down before her, she'd returned from the dream world she'd been sucked into.

"You ok?" Quil asked Veda and patted her hand as he settled at the head of the table.

Veda gulped and nodded, feeling clammy all of a sudden.

"This smells delicious," Veda said and heard her tummy rumble.

"Chicken rice bowls," Quinn answered. "My favorite."

Veda smiled at the sweet little angel clapping her hands and thanked Quil as he set the red bowl filled with fluffy rice, juicy chunks of chicken, and a small topping of freshly shredded cheese— it looked to be Manchago. The dish smelled heavenly, savory, and spicy.

Quil motioned to another tray set with smaller bowls of toppings, sour cream, pico de gallo, cilantro, caramelized onions and peppers, jalapeños, charro beans, and more.

"Wow, this is a feast," Veda told Quinn who giggled as she dug into the bowl she'd garnished with beans, sour cream, and cilantro.

Veda began to add the various delicious additions to her bowl, blushing when Quil looked at it and gave her a thumbs up.

"It's good to see a girl who knows how to eat."

Veda shrugged. "I didn't eat lunch today. Mam and I were—"

"You mean Grand Mam?" Quinn asked, getting a frown from Quil in confusion.

Veda laughed. "Yes, Grand Mam. Quinn met her at the hospital last week," she informed Quillan. "Mam is what we call our mothers in Ireland, you know?" she told Quinn.

"So Ireland is where you're from? Is that why Grand Mam talks funny."

"Quinn, this isn't 20 questions. Eat your dinner and let Veda eat hers," Quil insisted, more to give Veda a break than to scold his daughter, who was still shoveling food into her little mouth.

Veda grinned. "Yes, you'll notice every now and again I say things you don't understand or in a funny tone."

"Daddy does that too. He can speak three languages, can't you Daddy?"

Quil paused with a big bite of chicken and rice and gave a nonchalant shrug.

"Three?" Veda asked and felt a fleeting flutter at her belly.

When Veda's brows continued to rise in question, Quillan finally sighed and said, "English, Spanish, Siksika...well, Algonquian, as you might know it."

She'd known he was Native American but never which tribe. She asked, "Siksika? What tribe is that?"

"Blackfoot," he answered around another bite of food.

"Algonquian is where my name comes from, right, Daddy?"

Quil chuckled. "You always thought that, but it was your mama who pulled it from that word. She kinda just blurted it out one day and said it would go well with my name." Quil rolled his eyes and took another hearty bite of his food, getting a chuckle out of Veda who finally took a bite of her own.

Veda moaned as the melding flavors of salty, sweet, and spicy filled her mouth and hungry belly. "Oh my, this is amazing."

"You should try her carnitas, they're *my* favorite," Quil insisted. Veda almost laughed as he shoveled another bite in. "Sorry, I'm always starved after practice. That protein shake just doesn't do it for me."

Veda gave him a grin and took another bite. "So your father was Algonquian?" she asked after she chewed and swallowed.

She got a nod from Quil and didn't expect he'd say more. "My *abuela* and father raised me after my mother died in childbirth with me. They didn't get along well but loved me fiercely. Father didn't want me to forget my heritage and Abuela only spoke Spanish to me, so Pa decided to teach me the Blackfoot language too."

"*Abuela* means grandmother in Spanish, right?"

"Yes, she was the best woman I've ever known. A good Christian with a heart of gold and a penchant for cooking feasts."

This was the most Quil had ever told her about his life, well about anything really, considering he was a man of few words. Veda sucked it up.

"And your father?"

"The son of a Blackfoot chief who fell in love with the wrong woman off the reservation. He was banished, but if you saw my mother you'd understand. She had eyes like a jade sea and hair that was as black as night. Her skin was like honey and her lips like rose petals."

"She looked like me, right, Daddy?"

Quil smiled over at his daughter and gave her a terse nod. He failed to mention to Quinn that she didn't have black hair *or* green eyes because the child literally glowed at the prospect of resembling her beautiful paternal grandmother.

"It almost destroyed him when he lost her, and I didn't see much of him until I was about four. He took to the woods, grieving for that time. When he came back, he was as much a part of the wilderness as man; it took him time to reacclimate. He began telling me wild tales of hunting bears and beasts and how he'd communed with the spirit of my dead mother."

Veda stared at him in wonder… and shock. He was telling her so much about his life.

"My *abuela* didn't like that one bit. She was Orthodox Catholic, you see, and among other reasons, feared he would scare me by talking about such things." Quil shrugged. "He became a lumberjack, working long hours, but always pushed me to become an athlete in school and took pride in my talents on the field. He told me I was created to be a warrior, so a warrior I became. Warriors were my high school mascot." He gave her a smug wink and dug back into his food.

Veda grinned big and settled her eyes on Quinn when she laughed.

Sour cream smeared her little chin, and Quil's finger reached over and brushed it off. He chucked her little chin and got a laugh out of her.

Veda was about to take another bite of food when her stomach rebelled and a nausea pain hit her hard. Her fork hit her bowl with a clank and she covered her mouth, closing her eyes.

"V, you alright?"

She felt a hand come to her own as her left hand fell to her tummy. Her eyes opened quickly and she shook her head as she rose.

Quil must have understood, for he pointed to a door in the corner to the right of her. She took off for the bathroom, praying she got there before she painted the pretty blue walls in puke.

Once she'd wretched up the little contents she'd eaten that day, she sat down on the cool, tile floor, leaning her head against the porcelain toilet.

She could hear Juanita's loud voice in the background fussing at Quillan. Veda didn't speak or understand much Spanish but knew that Juanita was giving him hell when she heard the word "embarazada." She didn't remember much for the two years she'd taken that elective language in high school, but she did remember that word; it meant pregnant.

CHAPTER NINE

Quil left practice in a hurry to get to the chapel. He'd dressed in a suit, blue tie, and oxfords, not telling the guys what was afoot. He didn't want to hear it. It was none of their business. They would know soon enough as it was.

It was exactly one week to Christmas, and Quil couldn't believe he was getting married again. He'd sworn he would never do so... but that was before the prospect of another child seduced him into marrying the woman he'd impregnated. It was only right. His abuela and even his father would understand. He hadn't told them yet, either. They would also know soon enough. Tomorrow, he'd tell them tomorrow...after the game.

He smiled at the priest, at Becca and Pax who were their witnesses, at Veda's mother, Kathleen, who gave him a solemn one in return before his eyes fell on his bride.

Veda had never been more beautiful, covered in simple lace, face veiled by thin tulle. Her arms were bare, showcasing her colorfully-inked arms and chest. Her neck was bare too, save for a diamond choker that hugged her there. Her makeup was light, delicate, accentuating her most stunning features—plump rose lips and her sparkling emerald eyes.

Quil felt his stomach tighten and his heart overflow. He now understood why his father had abandoned all he'd known on the Montana Blackfoot reservation to be with something so akin to the Creator himself, something so heavenly, an angel in the flesh.

Quil gulped as Veda stopped before him. She would consider herself bad; he knew better. Inside her heart was pure, no matter what jewel or ink she decorated her body with to say otherwise, no matter how badass she appeared to be. A sweet soul lay beneath that tough exterior, and tonight, he would expose her. Like opening a treasure chest full of riches, she would reveal all her secrets.

He repeated the words of the minister, then Veda did. He noticed how reserved she was and figured it was because she still wasn't feeling well after last night's dinner. Clearly, that was the first time she'd been sick since her pregnancy. He'd taken her upstairs and laid her in her bed, fetching cool cloths to cover her head, chest, and neck with. He hadn't left her until he was sure she was alright.

Now, he was leaning in to kiss her and seal the deal. It was a soft kiss, but a kiss that was convincing enough to Veda that she was now his. His to control, his to dominate, his to break if she thought for one second about betraying him.

Quillan took her hand and smiled at her family and Pax, who looked unsure of what Quillan had just done. He walked his wife down the center aisle and out the doors of the church. He turned to kiss her again, more possessively this time, his arms wrapping around her small waist. God, she was such a tiny little thing. When he pulled back, he gave her a hard look.

"Are you sure you wanna do this?" he asked, even as he heard the rush of footsteps and the murmur of voices rapidly approaching them.

"I've never been more sure of anything in my lifetime."

He nodded and stilled himself for the flash of cameras as the press surrounded them in noise.

Veda sighed heavily as she sat on the toilet lid pondering her day. It had been a whirlwind of emotion. First, she'd married a man she wasn't in love with when she didn't even believe in marriage—not after what her father had done. Love was meant to be eternal, not fleeting; here one minute, gone the next. Her parents had seemed so happy in the beginning. She'd seen pictures, heard the grand tale of their meeting, the sparks, the love. *What a joke!*

She heard a faint knock on the door and Quil's deep voice asked, "V, are you ok?"

Veda cleared her throat. "I'll be out in just a minute."

She looked down at the racy piece of lingerie she'd bought herself for tonight. Another joke. They should have just consummated the marriage the minute they'd stepped over the threshold. It wasn't like this was the first time they'd been together. Hell, she was pregnant with his baby. What did it matter how they did it, so long as it was done?

But they'd both been overwhelmed—especially Veda.

She recalled the press closing in, Quil announcing their impromptu marriage, stating how they'd met and fallen in love on Halloween, how Veda was pregnant with his child, and how excited they were. Veda had plastered on her best fake smile, rubbing her husband's arm, and looking all the world to be the happiest bride on earth.

Then the first reporter asked the question everyone was dying to know.

"Mrs. Ry—Layton, so was it *you* who went to the clinic with Rebecca Ryan, your sister? Were you the mystery girl?"

"I was," Veda had looked up to Quil, as if seeking reassurance. He'd nodded for her to go on. "I went to the clinic with the intentions of having an abortion."

Chatter had overwhelmed her and flashes had blinded her.

Quillan had quieted them down and another reporter asked, "Why would you do that if you two were so happy?"

Inner rebel Veda took over then. "Because this *is* the 21ˢᵗ century and women have options. Options that I wasn't given at the age of sixteen."

She'd proceeded to tell them the story of what happened to her, how she'd been treated, the story of her fall from grace, when her innocence had truly been taken away from her—murder by her own hands. Veda had cried—true, genuine tears of regret, pain, and hate —revealing the deepest, rawest side of herself for all to see. And when she was done, the reporters all sighed heavily.

"So, why did you decide not to abort this child, Mrs. Layton?" A blonde reporter asked with tears in her eyes.

"Veda and I made that decision together," Quil piped in then looked to Veda to finish.

"I realized it wasn't just my decision to make." Veda gave Quil a soft smile. "Although having an abortion is no easy matter for either party involved. However, women need to know all their options when they have an unplanned pregnancy and that it doesn't make them a bad person if abortion is indeed one of them."

"So, you *support* abortion, Mrs. Layton? Even after what was done to you as a minor?" A male reporter had smarted off. "Isn't Mr. Layton here actually a pro-life advocate, along with your sister's fiancé, Paxton Guthrie, your soon-to-be brother-in-law?"

"I am pro *decision*, sir. I support the right for a woman to be able to decide for herself, so I guess I'm a supporter of both life and the alternative."

Another million flashes blinded her once more, and she'd felt herself being pulled to a limo.

Quillan had given her a slow smile then and nodded. "Well done, *Mrs.* Layton."

She'd laughed heartily then cried, sobbed even. God, those damn pregnancy hormones were a bitch! Quillan had pulled her into his arms and comforted her, and when they'd pulled up to his house, he'd seen her inside.

She'd come to her room to rest and freshen up, and now, was the grand finale for the evening—the consummation of their marriage.

Veda popped up off the toilet lid and looked into the large mirror on the wall, beyond the grey and white-marbled countertop. Her eyes looked tired, but she still had every ounce of makeup in place just as she had hours ago—these celebs had it easy. She was indeed grateful for make-up primer, spray, and waterproof mascara though.

She straightened the thin, see-through lace teddy and rubbed her lips together to smear her rose lipstick into place. Her hair was up and off her neck, clipped up with a claw-like clip.

She took one last look before turning and opening the door.

Hades lay on his back, looking far too comfortable for his own good, his boxer briefs covering his hips. A glass of wine sat on the nightstand beside him and he eyed her with growing interest as his caramel eyes moved from her face, down her chest to her legs. He gulped but said nothing.

Veda lowered her eyes, for she felt like his were actually burning lasers scorching her skin. They fell to the sheets and comforter of the massive sleigh bed—dark purple, the color of royalty, embellished with deep gold. It was fitting for Hades, the god he was.

Quil's hand gripped her wrist as she stopped next to the bed.

"Would you like a drink?"

Veda only nodded, not trusting her voice. Why was she so nervous? She'd already slept with him, several times? Why would this time be any different? It didn't mean anything, despite the platinum band on her finger searing her flesh at the thoughts of falsifying such a sacred union.

A glass of deep red was handed to her and she turned it up, gulping down the contents before handing the glass back to him. To her surprise it wasn't wine, it was sparkling red grape juice. The sentiment touched her and she hoped she could keep it down, unlike her breakfast that morning.

"Are you hungry?" Quil asked.

Veda shook her head and looked his handsome face over. At least she was gonna have a great view while defiling herself. "Let's just get this over with."

Quil scoffed, then his face went grave as Death himself. She was pulled roughly atop him. Her thighs splayed involuntarily—straddling his hips—as his big palms gripped her bottom unmercifully and squeezed. She gasped, as much for the surprise of her desperate arousal as from his actions.

"I'm calling the shots now, *dama serpiente.*"

He leaned up, licking her nipple through the lace as he rocked her hips on his, his long thickness rubbing against her pierced clit, making her moan.

"I see you still burn for me, lover."

Burn. Yes, she burned, and with a heat hotter than any she'd ever felt, her womb humming to have him buried deep within her once more.

She might as well enjoy this, she figured, as her hands moved over his tightly-muscled abs and chest, running her fingertips over his small peaked nipples and getting a shiver out of him. He moaned unabashedly and gave her a devilish grin before suckling at her lace-covered nipple and biting down into the barbell impaling it. Veda gasped again and cupped his head, running her hand through his jet-black locks.

"Fuck, Quil, I want you."

"Mmm, yeah? You want this?" He thrust himself against her hips, his hard flesh poking her inner thigh.

"Yes, I want it." She moved her hand down to his erection, scooting her hips back so she could slip it from the opening of his boxer-briefs. His impressive member popped out eagerly and jerked in her small hand as she began to grip it in her fist and pump it.

"Mmm, yeah, baby. Stroke me."

She became mesmerized with the big cock in her hand, the veiny flesh rigid and wanting. It gave another sharp jerk again as she traced her other fingertip over the opening at the head and watched liquid bead at the tip there. She moaned aloud and moved out of his hold, lowering her head to lick the precum from him. He grunted as she sucked the tip of his cock into her mouth and pulled back, watching his eyes as she licked her tongue over the head again.

"Fuck," he groaned as his hand moved to her hair, gripping the clip lightly and tugging gently. "Take it all down, *chica mala*."

She gave him a naughty smile and did just that, gripping the base with her hand and fiercely sucking his girthy length down her throat, using her tongue on the underside. He ate it up as she feasted on him, his head lolling as she coaxed him closer and closer to his most vulnerable state before he was pulling her by her hair off him and jerking the crotch of her teddy aside.

He slammed her down hard on his hips, his thick erection penetrating her opening with violent possession. As much as the initial burn hurt, she found herself rocking with him as his mouth moved to her bare throat, sucking and licking, his thumb stroking at her clit piercing.

"Oh, God," she whimpered as his teeth bit into her flesh, his palms gripping her bottom with strength.

"Hades, baby. I won't tell you again." He smacked her ass even as his fingers stroked harder against her swollen bud, getting another gasp out of her.

"Mmm, yes... Fuck, I'm gonna come."

And she did, with a violent spasm that shook them both as he brought her up and down on his cock. She screamed in pleasure and his mouth took hers, his tongue thrusting with the rhythm of his hips.

"Mmm, mmm, oh, oh," she groaned as she came down, her sex still clenching him.

Quill's chest heaved as he looked her over and gave her another devilish grin.

Suddenly, she was pulled from him and flipped over on all fours. She felt the clip jerk from her hair and his fist replace it as he entered her again. She gasped even as the feel of his cock inside her once more made her desire soar. He pushed her head down to the mattress as he took her from behind and fisted her mane, the pain and pleasure warring within her. She moved her hand in between them and cupped his scrotum, tickling him with her long nails.

He groaned in pleasure and ran a hand up her laced back before she felt the fabric tear around her. A massive warm palm moved delicately over her now bare flesh and made her shiver, her sex gripping him in an intimate hug that had him groaning again.

"Oh, baby, you feel so good, so *damn* good." His thrusts became harder, more desperate before, once more, he was turning her over, her weak and needing body wrapping around him as he covered her.

She'd forgotten how tall and big he was, how much he towered over her, but it didn't matter as he held her tightly to his chiseled frame, her body aligning perfectly to his. She moaned as his manhood began unraveling the very fabric of her as it stroked her inner walls with the expertise of a skilled lover, like being truly touched by the gods.

Her grip on him tightened, her legs pulling him ever closer as her hands clawed at his back, seeking, reaching. His hips hit hers violently, the flesh slamming together in deafening smacks as his palms moved to her bottom, spreading her wider. And she couldn't fight the need to join him in the Underworld, for she was lost to his allure. The darkness within him matching her own as he climbed, higher and harder, pulling her down, lifting her up, breaking her down, and pushing her to her climax, to his climax, to *their* climax. It was bittersweet, the giving, the taking, the yielding and the overpowering. He was her torture and prize all at the same time and as she looked up at his ridiculously handsome face covered in sweat and red from their love-making, she realized this hot lust between them was getting worse and not better... for both of them.

Their bodies quivered, their sexes still linked and throbbing in the most intimate of embraces. Quil didn't move, didn't speak, just breathed hard and heavy as he returned from his release, cupping her face and looking her over.

"Did I hurt you?" he whispered after long moments had passed.

Veda just shook her head, running a hand through his soft, thick mane of black.

"You. I don't know what it is about you, V. But I..." he trailed off and looked away, as if embarrassed.

"Say it. You can tell me," she insisted, loving how he had begun to open up to her as of late.

He smirked before his eyes fell back to hers. "It's kinda morbid."

Veda gave a sharp cynical laugh, getting a moan out of Quil. "Try me," she smarted.

"It's just...well, when I see you, there's this overwhelming need within me to..." He looked down again and she had to shake him to get him to confess. "To possess you. To *own* you. To break you." He gulped, shame hitting his face.

Veda could've laughed because she understood. She'd felt the same way when she'd first seen him in the club. The need to corrupt him. Soil him. Scorch him with her invisible brand. When Quil began to withdraw, she held tight and ran her fingertip from his bearded chin to his cheekbone, watching his jaw clench and unclench.

She grinned. "Quillan, you're a warrior, remember? Your first instinct is to conquer, is it not?" She laughed lightly, getting a smile out of him.

He looked her face over again, his palm moving back to her face, cupping gently. "It is, V, but the problem is that I'm notorious for just that." When Veda frowned in confusion, he said, "I've destroyed every woman in my life. I honestly don't want to destroy you too."

QUIL HAD a hard time sleeping that night as he lay spooned against Veda, tucking her tightly into his arms. She was so soft and small—and sweet when she was sleeping. He'd been truthful when he told her he didn't want to destroy her, but the women of his past had bore witness to the truth. First his mother; he'd killed her while birthing him. Then Rian; he'd destroyed her by planting a defective seed within her, breaking her heart for all eternity. Then Quinn, sweet precious Quinn, the daughter spawned by said defective seed, a defect that would lead to her untimely death because her body didn't work like it was meant to. Now he had Veda to worry about. What unforeseen and unfortunate event would she succumb to at his hand? And their unborn child?

Quillan knew his thoughts might be irrational and paranoid, but marrying her without question had got him remembering things about Rian he didn't want to remember. The addiction that had destroyed them all for a time, the pain, the anguish, the anger, the hate. Hate for the woman who'd loved a substance more than she'd loved the people who adored her more than life itself.

He knew Veda had no such unhealthy addictions, despite her rebellious nature. She also had a heart as big as her attitude, and he was starting to enjoy her company, much to his chagrin. She was a feisty and fierce little warrior who became straight goo in his hands when he touched her, and he loved the effect that touch had on her. It turned him on unlike anything he'd ever felt before. That was another thing that scared him—he was starting to have feelings for her.

But how could he not? She was pregnant with his child. Very early on, but still.

His hand settled on her lower belly and stroked her naked flesh there, getting a muffled moan out of her. He grinned and began to move his hands over her, admiring the softness of her skin, the plumpness of her breast, the curve of her hips and ass. She was gasping, grunting, and still half asleep when she reached for his solid erection and pulled it to the entrance of her body. Her heat never failed to still his breath—so hot, so sweet, like dipping into a silk-wrapped hot spring; he couldn't get enough, couldn't get deep enough into it.

He grunted as one palm moved beneath her to cup her breast, the other to her throat, lightly holding, not squeezing as his hips thrust against hers. Her hand held the back of his thigh as she lowered herself onto him, making his cock reach even deeper inside her and making him groan in sweet agony.

"Fuck, Veda," he muttered into her ear as the hand on her breast lowered to the delta of her thighs, tickling the jeweled flesh between. In seconds, she was coming, her womanhood clenching him hard. *Madre de Dio*," he whimpered and attempted to hold himself back but couldn't. "I can't stop myself."

He bit down into her shoulder as he hammered into her, harder, faster, mindlessly needing to claim this woman he was inside despite that he was already claiming her, every inch of her as his hands gripped her selfishly. Her cry of pleasure matched his own as he spilled himself inside her, sputtering and whimpering, a man at the pinnacle of a blissful weakness second only to death.

"Mmm, Quillan," she lazily murmured, still half asleep as she leaned back to kiss his jaw.

"Persephone," he chuckled beneath his breath.

"Huh?" she asked, amused.

"Persephone. That's you."

He had her full attention as her vibrant green eyes bounced between his. He gave her a grin of equal parts happiness and fatigue, the grin of a lover following his climax.

"Persephone was the goddess of fertility and Queen of the Underworld."

"I *know* who Persephone was." Veda giggled. "It's only fitting since you kidnapped me and forced me into marriage, I guess." She scoffed and elbowed him lightly in the ribs.

"Some miserable hostage you are indeed," he answered back and lightly squeezed her breast again, getting a sexy moan out of her. He kissed the crook of her neck, licking the sweat there and savoring the shiver that ran through her. "Guess it's time to pull out the pomegranates now."

Veda laughed heartily and Hades joined her. *Yes, lots and lots of pomegranates,* he thought as she turned in his arms and began kissing him with passion.

CHAPTER TEN

"Where's Daddy?" Quinn said as they took the elevator up to the luxury box, Becca in tow.

"Don't worry, sweetheart. We'll get to see him before the game, ok?" Veda answered and pulled Quinn's head to her hip. Quinn looked anxiously around at the large hallway they stepped into, their footsteps echoing on the tile floors.

"Whoa, this is big!" Quinn's little voice echoed as well, getting a giggle out of her, but she was focused on the field in front of her lit up by the sun, the uprights glimmering yellow where the rays touched them.

Veda followed Becca as they moved into the heated box that was the size of a banquet hall. She smiled over at Valeria and Skyla, who both looked at Veda apprehensively. Madi's face was more passive; she could be loathing Veda's attendance and Veda wouldn't have a clue, but she'd come to realize that was just Madi's way. Becca hugged them all and reintroduced Veda and Quinn to be polite. Veda, in turn, nodded to them all.

It was Madison who spoke first. "Veda, congrats are in order."

Madi handed her a flute of what appeared to be champagne and clinked her own glass with Veda's.

Quinn ran over to the window then to look for her father and Madi whispered, "To a happy marriage and a healthy baby. It's sparkling grape juice by the way." Madi called over to Quinn. "Quinn darling, would you like a glass?"

Quinn looked up at Veda in question, who nodded eagerly at her. Quinn smiled and nodded vigorously before taking a flute of juice from the tray Madi had brought over.

"That was quite a speech you gave yesterday," Brooke Taylor said from the corner of the room, next to a large silver platter of bacon-wrapped shrimp with a warmer beneath it.

"Thank you."

"I don't think there was a dry eye in America."

"Brooke," Madi turned her head, blonde hair up in a French twist, warning her sister.

"I'm serious!" Brooke stated with a shrug and approached. "I know my eyes weren't. Were yours, sister?"

Madi gave Brooke a withered look.

"It's a shame your husband won't let you work with me anymore." Brooke pouted. Veda wasn't sure if it was real or she was being sarcastic; that was just Brooke.

"It was...what was best for all involved," Veda retorted, barely audible in the murmur of voices filling the room.

"Sure. I guess."

By this point, Madi had taken Quinn over to talk to Sky and Val, who oohed and aahed over her cute little Gladiators cheerleading outfit.

"Brooke," Veda began but was interrupted as Brooke separated the distance between them.

"Look, I get it," Brooke gave her a sly grin, "your husband is a possessive man. I would be too if I had a looker like you on my arm, don't get me wrong." She winked and reached out to lightly grasp Veda's arm. "I'll cut my losses. If you're happy, that's all that matters.

If it's what you want, then it is what it is… but never forget that if you want to work with me again, I'll gladly take you back under my wing."

The insinuation was not missed on Veda; she gave her a slow grin and thanked her.

Working with Brooke hadn't been difficult. She was easy-going, fair, and even fun. It was what happened after their photo-shoots that had given Veda pause. The bribery. The push in a direction she hadn't wanted to go. Not that she wasn't wild and crazy—and explo-rative—when it came to sex, but she'd attempted being with a girl before and it just wasn't enjoyable for her. The entire time she'd wanted a man, a real penis, because nothing felt like the real thing. Brooke was a beautiful woman with a beautiful body, but clearly, TJ hadn't been into her little stunts and his lack of interest in Veda's attendance only made the entire awkward situation even less plea-surable.

Both times that she'd been present while they were doing their thing—since she'd been hesitant to be an active participant for all those reasons—she'd just sat on the chaise in the corner and touched herself for Brooke's benefit, she assumed, because TJ was focused on Brooke and nothing else. Veda herself had closed her eyes—and attempted to close her ears—and thought of Quillan.

She was glad now he'd put a stop to it because she had planned to do the same herself. The knowing grin Brooke now gave Veda said she was all too aware of that fact as she walked over to the bar to get a drink.

The mood seemed to lighten as Veda came over to where Quinn was telling Madi about their plans for Christmas weekend and how excited she was to get to see Val and Linc's twins again.

Madi nodded for Veda to accompany her to thick leather seats overlooking the expanse of the ever-green field ahead of them. She looked straight ahead and sipped her flute of bubbly juice, looking as elegant and refined as ever, a true born leader, Hera—the queen of the gods.

"You have redeemed yourself, Veda. And your sister's reputation."

"I didn't just do it for us, contrary to what you believe." It was important for Madison to understand that fact.

"I know." Madi turned her Caribbean blue-green eyes to her and gave her a warm smile. Maybe she wasn't just a rich bitch after all. "But I'll thank you all the same." She gave Veda a brief nod. "I've been told that you've been contacted by both Pro-Life and Planned Parenthood now to speak about your ordeal."

Veda answered with, "Yes, apparently I captured the audiences of both. Sympathy from the Lifers for my decision being a forced one and gratitude from Planned Parenthood for not throwing women who have had abortions to the wolves."

"Fitting and good publicity—for all of us," Madi added, not seeming to sound smug, of which she didn't. "That should get you a name for yourself apart from your marriage to a pro-football star. We all need our own things too, ya know?" Madi winked and Veda nodded, sipping her drink.

"Veda, can we go down and see Daddy now?" Quinn came over and asked, biting into a shrimp and discarding the tail on her plate.

"Let's eat a bite real quick, huh, kiddo? I'm starved." Veda patted her rumbling belly, getting a giggle out of Quinn who said, "Alright."

They moved around the buffet of indulgences Veda rarely got to sample before marrying a rich man: prosciutto-wrapped figs stuffed with goat cheese, pan-seared scallops tossed with linguine, sea bass baked in lemon butter and shallots, sweet potato bites, mini beef wellingtons and a mixed green salad with a cranberry vinaigrette that was to die for.

Even Quinn was begging for seconds, making all the women laugh at her enthusiasm. Madi told her to knock herself out and Val said, "A kid with great taste!" as the little doll ran back over to grab herself more shrimp and sweet potatoes.

Becca sat next to Skyla who seemed reserved—more reserved than at the Halloween party—probably because she was still reeling from the loss of her baby.

Even though Veda was only in her first trimester, she couldn't imagine losing this baby, despite that she'd gone to the abortion clinic to do that very thing. She was so glad Quillan was so excited. It made her heart soar.

Speaking of Quillan, Quinn set her plate aside and ran back over to Veda, begging. "I wanna see Daddy, please?"

Veda laughed and stood. "Alright, baby girl, let's go see Daddy." She took a hot towel from the maitre'd who'd walked over and began to wipe Quinn's hands, all too aware of the eyes on her.

"Daddy, huh? Taking after Val, are ya?" Brooke smirked.

Val blushed, and Veda's brows drew in confusion.

Madi snorted but it was Sky, who said, "Ladies, looks like Becca's twin is gonna fit right in with us."

They all laughed and stood to head down to the tunnels.

QUIL'S TEAMMATES were quiet as they suited up for their game against the Packers. It didn't really matter if they won or not; they were still going to the playoffs, either way. The tension wasn't high, but Quil was aware that none of them seemed too thrilled with him since he'd spontaneously married the cantankerous bitch that had insulted them all the day after Halloween in Paxton's kitchen.

Brett gave him the once over as he adjusted his shoulder pad.

"Alright Cap, what's on your mind?"

"Not much. Just wondering why you'd lock yourself into a loveless marriage." Brett turned away from him and dug in his locker for something.

"I never even expected to marry again, you know? It's not like it was planned. Fate has a way of kicking you when you're down, as you well know."

Brett frowned as he turned around. "Still Quillan, I guess I expected more from you." He shrugged.

"You think she's out for my money."

"Isn't that kinda *obvious*?" Brett smarted.

"I think she might have been, in the beginning. But not anymore."

"Is she really even pregnant or did she just make that shit up?"

A flicker of doubt rippled through Quil as that thought crossed his mind. *Holy shit!* He'd never really had any proof, had he? He'd seen the news coverage of her going into the abortion clinic. She'd told him she was. But there was no *physical* proof of that claim. He'd not seen a pregnancy test and she hadn't been to the doctor to verify it. Jesus, how dumb was he?

Brett's brows rose as if to say, "Told ya...idiot!", and he turned back to his locker.

Pax brought Quil out of his stiffness, patting his back with a laugh. "Is Hades here with his horse-drawn chariot? 'Cause Poseidon is ready to fill the Gladiator's sea with green and gold blood."

TJ rolled his eyes upward as Travis grinned at Paxton's enthusiasm.

"That's right, bro. Let's get our god on!" Travis smacked Paxton's fist in a fist bump. Trav was starting to get back to his old self again, which was nice to see.

Linc came up then and nodded to them all. "Pax and I are gonna steam roll 'em."

"See to it that you do, defense. I'll take a grilled cheese sandwich, please?" Brett insisted, getting a laugh out of all of them.

"Daddy!" came a little squeal Quil was accustomed to hearing and he turned to see his daughter and new wife in tow, his heart hammering at Veda's subtle smile.

God, he really hoped Brett was wrong... but what if he wasn't?

Quillan hugged his child to him, her little arms barely wrapping around his bulky, pad covered frame.

"Daddy, you're so...puffy," Quinn patted at his chest pads and he laughed.

"I know. It's so I don't get hurt from all those big lugs like Uncle TJ here."

Quinn frowned and looked over at TJ, who shrugged. "Do you like my outfit? Veda said it looks authentic, does it?"

Quil grinned and looked his brown-haired doll over. "It does, indeed."

"What does authentic mean?"

"It means you look like a real cheerleader," Veda ruffled Quinn's thick curls and smiled up at Quillan, making his heart rate double. She looked beautiful today, dressed in a simple, form-fitting, long-sleeved black dress, leggings, and boots.

"And you'd know, wouldn't you, V? Since you *were* one and all." TJ came by and smacked Veda's bottom a little more familiarly than Quillan liked, and he held back a growl. Brooke had said she hadn't participated in the threesome, but Quil was starting to doubt her words as TJ's smirked back at her. Had TJ not been his teammate and them about to play a game, Quil might've knocked that smile clean off his face.

Veda blushed and looked down, giving Quinn a forced smile.

Quil's attention was drawn to the sound of Travis pushing his fiancée against the locker in a searing kiss. He moved his head into the crook of her shoulder and whispered something only the two of them could hear. Sky closed her eyes, emotion seizing her features. Quil felt a pang of guilt, knowing how upset they were about the loss of their unborn baby. Perhaps, in time, she could get pregnant again.

Brett's throat cleared, pulling Quillan's head back around.

"Good luck," Veda said with a sly smile.

"Thanks. I'm glad my ladies came to see me before warm-up." He grinned at both Veda and Quinn before Veda reached up on her tip-toes to kiss him on the cheek.

The women hurried off then; Hera the last to see her king off to battle, blowing him a kiss that he "caught" and tucked into his jersey, getting a laugh out of the lovely Madison. Quil couldn't help but smile at the two of them; a second chance romance indeed.

"Alright—huddle up, Gladiators," Brett insisted. "We got a game to win."

With that, they followed their captain out the tunnel and into the Colosseum.

THE MORE QUIL thought about what Brett had said, the madder he got. What if he was right, what if Veda had lied about this whole thing? But why would she? His anger fueled his drive to win and he found himself the receiver of the game ball tonight with seven receptions, one hundred and twenty yards, and two touchdowns. He'd also blocked for two big touchdowns that Trav had ran in tonight. And the defense had smeared the field with cheese as they'd bragged that they would.

Quil couldn't share his team's celebratory happiness, though. He was too busy stewing. Pax noticed his mood first.

"Oh, Hades... Always brooding, brother." He laughed and patted Quil's shoulder, but quickly saw that Quil wasn't in the mood. "Damn, sorry, I didn't realize you were on your period."

"Can it, merman," Quil grumbled and threw his helmet down onto the bench.

"What do you have to be so mad about? You do realize we *won* the game, right?"

"When I get reincarnated, I want to come back as *you*, hippie boy —with not a damn care in the fuckin' world." Quil whipped around and headed for the shower room, aware of Paxton's pout.

He heard Trav ask, "Who pissed in his Cheerios?"

"Ah, you know Hades," Brett answered, "Always in a bad mood lately."

Quil was ready to slam his fist into the concrete, despite that he knew it would hurt him more than the damn concrete. But dammit, he was amped up and ready to fight; the game had not calmed his adrenaline one ounce. He was mad, he was hurt, and he was starting to feel something for the naughty little taboo wife of his.

After a cold shower, he threw some gel in his hair, brushed his teeth and dressed, spraying some cologne on and dumping his towel into the hamper. Then he headed up to the luxury box.

Seeing his sweet daughter passed out on the leather chair softened his heart some. So did Veda's bright green eyes, smiling up at him. "She tried so hard to stay awake to see you...but she just crashed."

The way Veda stared down at Quinn made Quil gulp. She ran her small hand through his daughter's thick locks, grinning sweetly down at the little snoozing angel.

"She was adorable tonight, Quil, watching you score your touchdowns. I videoed her. I'll have to show it to you."

"Yeah. Later. Let's go." Quil looked away as his tone hardened.

Veda stood, and he moved to scoop up his daughter, resting her head into his shoulder.

Veda followed as he bade a good night to Jerry, their GM, and the others left in the luxury box. She didn't say a word as they walked out to his Land Rover, and he strapped Quinn into the seat.

Quil tried to keep his anger at bay, but as he drove to his house, it built within him like a volcano. Once they'd gotten inside and he'd laid Quinn down in her bed, he rounded on Veda.

"I'm gonna ask you once and only once, and so help me God if you don't tell me the truth, I will *fucking* ruin you!" He backed her into the wall adjacent from Quinn's door, pressing his hand above her head, caging her in.

He gave her credit; she blinked in surprise but didn't cower as most women would in that instant. "You enjoy threatening me with destruction, don't you?"

He continued as if she hadn't spoken, "Are you really pregnant with my child or has this whole thing been a sham?"

Veda balked then and gave him a soft, humorless laugh. "Do you honestly think I would marry you if I didn't have a *damn* good reason to do so?"

"Answer the question, Veda. Yes or no!"

Her eyes narrowed as she growled, "Yes. I'm fucking pregnant. And with *your* baby."

"Where's the proof? The bloodwork, the ultrasound?"

"I don't have any of that!" She whisper-yelled so as not to wake Quinn. "I have my first doctor visit next week."

"So… let me get this straight… you don't know for a *fact*?" His face felt like it might melt off with the rage building within him.

"No. I don't… but I took three pregnancy tests back to back, I can't stand the smell of lunch meat without gagging, and I have a ridiculous craving for pickles swimming in ice cream. Not to mention that I've missed two periods, and I'm that girl who's like clockwork."

Quil inhaled deeply, feeling some sense of relief. It was early on—he'd known that when he'd decided to up and marry her—but he'd had a knee-jerk reaction to this whole situation, and that had been completely and regrettably irrational.

A sneer took Veda's face then. "Who is it you're angrier at right now, Quillan? Me for not having proof of my claim or yourself for being stupid enough to marry me without it?"

He felt his jaw tick and his upper lip quiver as he took her chin in his grasp and leaned down, his nose touching hers. "You think you have the upper hand here?"

She said nothing, just squared off with him, not blinking. She had balls, he'd give her that. A vile thought planted into his head, and his stomach clenched as he decided to roll with it. She wanted to poke the bull, she'd get the horns.

He pressed his frame into hers, his body holding her captive against the wall as he unbuttoned his slacks. "You'll do well to remember who wears the pants in this house, V. Baiting me will get you nowhere. I'll teach you what happens when you fuck with the wrong god, *dama serpiente*."

With that, he peeled her leggings down. She didn't rebut him, didn't object, and when he jerked her panties down, lifted her and penetrated her, she didn't even cry out.

He was aware of two things at that moment. One, how his anger dissipated as easily as it had come on and two, how sweet it felt being inside her once again. Nothing else existed in that moment but the need within him to dominate her, and he thrust hard to answer that need. Finally, a muffled moan answered him.

"Shit, baby," he murmured as he gripped her bottom and nuzzled her neck, licking at her pulse point, his teeth nipping at her collarbone. "Mmm. My *chica mala*. It makes you mad that you want this too, doesn't it? Who do you hate more right now? Me or yourself?" he asked as he pulled back a little, rocking his hips seductively, loving her with his rock-hard member. He stared into eyes as fierce as his and grinned in triumph at the inner battle he saw there.

Quil moved a hand to lightly grasp Veda's throat, cupping without restricting. Her hands stayed at her sides. She wasn't going to submit to his power.

"You forget who you married. I'm Hades. I walk through darkness daily. The outsider of Mt. Olympus. Not unlike you, *mi esposa*." He continued to plunge and withdraw inside her, watching as her frustrations turned to pleasure, evaluating her resolve as she fought to hold herself back. "Touch yourself, Veda, come for me. Fall with me, *pequeña rebelde*."

Her chin went up defiantly, even as her eyelids fluttered in pleasure and she stifled a moan.

"Do it, Persephone," Quillan murmured. "Succumb to your dark god, your lover, your husband." His mouth lowered to her cleavage, licking and sucking as he thrust harder and higher, seeking Heaven within the center of the most frustratingly amazing woman he'd ever known. He moved his hand from her throat and stroked her wet folds with nimble fingers, his pace picking up as she began to whimper in equal parts lust and resistance. He felt her shudder as they both surrendered to the flames licking at them. He bit into her shoulder and roared his release, his climax coming fast and violently upon him. The force of his thrusts crushed Veda into the wall as the spasms of his orgasm rendered him captive.

When he finally stilled, he stepped back, shocked by his aggressive behavior. He set Veda down quickly and looked her over for any sign of damage. He saw streaks of tears running down her cheeks and, in a flash, he was slapped, his head whipping to the side. The sting was sharp, but it was the realization of what he'd just done that burned him.

"Don't *ever* touch me again," Veda stated deathly calm, "or you'll no longer be bragging about being the king of the dead, you'll be *among* them."

VEDA HURRIED off to the solace she needed and closed her suite door behind her as she moved inside the room. She sank down, as if melting, bracing herself against the wood—whether to keep Quillan out or herself in she wasn't sure.

She'd been outraged by Quil's cruelty and appalled by her attraction to his violence. The anger within him had matched her own, their passions equal in their resolve, their desire for pain and pleasure indistinguishable. She wasn't sure if she'd been more sickened by her need for his darkness or that she'd been unafraid of him.

Pain wasn't something Veda was unfamiliar with; she'd learned to live with it, learned to turn her back and accept the flogging life had given her, learned to lick her wounds in private and simply move forward. But this was something different. This was a pain she was starting to relish, an unhealthy pain. Quil had enjoyed hurting her, overpowering her, angering her. And she'd enjoyed it too, every second of it. His anger, his desire for her, his need to punish her.

She'd always been the evil twin, the bad girl—now she was proving it at every turn.

She pulled herself from the floor and moved into the bathroom to shower, wanting to wipe the proof of her sin away, even knowing she couldn't. The stigma would still be there no matter if she washed for a thousand years.

But she'd made a point tonight—that Quil couldn't continue to use her as his puppet—and hopefully, he'd taken heed of her warning.

She shucked her clothes and entered the water, letting it cover her face and hair, basking in the warmth. Her anger hadn't fully dissipated, and she once more cursed herself for getting pregnant with that asshole's baby. She was going to be cursed with his presence forever now. She would never be free of him.

She leaned into the water and let it pound her relentlessly, cloaking her in safety, enclosing her in a bubble where nothing existed but peace and determination.

"I'm sorry, little one," she apologized to the unborn child in her womb, stroking her hand over the no longer flat belly. She wondered once again if she'd made a mistake in keeping this baby, for perhaps even death would've been better than being born the child of the very Devil himself.

CHAPTER ELEVEN

Q uil looked Veda over on Christmas morning, seated on the couch, faking it for Quinn's sake.

"I love them, Veda!" Quinn squealed at the Disney pajamas Veda had gotten her.

"Oh good, I'm so glad," V stated in relief as Quinn ran to hug her.

"Daddy, look! Pocahontas… like you."

Quil couldn't hide the crooked grin snaking up on him. Pocahontas was her favorite because she was a Native American, like Quil's dad had been. The many stories she'd pried from over the years about her grandfather Machk—Mac for short.

"What do you tell Veda?" he asked Quinn who then turned and thanked Veda.

Her eyes had big dark circles under them and she looked sickly, like she might hurl. The last few days had been tough for them both. Quil had hurt his ankle at practice. Veda had had morning sickness something awful and couldn't keep anything down. She also hadn't spoken to him in that time either, which made life even harder for them both. Quinn was none the wiser, and her enthusiasm was the only thing good about the day.

They had plans to meet up with Becca, Pax, Kathleen, and Walt for lunch and head to Madi and Brett's for dinner. Quil knew V didn't really want to do either but would, just to save face.

Quil had felt bad for their last sexual experience but wasn't one to grovel, so he hadn't. Veda didn't seem to want an apology anyway, so who was he to push the envelope. She'd known marrying him wouldn't be a walk in the park, and he didn't really intend for it to be anyway. She should have thought about that before she'd agreed to marry him and before she'd spread her legs to him.

He knew he was punishing himself as much as he was her and knew his thoughts and feelings on the matter weren't exactly sane or healthy. The whole situation was fucked and fucked up. There was nothing more he could say on the matter; no other word could do it justice.

Until the baby was born, their lives were intertwined. They had to coexist together.

For now, he smiled at yet another gift Quinn opened.

He tried to focus only on his daughter, on her happiness, for if he didn't, he would be condemning himself. He'd known he'd been too rough, too violent, too dominating when it came to Veda. He knew he was on a precipice when it came to her. A precipice where his very soul hung in the balance. He took a side glance over at her and realized she was doing the same to him.

Great! This day was going to be as painful as the rest had been. He stood, took her empty coffee mug and walked into the kitchen, needing a moment to breathe.

He wasn't prepared when he turned and there she was, looking up at him from her perch of five foot two inches tall.

"I don't need you to wait on me," she murmured as she opened the fridge and pulled out her peppermint mocha creamer.

"Well, excuse the hell out of me if I was just being nice," he smarted.

"You aren't *nice*. You're the damn Devil himself in the fucking flesh, and we both know it."

Quillan smirked and rolled his eyes then. But scowled when her frown deepened. "You knew you were dancing with *el diablo* the night of Halloween, *dama serpiente*."

She shook her head, but he cut her off before she spoke. "I warned you. *El diablo* lies and manipulates. He comes in the form of the most beautiful thing you've ever seen. Perhaps *you* are him yourself."

She swallowed hard, and those green eyes pierced his soul once again. "Wouldn't be the first time I've been accused of that."

She turned on her heel, grabbed her coffee, and moved back into the living room.

Later, when they were all showered, dressed, and piling into his vehicle, he glanced over at her with her elbow on the window, looking like a lost soul, crestfallen on this sacred day. Quil's heart-strings pulled, feeling the need to remedy the void between them.

"So," Quil started, looking back to see that Quinn was watching her iPad, earphones on her head, "you said your father was the one to force you into your abortion..."

Veda's head turned sharply to look at him, her sad eyes begging for relief. "If you don't mind, I'd really prefer *not* to talk about my father today."

"I'm sorry." Dammit, why did he suck so much at talking to people? Now, he knew why he was such an introvert. "I've just been wondering why. You never told me the whole story."

Veda huffed out and looked out the window again. Quil saw her lips quiver and she swallowed hard. He didn't think she would answer him but said, "He thought I was evil."

"Evil?" Quil couldn't hide his smirk. "Like...really?"

"Yes, really!" she stated loudly and jerked her head to look back at him again.

When he came to a stoplight, he glanced back at her, watching the war within her battling—pain versus anger.

"Why?" he couldn't stop himself from asking.

"Because he was fucking crazy. After my sister Sarah died, then our mother was diagnosed with the same illness, he thought we... well, *I* was cursed. A bad omen. Becca was perfect, you see. In his eyes, she was practically a nun and I was the spawn of Satan because I wasn't like her. I was her 'fetch'. I talked back, enjoyed the company of boys, and listened to heavy metal, loved dancing and being a normal teenager. I was Becca's doppelgänger, and I had to be cleansed of my sinful ways, especially once I caught him cheating on mam."

"Jesus Christ," Quillan murmured and hit the gas after getting a honk from behind them, realizing he'd frozen at Veda's words. He said nothing for a time as they rode into the city, navigating the side roads to Kathleen's apartment, where they were to have lunch with Veda's family. Finally, Quil was the first to break the silence. "Abortion is just as wrong as adultery and premarital sex is... according to the Catholic faith."

"Yeah, and so is birth control. So where does one find a happy medium?" The cynicism dripping from Veda's lips wasn't lost to him.

"You consider yourself Catholic?" he asked.

Veda shrugged. "I go to church for my mother's sake."

Quil couldn't help but grin. "I get it."

"Your *abuela*?" Veda asked.

Quillan nodded. "I find a peaceful existence between the spirit she calls God, but I can relate to my Blackfoot father's faith. So long as I can pray and feel good about it, it shouldn't matter what I call our Creator."

Veda gave a subtle nod and was quiet again for a time before she said, "I think my father used religion as an excuse for his own mental sickness. Sarah's death and Mam's diagnosis were very difficult for us all. Then when I got pregnant, I think that was the final straw."

"So you forgive him for what he did to you?"

"How can I still be mad at a dead man? What would that accomplish? Besides, how can I throw stones at sin when I'm living in the bosom of it?" Again, the acid that dripped from those beautiful lips gave Quil pause.

"You aren't the only one who's familiar with being an outcast, you know?"

"Oh?" she snorted and turned her head to look out the window again.

Dead leaves swirled across the street ahead of them, dancing in the rays of brief sunlight that streamed desperately from the clouds of an overcast sky.

"I was an outsider to the Blackfoot, a disgrace to the small-town Catholic community of High Mountain, Montana, and an abomination to my chieftain grandfather. Ya see, I was a bastard born to an unwed couple from two separate worlds, the product of forbidden love. Evil incarnate."

Veda gasped as she looked over at him in surprise, realizing what he was saying.

He gave her a slow grin and took her hand in his.

"You and I aren't so different after all, Veda." He brought her knuckles to his lips and kissed them lightly as he put the car in park.

MADI AND BRETT'S house was loud and boisterous as Quinn, Quil, and Veda entered, her arm in his. The cacophony quieted down as people took them in—man and wife—their first holiday since their wedding.

The murmuring was brief and the eyes fleeting before Quinn ran in to find Lincoln and Valeria's twins, the loudness returning when Brett and Madi came over to greet them. It was Madison who smiled warmly.

"Welcome, Mr. and Mrs. Layton. Please make yourselves at home."

"Thank you, Madi," Quil stated with a nod.

"You have a lovely home," Veda noted, looking around at the warm and cozy farmhouse, surprised by its lack of opulence.

"Thanks, Veda. We're glad to call it ours," Brett answered and smiled down at his wife.

The look stilled Veda and she gulped, looking away. Her emotions were high today. After a gathering at her mother's apartment, the enjoyment of seeing her sister and mother so happy, and Quil's confession in the car, Veda felt as if she'd been dowsed in a heavy dose of softness. What was happening to her tough exterior? Was pregnancy causing it to crumble?

She didn't get a chance to think that concept over as Quil pulled her forward, and Brooke Taylor zeroed in on her. Veda's grip on Quillan's arm tightened involuntarily.

"Well, well, doesn't pregnancy become you, *Mrs.* Layton?" Brooke smarted.

"Brooke," Quil grated out in greeting.

"I bet those hormones are pumping a mile a minute in that sexually-primed little body of yours." Brooke gave her the once over, making Veda blush.

"Whatever is going on in my wife's body is no business of yours."

Veda was momentarily stunned by the overprotective words and stance Quillan took in that moment.

Brooke gave a humorless laugh. "Well, just keep in mind my invitation still stands, Quil. Anytime you two wanna come over and perform for me, I'd *love* to watch."

Ah, Brooke Taylor, little miss bad-ass, rich, broken, crying out for attention... Veda needed to call her bluff.

"Mmm," Veda cooed and ran the opposite hand that wasn't gripping her husband up his linen-shirt covered chest. "Now there's an idea, Hades. We've been looking for new adventures in the bedroom. Perhaps we *should* let her watch us." Veda's brow went up and didn't miss the instant shock on Quil's face. "We could show her a thing or two." Veda bit at her bottom lip and gave Quil the mother of all, 'fuck me right here and now, baby' looks.

Quil understood immediately what she was doing and played

along. He shrugged even as he pulled Veda into his arms. "I don't know, *dama serpiente*, we might frighten her."

He enfolded her in his big arms and she shivered as his hard chest hit hers. His head lowered and he took her lips, possessively. She hit her tip-toes and arched herself into him, the snake wrapping around the tree in the garden of Eden, gripping his neck and arm like her life depended on it as she thrust her pierced tongue into his mouth. He moaned hungrily before nipping her lip with his teeth as he pulled back.

"No one frightens me like you, my god of darkness," Veda cooed as she contorted her face into a sexy smirk. "Let's fuckin' do it."

Quil's eyes darkened as he looked her over in undeniable interest before he looked back at Brooke and said, "When and where?"

Brooke looked like she'd been slapped, tilting her chin before walking abruptly away.

Quil pulled Veda back into his arms for a brief victory hug and whispered, "That was fucking brilliant, V. Why didn't I think of it before now?"

Veda grinned into his handsome face and gave a light shrug.

"Looks like the fates are cruel bastards, aren't they, brother?" Travis Redmond's jovial voice called to them as he slapped a hand into Quil's.

Quil gave a snort and returned Trav's half hug. "Merry Christmas, Ares."

"Merry Christmas, Lord and Lady of the Underworld." Travis nodded to Veda who returned it.

"Veda, you look great!" Sky said with a smile. Veda didn't think her fitted plum V-neck dress did wonders for her, but what did she know?

"You too, Skyla." ADA Larson was as beautiful as always, her fire-red dress complimenting her vibrant hair.

Lincoln Porter and his wife, Valeria came over then, Linc pulling a screaming toddler with him. "Here, Uncle Travis, do something with your rowdy nephew. He's kissing Quinn."

Quinn ran at Veda's hip then, giggling up at her as she wrapped her arms around Veda's leg. "He got slime all over me." The little doll wiped at her cheek and looked back to the twin who was puckering his lips again, getting another adorable laugh from Quinn.

"Raising 'em right, I say," Travis retorted with a grin. "Already carousing with the ladies—Len, my man." Travis gave the baby boy a fist bump, and he gave his uncle a toothy grin which got all the adults laughing.

Becca and Paxton were the last to come to the party, and Veda wondered what had kept them until she realized her sister's dress was slightly unzipped in the back. She tried to hide a grin as she moved slowly over to her and subtly zipped it up, patting her hand on her twin's shoulder.

"Careful, sister. You keep up like that and you're bound to be the next in line with a bun in the oven."

Becca blushed, her pinkening cheeks highlighting her blue dress. "Oh my, I—"

"Don't worry, I get it. And I am happy for you both. I can see it on your faces. I was wrong about him, and I'm sorry," Veda admitted. Becca pulled her in for a hug; when she pulled back, there were tears in Becca's eyes.

"Oh Vey, I'm the sorry one. I—"

"Water under the bridge, ok?" She pulled Bec's head to her shoulder and kissed her hair.

Becca smiled big when they pulled back again, and Veda said, "We're overdue for a sister day."

Becca just nodded eagerly and took Veda's hands as they rejoined the group.

The banter was lighthearted, the conversations were entertaining, and the meal was decadent, set up in stations—prime rib, lobster and shrimp, veggie lasagna, scalloped potatoes, salads of all types, rice, roasted veggies, rolls, and desserts that looked too good to be real.

It was a beautiful Christmas evening. The team was headed for their last regular season game come Sunday before heading to the playoffs. They got a bye next week thanks to the upcoming wild card playoff game, since they'd clinched the division title. Quil wouldn't be playing on Sunday due to his ankle, so he had a couple weeks before their championship playoff game; plenty of time to heal up to one hundred percent.

Everyone finished dinner and dessert and was scattered around. Some people talked, some played games, and everyone was drinking—save for Madi, Linc, Val, and Veda—and having a good time. Most of them moved into the large living room to watch the Colts play the Chiefs, then Brooke and TJ got into a shouting match.

"You don't fuckin' own me, asshole," Brooke huffed as she pulled out of his arms. "Just because we've fucked a couple times doesn't mean you get to tell me what the hell I can and *can't* do." Hands went to her hips, and she turned and pointed her finger in his face.

TJ Rawlins' eyes darkened and he gritted his teeth as he stepped forward. "This isn't the time nor place, Brooke. But since you brought it up first," the smirk on TJ's face was almost cruel, "then I guess that means you won't be banging on my door at 2 AM crying and lonely, begging me to take you to my bed, will it?"

The shock on Brooke's face must have matched everyone else's, but she quickly recovered with, "Ha, you fuckin' wish, you big lug. Like I need you!"

TJ laughed then as if just being told a funny joke. "You're something else alright, you fake. You want everyone to believe you're some bad-ass bitch, Brookie. Well, guess what, guys? It's all a bunch of bullshit."

"You wouldn't know real if it slapped you in the face, you dumb jock. Now I remember why I don't date football players."

She better be careful, she's surrounded by football players! Veda thought.

"Because you're all a bunch of *idiots!*" Brooke shouted and shoved hard at TJ's barrel chest. He didn't move, not an inch.

"I know what you're trying to do, Brooke, and guess what? It ain't working, baby."

Brett stood then and moved toward them, attempting to calm the storm raging inside his house.

"Brooke—" He barely got her name out before she rounded on him, her inebriation worse than they'd all originally thought.

"And fuck you too, Brett. Stay the hell out of this. You're the biggest idiot of 'em all!"

Brett frowned, not understanding why she'd called her brother-in-law that—obviously.

"You've been blinded by love your whole damn life. Madi practically had you balancing on a fucking ball, like a damn elephant in a circus, never able to live your life to its fullest because you were literally held captive to her. It's *disgusting!*" Brooke spit out.

Madi's face gaped in a big O as she came to stand behind her husband. His forearm stopped her from moving closer as Brett held his ground and practically growled.

"You know what's disgusting, Brooke? Your attitude. Stop throwing love back in the faces of others simply because you haven't felt it for yourself," Brett replied.

"There's no such thing as love. It's an illusion. You're all under its spell." Brooke looked around at all the seemingly happy couples, envy and anger flooding her red face.

Veda rolled her eyes. This chick was fucking nuts! She had to be on drugs or something.

"No such thing?" It was TJ who answered her. "Grow up, Brooke. You aren't a teenager anymore. I'm sorry for what happened to you —God knows, baby—but it's time to stop running like a scared little girl. The jig is up, sweetheart."

Brooke laughed, short and maniacal, before stepping forward and slapping TJ hard across his face. "Don't you dare—"

"You know the difference in me and you, blondie?"

That shut her up for a minute.

"I'm not afraid. Not of you. Not of love, and certainly not of doing this." He grabbed her, pinning her arms to her sides as he kissed her hard. She grunted in protest, and Veda saw Jerry step forward only to halt as TJ pulled back and bent to scoop Brooke up in a fireman's carry, pulling her body over his neck and shoulders.

Brooke squealed but couldn't fight the huge offensive lineman of a good six feet six inches and close to three hundred pounds of solid muscle holding her. She began to mutter a string of curses that would have a nun fainting as TJ gave them all a nod and said, "Y'all have a Merry Christmas. I got an angel who needs a tree shoved up her ass in the worst way."

With that, TJ hauled a flailing and screaming Brooke toward the door, leaving everyone's faces aghast.

It was Amelia Taylor who spoke first, elbowing her husband as her pink and stunned face grew stern. "Jerry, surely you're not gonna stand for that kind of behavior from—"

"Oh lighten up, would ya, Millie?" Jerry Taylor, the team owner, turned to his wife and took her shoulders. "Clearly that man is in love with our daughter. Can't you see that?"

Amelia's hand went to her chest. She'd been rattled by both TJ's words and his actions and didn't really know what to say.

Madi gave a little laugh. Brett turned to embrace her then, his face breaking into a grin. "I never thought I'd see the day when Brooke would meet her match... but well, looks like that day is today." Madi turned to eye her parents in return.

Quil stepped up and patted Jerry's back. "Well sir, I'll admit: I'm glad I joined the Gladiators when I did...there's never a dull moment among *this* crowd."

Jerry laughed heartily. "You can say that again, Hades."

THAT NIGHT, Quil was getting ready for bed, debating whether to go to Veda or stay in his own room. It was Christmas, and he'd gotten a gift for their baby. He knew it was still early and anything could happen, but he hadn't been able to resist talking to the coordinator of their uniform design and getting her to make a tiny jersey. He'd had it gift wrapped in beautiful red foil wrapping paper and a gold bow.

His desire to make amends won out and he padded down the hallway to Veda's room, clad in only his PJ pants. He knocked lightly and didn't miss the pounding of his heart against his ribcage.

She came to the door moments later and gingerly opened it, looking surprised to see him standing there. He noted how her eyes flitted languidly over his bare chest and lower, making his body break out in feverish desire.

"Quil?" she asked, as if to say, "Why are you here?"

He stood his ground, trying to keep to the task at hand, remembering how cruel he'd been just feet away as he'd roughly taken her just days ago.

"Uh, I uh, I have a gift... it's...it's for the baby." Quillan pulled the gift from behind his back and presented it to the woman who'd made him a father for the second time. He still had no proof but didn't need it; he knew she was pregnant, knew she was carrying a healthy baby boy—he'd had dreams of his face and his name.

"Oh wow, Quil, I..." she trailed off, gulping hard as she took the present from him.

"Open it," he insisted with a smile.

She did, pulling the bow off and tossing it down along with the wrapping paper. She opened the box and pulled the tissue paper away to reveal the tiny Gladiators jersey inside with Quil's number, 87, on the back of it. He'd had it customized with the name, "Layton Jr."

Veda covered her mouth, and when she looked up at him, tears glistened in her eyes. "Oh, Quil, this is... this is the most adorable thing I've ever seen." She gave a little giggle that warmed his hard heart, and he grinned in return.

"I know we haven't named him yet and we..." he trailed off as she frowned. "It'll be his first of many to come," Quil finished.

"And what happens if it's a girl?" she asked, a brow raised.

"I assume it's just as fitting for a little girl to wear her daddy's jersey as it is a boy." Quil shrugged lightly.

Veda gave a sly smile and nodded. "Thank you, Quil. This... this means a lot."

He nodded in kind and looked her over. She was clad in dark purple silk PJs; she wore purple and black a lot for some reason. Her hair was down, framing her porcelain face in ribbons of obsidian strands. *Obsidian*, like her stage name had been; suddenly he wanted her with a hunger that wouldn't be quieted.

"Did you wanna come to Santa's bed tonight, *seductora*?" He gave her a slow grin.

"And why would I want to do that? I thought I'd made it clear that I didn't want you touching me again." Her big lips puckered even as she crossed her arms over her chest.

"Oh c'mon, V, we both know that's not the truth." Up until the last time, she'd enjoyed sex with him... hadn't she?

He stepped forward, taking her off guard, and moved to embrace her. "Say I'm lying and I'll leave."

"Quil..."

He fed on her reaction. He knew he'd been rough in the past, but she seemed to enjoy the dark side of him he'd not shown anyone prior to now. He couldn't figure out for the life of him why he loved to hover at the border of pain and pleasure with her. He had his suspicions but owning her was as vital to him as breathing; and, in that moment, he needed her like he'd never needed anyone. She was his addiction, he realized again.

He scooped her up and pulled her into his arms, kissing her with fierceness. She grunted but wrapped her arms around his neck as he fell with her to the bed, easing between her legs.

"Fuck, Veda... I want you. God, I can't help myself..." Quil trailed off again as he kissed her creamy, ink-covered skin, over her exposed collarbone, then moved his lips back to hers. He kissed her with a passion that frightened him. "Tell me I'm the only one, and I'll stop."

He hovered over her, waiting with growing impatience as she eyed him. He watched her struggle, knowing Hell would freeze over before she admitted that she wanted him.

He smirked. "You are the most frustratingly stubborn woman I've ever known."

"I'm Irish." Veda shrugged. "Besides, you love it."

It was true. She had him spitting mad one minute, ready to fuck her brains out the next.

"Can you give me a Christmas present then?" When her head tilted, he said, "Indulge me."

That got a brow raise out of her. She was always up for a challenge.

He pulled her to a half-seated position in the bed, relaxing her head against the headboard, her back against the pillows, and pulled his boxers down.

"I wanna fuck that beautiful mouth of yours, V."

"You're pushing it tonight, dark one." A seductive grin flirted at her lips and his entire body tingled in anticipation.

"I love pushing the envelope with you. Now lift your arms, *dama serpiente.*"

He couldn't help but quiver as he thrust the head of his cock to her lips and pulled her arms up, pinning her wrists at the headboard as he cupped her head with his other hand. She lowered her mouth to the tip of him and took his entire length down easily. "Oh, yeah. Suck your god's big dick, baby girl. Mmmm, yeah." He encouraged her on as her emerald eyes looked up at him and he began to fuck that enticing mouth of hers, feeling her tongue ring sliding up and down his shaft. "Oh Jesus," he whimpered as her pace increased, and he pumped into her. Tears began to flow down her temples as she took his girthy member deep down with ease. Quil grunted and groaned and whined, feeling the tingling begin in his lower belly. His roar was beastly as he spewed himself into her long, alabaster throat, pistoning his hips against her.

He came down from his blissfully beautiful high and stroked her cheek, wiping her tears away as he pulled back then wiping the drool from her mouth as she caught her breath and licked her lips.

"Mmm, that was incredible, *chica mala*. I knew you could relinquish control for Hades," he murmured as he moved, aligning his body back to hers and kissing her once more. "I'm gonna make love to you now, baby."

That's when he felt her shudder as if electrified. "Stop," she commanded.

Quillan pulled back with a frown. "Wh—?"

"Get off me, Quil."

His frown deepened and anger began to overtake him. Why was she acting like this?

"You don't know *how* to make love to me," she answered his unspoken question. "All you want is my submission, to control me, and I'm fecking sick of being your toy to use and abuse as you see fit. All you do is butter me up so you can sink your hooks back into me again. I have feelings, and I'm tired of being your whore. I'm not gonna allow you to keep hurting me and using sex as a way to punish us both."

So, she'd figured him out—his warring emotions where she was concerned.

"You're my wife. I can—"

"Yes! I'm your wife, but only *legally* and don't forget that." A dark shadow flashed in her eyes, reminding him of his own darkness, hidden deep inside him.

He smirked. *Good for you, Veda. Make me work for it.* "You can't keep me out of your bed forever."

"Maybe not. But seven months isn't forever, now is it?"

"You wouldn't—"

"Try me!" she smarted back and shoved at his chest. "I told you not to touch me again."

Damn! She was as serious as a heart attack. Quil felt the blow hit him where it hurt.

"I've had enough men hurt me for one lifetime. I'm done."

Quillan looked her over, feeling a pang of regret, anguish, and pain shoot through his heart as he began to move back off her, as she'd asked. He wouldn't force himself on her. He wasn't the best guy in the world, but he sure as shit wasn't going to be *that* guy...not again, anyway.

He wordlessly drew his pants up and turned to leave, all the while wondering why he was so distraught by her words, wondering which was worse: that she was telling the truth about how he'd treated her or that she was kicking him out...for good.

CHAPTER TWELVE

The weekend passed with a dull pace, their final regular season game behind them. Quillan's heart felt broken in half and he couldn't understand exactly why. Nothing Veda said was untrue. He'd been cruel, mean, and even forceful. He could even admit to himself that he'd used her, but she'd seemed to enjoy their violent delights as much as he had. She wouldn't be able to lie about that. So, why had she suddenly decided to punish them both by going without the sex that had gotten them here in the first place?

Because she's sick of your shit! his heart told him. Which only served to worsen his mood.

On Tuesday, for Quinn's birthday, they'd taken her to see the elephants at the Atlanta Zoo, along with Linc, Val, and the twins. It was busy and crowded, and he and Linc had been stopped by far too many fans far too many times. Quil had been a good sport, plastering on a fake smile for countless pictures and signed dozens of autographs.

But he couldn't help the genuine grin on his face as Quinn looked up at Veda and asked, "Are there elephants in Ireland, Veda?"

"Nope," V giggled and shook her head. "Aside from the zoos we have there. They're native to Africa and Asia."

Quinn took her hand as they walked ahead of him. She and Quinn had grown even closer as time passed, and it warmed his heart to see them together as they were now. It was adorable, Quinn leaning her head against Veda, Veda stroking her hair. It stirred something inside him that he hadn't felt in far too long; something that frightened him.

He looked away, overcome with a sense of dread so poignant it threatened to destroy him. He couldn't do this again. This was too familiar: wife, daughter, the promise of a good life on the horizon. It had all been taken away from him. Losing Rian had awakened him to life's cruelties, and one day he would lose Quinn too. What would happen when that day came? He'd prayed and prayed, but knew her time would eventually run out.

"Veda, can we go shopping tomorrow?"

Veda gave her a little laugh, "Sure, we'll have to go after lunch though. I have my appointment tomorrow, remember?"

Quinn nodded vigorously.

That's right, her appointment to the female doctor is tomorrow, Quil reminded himself. Veda had originally invited him to go along with her, but she hadn't mentioned it since. The disappointment that thought conjured in him made him frown.

They continued into the indoor reptile exhibit while Linc and his family headed toward the pandas. Quil couldn't help but smile, remembering meeting Medusa that fated Halloween night. *Dama serpiente.*

He saw Veda smirk as Quinn ran at the cobra enclosure and gaped, "Whoa, Daddy—look!"

The sleek and onyx scales of the cobra shimmered as half of him stood erect. His raised body was about the height of Quinn, ready to strike, his hood wide, beady eyes staring into hers.

"Deadly," Quil answered.

"Fascinating," Veda quipped, her eyes piercing his before returning to the snake.

She *would* find him fascinating, Quillan thought, as he recalled the snake tattooed across her lean back.

"Oww," Quinn whimpered and looked down at her tummy.

"Baby, what's wrong?" Quil asked. "He can't hurt you, he's behind glass." Quil noticed her eyes were intent on the cobra, staring at her as if he meant to devour her whole. But Quinn gripped her tummy suddenly and cried out again.

Veda squatted before her, and Quil stepped up behind her as Quinn leaned forward and began to sob. "Honey, what is it?" Veda asked as Quinn fell into her arms.

"Oww, it hurts, Veda. It hurts so much."

"Oh, honey," Veda soothed and began to rub at Quinn's tummy. She looked up at Quil then. "Think it was the ice cream?" she asked, her eyes full of concern.

Quil shrugged, not sure. She didn't eat ice cream often, so perhaps it could be lactose intolerance. That caused bad belly aches...right?

"Baby, come here." Quil motioned to Quinn, but she gripped Veda tighter in a death grip, ignoring her father.

"I want Veda," Quinn whimpered. Veda gave him a regretful grin as she moved to stand.

Quillan didn't want her lifting Quinn, even if she was small for her age. It probably wasn't good for the baby, but he didn't have time to protest as Veda walked with her toward the ladies' room. "I'm gonna see if she needs to go potty. Wait here."

She moved off, and Quil sighed heavily. Deep down he was grateful for Veda but, at the same time, he felt passed up; it had kinda hurt his feelings that Quinn had wanted her instead of him.

He waited for a ridiculously long time, his mind going in all directions and his worry increasing as time passed and the two didn't come out of the bathroom, even when Linc and Val rejoined him. Quil explained to Val what had happened, then sat and leaned forward, placing his head into his hands. What if something was wrong? What if Quinn had an infection? What if—?

Suddenly, Veda came out with a pale Quinn, a wet paper towel across her forehead.

"Shit, is she ok?" he asked and moved to take Quinn from Veda. His daughter fell limply into his arms, and he cradled her to his shoulder.

"Easy, she vomited. I think we need to get her home."

"Aww, poor love," Val cooed and patted Quinn's back, motioning to Linc to corral the boys so they could leave too.

"Damn ice cream," Quil murmured and kissed Quinn's forehead as she muttered, "Daddy, I don't feel good."

"I know, baby, we're going home."

Once they were home, Quil got her to bed and called Quinn's doctor, Dr. Parastatidis—aka Dr. P—who told him to try clear liquids after the vomiting had stopped for a couple hours, and to let her rest, but to call for any questions and take her to the ER if she got worse.

Veda was sitting in the rocking chair next to the bay window when Quil walked in.

He relayed what the doctor had said when she looked up expectantly.

She nodded and looked back over at the sallow angel sleeping contently in her Pocahontas PJs that Veda had bought her for Christmas.

"I can take first watch. I'm sure you're tired."

Veda shook her head. "It's ok. I—"

"It's fine, V. She's my daughter so..." Quil trailed off, not wanting her to feel anymore put out than she already was, but he could immediately see that he'd said the wrong thing...or perhaps she'd just taken it the wrong way.

"Dammit Veda, I just meant—"

"It's fine. I'll be in my room if you need me."

"Veda," Quinn murmured and reached her hand out to Veda.

"I'm here, sweetie." Veda moved to the bed and took the small hand of his daughter's.

"I love you."

Veda grinned even as Quil's heart splintered. "I love *you*, sweet girl. Get some rest. Ok?"

Quinn nodded, and Quil moved to apologize to Veda, only to have her hold her hand up and see her way out.

Quil took the seat she'd just vacated and felt like a real asshole. He had to fix things between them. He had to. Some way. Somehow.

VEDA DIDN'T SLEEP WELL, tossing and turning as she worried about Quinn all night. She was reluctant to leave her, even if it was with Juanita, her nanny, and only long enough to go to her doctor's visit.

Quinn had begun to develop an attachment to Veda and she to the little girl, which should worry her, but only made her happier. Veda figured it was because things were so tense between herself and Quillan. She knew she had been straddling the fence where their sexual relationship was concerned—yearning for his fierceness one minute, pushing him away the next—but she couldn't keep up the charade. She knew what the problem was; she was starting to have feelings for him, and therein lie the biggest issue of all. Quillan was all kinds of fucked up. Veda just thought she had demons; Quil *was* a damn demon. With his broody demeanor, dark sexual side, and deep secrets.

Who was she kidding? Veda had more secrets she was still keeping from him...

She smiled at the nurse who led her back to an exam room.

She was instructed to disrobe and put on the gown provided. She'd already given a urine sample and her finger had been pricked; her vitals taken upon entry.

She did as she was told and gave the nurse a brief medical history when she came back in.

Veda sat awaiting the doctor to enter next, her nerves beginning to get the best of her as she let her mind drift back to Quinn and Quil.

A set of three knocks came at the door, and Veda's heart leapt into her throat as she saw Quillan Layton—tall and broad god that he was—entering.

He closed the door behind himself and shuffled his feet, looking sexy as all get out in a tan sweater and dark khakis, his thick, black hair styled and his beard cut close.

"You, uh, said I could join you at the doctor visit if I wanted and..." he trailed off.

She simply nodded, suddenly grateful to have him there with her.

He gave her a gorgeous smile and came to sit beside her.

"Nervous?" he asked.

She nodded.

"Don't worry. The doctor will just do a quick pelvic exam and hopefully an ultrasound so we can see the baby."

She gulped, even more nervous. The ultrasound was gonna make this all the more real.

Her gut tightened as the ob/gyn came in, Dr. Bart Westmoreland. He was a young Black man with a kind smile and deep brown eyes with dark-rimmed glasses sitting atop his nose.

"Mr. and Mrs. Layton, congrats on your upcoming bundle of joy are in order."

Veda smiled over at Quil who'd been frowning at the doctor as he entered. It didn't take but a minute for Veda to realize that it was because he was a man, not a woman as Quil had been expecting. She stifled a laugh as the attractive young doctor shook the surprised Quil's hand then Veda's.

Dr. Westmoreland began asking Veda a series of questions, including Veda's last period, of which coincided with two weeks prior to Halloween she suddenly realized.

"We're pretty sure we got pregnant on Halloween night," Quil insisted.

"That sounds about right," the doctor smiled. "So that would make your due date probably be in July."

"Great! Summer time. Can't wait," Veda gave a mock smirk, thinking how big she would be by then...and how hot in the summer humidity.

"Best time to have a baby," Dr. Westmoreland winked. "I'm a Cancer myself." He looked down at her chart in his hands. "You've had an abortion in the past, huh?"

Veda's head lowered and she felt Quil take her hand and squeeze it lightly. She gave him a quick, grateful smile before she looked back up to the doctor and nodded. "When I was sixteen. It was...regretful."

"No need to feel apologetic, Mrs. Layton. You'll get no judgement from me on the matter. I just want to assure you that you can still have a safe and healthy pregnancy and delivery. I don't see that you yourself have any significant medical history, but I'll have a panel of labs drawn to be sure there's nothing concerning. Now, you lost a young sister to lymphoma? And your mother also has it?" He looked up at Veda then, who nodded in response.

"I have anemia, and my daughter has beta thalassemia major," Quil added.

"Oh wow," the doctor's attention perked up some. "Well, that's all pertinent information to relay and I'll be sure we run some genetic testing as well." The doctor jotted some things down, scratching away on the paper attached to the clipboard. "Now, let's do an examination and we'll get an ultrasound."

Veda only nodded and the doctor stood and set the chart down. He then washed his hands thoroughly and knocked lightly on the door, signaling for the MA to come in before he gloved up and approached the table.

He started with Veda's neck and glands, then listened to her heart with a stethoscope. He examined her breasts, his brows raising as he noted that her nipples were pierced but not saying a word. She found that amusing, Quil did not.

Dr. Westmoreland moved his hands over her abdomen, examined her legs and arms for swelling, then had her lay back and put her legs in the stirrups to give her a pelvic exam.

She pulled in a deep breath as she tried to calm her anxiety. That's when Quil stood and placed a hand on her bare tummy, reassuring her. He grinned and she reached for his hand, telling him without words that she was glad he was there as she looked up into his deep caramel eyes. God, he was such a beautiful man, even if he had more baggage than she did.

She heard the doctor tell her to open her legs, and she reluctantly attempted to relax and do as he'd asked. She heard a sharp intake of breath and looked down to see the doctor clearing his throat uncomfortably.

"Something wrong, doc?" Quil asked.

"Uh no, I'm sorry. Just...a first."

Veda couldn't stifle the laugh welling within, realizing he was talking about her clit piercing. Quil frowned again and looked off, his grip on her hand tightening. She stroked his knuckles with her opposite fingertips, not sure if she were comforting him or vice versa.

When the time came for the ultrasound, Veda was sure she would pass out as the tech moved the wand over Veda's tiny little "baby bump" to reveal a little blob on the screen.

"There's your little peanut," she giggled and pointed.

"Where?" Veda asked as she squinted her eyes to try to figure out what she was looking at exactly.

"See the flashing?" Quil asked. "That's the heart."

"Oh...wow," Veda whispered in awe. There it was. The baby. The one Quil had given her that wild Samhain night.

She looked over to her handsome baby daddy who gave her a sexy crooked grin, unshed tears glistening in his eyes.

She was shocked when he leaned down and kissed her, softly, sweetly, as light as a feather.

"Hmm," the tech said in deep thought, pulling Quil's attention away from Veda.

"What is it? What's wrong?"

"Well, Mom and Dad, looks like you need to be prepared."

Oh God! No. What does that mean? Veda gripped Quil's hand in a death grip and heard him audibly gulp beside her. Her panicked eyes looked into his then and she saw the disappointment so visible there.

The tech smiled over at them, broadly. "Oh, nothing's *wrong*! You just need to plan ahead...to double everything."

"D—double everything?" Quil asked dumbfounded.

Oh shit! Veda knew exactly what the sonographer was going to say before the words ever came out of her mouth.

"Yup! You're having twins."

"TWINS! HA HA! HOW ABOUT THAT?" Travis laughed and slammed Quil's back the next day at practice. "Congrats, man. That's awesome."

As awesome as it was, Quil could see the envy on his friend's face and it ate into him.

Seeing the second embryo come into view had been surprising and his heart had swelled as he'd looked back into Veda's over-whelmed face. He'd felt a dam opening up within him, emotions he hadn't felt in so long breaking forth as he'd chuckled happily and looked back at the screen.

"Oh my God," Veda had whispered in awe, and Quil had squeezed her hand.

"What on earth are you gonna do with twins?" Pax shook his head in shock.

"Uncle Pax is gonna be busy, looks like," Brett mumbled and slugged playfully at Pax's middle.

"Yeah, that's right *Uncle* Pax. Daddy Pax isn't gonna happen for a while and don't go rubbing bad juju on me," Pax held his hands out in protest. "Me and Becca are taking things slowly."

Linc laughed. "You *do* realize Becca's a twin, too—you never know!"

"You go to the meditation room right now, Lincoln Porter! Do some Hail Mary's or whatever it is that you do in there." Pax was frantic as he pointed to the quiet room with calming music and floor mats adjacent to them. "I mean it. Right the hell now!"

All the guys were laughing by then, including Josh and TJ, whose mood had lightened over the last several days following Brooke's change of heart.

"Alright guys, let's get our heads in the game now. We gotta be ready for next weekend's Division Championship game." Brett reined them in even as he nodded over to Quil.

Quil was happy, really happy for the first time in a long time, and he sensed a change in the cosmos. Perhaps this year was his year, finally. He had things to look forward to, his anxiety placated for the time being.

They had a light practice viewing film tape, discussing new routes, and planning their attack on Tampa Bay next Sunday with well-executed precision.

They'd taken a break after lunch before a meeting, when Brett pulled Quil to the side.

"I just wanted to tell you that I'm sorry for being hard on you, Quil." When Quillan frowned in confusion, Brett elaborated. "You know, for the things I said to you about Veda and not taking things seriously after the Halloween party."

"Ah, no worries, Cap. I know you were just trying to keep me in line."

"Well, I was wrong and for that I apologize. I didn't realize what you and Veda had. I thought it was just..." Brett trailed off, looking down at his feet.

"I get it. I wasn't sure of her intentions in the beginning, either.

She led us all to believe that she was a...well, a..." Quil trailed off, shrugging.

"I just know that when I was having a hard time, you gave me the pep talk I needed to move forward. I owed you, at least, the benefit of the doubt. I just had my sights set on the Super Bowl and didn't want anything altering our paths."

"I know. Sometimes we need the hard truth to shake us in the right direction." Quil gave his QB a knowing grin and slugged at his shoulder. "I'm grateful to be a part of this team and to have you as my leader, Brett. Truthfully."

"Aw, don't be going and getting all sappy on me, Hades." Brett playfully elbowed Quil then, getting a chuckle out of him. "But it's good to see a smile on your face. Tell Veda to keep that coming."

"Now Zeus, if I smile too much I can't bring Hell with me when I ride that pale horse of mine. That wouldn't be very fitting on the face of *Death*, now would it?" Quil smirked.

Brett burst into laughter and Quil followed suit, and they headed back out to the practice field.

VEDA WAS on cloud nine as she listened to Quinn rambling on the way back from the hospital cafeteria, thinking about how surreal it was that she and Quil were going to have twins. Twins! *Imagine that!*

Becca had been overjoyed when she'd told her that morning on the phone. "Oh sister," she'd said. "This is wonderful!"

They'd laughed, cried, then planned a day for shopping; Rebecca couldn't wait to buy her nieces/nephews their first presents. Veda wouldn't rain on her parade and inform her that Quillan had beaten her to the punch. Although, now he'd have to buy a second jersey for the other baby.

Quil had looked at her differently following the visit; he'd been smiling more, and the joy on his face was contagious.

Veda and Quil had plans to go to her mother's apartment tonight and tell her the exciting news. Quinn would be staying with Juanita again.

For now, they were heading back to the volunteer center to grab gift baskets for the pediatric chemo patients on the second floor. Quinn took her hand as they stopped just outside the door, waiting their turn to go inside.

Suddenly, Quinn took hold of her stomach again and whined.

Veda frowned, wondering what she'd eaten this time that had upset her sensitive tummy. She then watched in horror as Quinn began to go limp and started falling, her eyes rolling into the back of her head.

She screamed out as she caught the little seven-year old before her head could hit the ground, Veda's knees hitting the floor hard. She immediately went into action, feeling for a pulse in her carotid artery. Her pulse was there, if not strong, and Veda began yelling at the volunteers in front of her to call for help and get a doctor.

She cradled Quinn's head and felt tears stream down her cheeks as she put a hand to Quinn's small chest to check her breathing. The little girl's chest was rising, albeit it not deeply.

"Quinn, baby... Quinn, can you hear me?" she called to the brown-haired angel, but no answer came.

She thrust her fingertips into Quinn's neck again, verifying that a pulse was indeed there. She wasn't in cardiac arrest—*Thank God*—she'd only passed out.

A nurse moved in, squatting beside her. "What happened?" the lovely Asian girl in coral scrubs asked.

"One minute she was complaining of a stomach ache, the next she was passing out. I don't understand. We just ate and—"

"What's her name?"

"Quinn. Quinn Layton. She's seven years old."

"Any history of medical problems?"

"Yes! She has Cooley's thalassemia."

"Ok," the nurse frowned as she began evaluating Quinn's pulse and breathing, as Veda had done moments before. "Ok, her pulse is too slow, we need to get her stabilized. Where are her parents?"

"I—" Veda gulped hard, realizing she *was* Quinn's parent. "I'm her stepmother. She's here with me. She got her blood transfusion earlier today. We volunteer in the afternoons. We—" Veda's mind went blank as she became surrounded by nurses and a doctor.

The doctor listened to Quinn's heart even as a gurney was pulled up and she was moved onto it and raised. They began moving down the hallway and Veda followed, stupefied.

"Ok, let's get her to the trauma bay."

"Tr—trauma?" Veda croaked out.

"Who does she see for her thalassemia?" the nurse asked Veda as they moved through a set of double doors and into a cold back hallway.

Oh, he had a Greek name... What the hell was it? Parakeetis? Dammit, why hadn't she paid more attention!

"I—I need to call my husband." Veda quickly pulled out her phone only to get side-swiped as the doctor's voice changed.

"Shit, she's going into shock. We're gonna need to get a line. Ma'am, I'm gonna need you to step out." The doctor motioned to one of the many nurses to see Veda out of the large room they'd wheeled her into.

"Wait!" It was right on the tip of her tongue. "Dr. P. She sees Dr. P for her anemia. He's a hematologist."

"Oh ok, great. I'll contact him." The nurse assured her even as she began to escort Veda out.

"Please?" Veda begged, not sure what she was asking for.

As the doors closed and she was outside the room looking around a busy nurse's station, hearing commands, machines, and footsteps, she began to pray.

Oh, God, please, don't let anything happen to my sweet little Quinn.

She folded herself against the wall and slid down, hugging her knees. This was what Quil had been talking about when he said Quinn's health was waning, and he wouldn't have her forever; but the thought of Quinn not being in existence was unfathomable. Veda continued to beg, plead, and cry, all the while aware that the voices behind the door were getting louder. More people were coming in, some in a hurry and some with big equipment.

Veda was on the verge of panic when a man in a white coat came hustling out toward her.

"Mrs. Layton?"

"Yes!" She popped up, her heart threatening to bust out of her chest. "I'm Veda Layton, Quinn's stepmother."

"She has a ruptured spleen. We must operate immediately."

Oh, Jesus! How could she make that decision?

"Please, I need to call my husband." She grabbed for her phone again, only to be halted.

"Ma'am, we don't have a lot of time here. I need consent, and I need it *now*. If we don't hurry, she could die."

A clipboard was handed over by a nurse. "Just sign on the line, please?"

Veda robotically signed the document put before her, stating. "Do whatever you need to do. Save my daughter's life."

And with that she handed Quinn over to God, for everything else was out of her hands now.

CHAPTER THIRTEEN

Quil walked through the doors of the hospital, heart in his throat and fear gripping his soul.

"Where is she?" he huffed out as he tried to catch his breath.

"In surgery," Juanita replied.

"S—surgery?" Quil thought he might pass out and staggered. "How?"

"Veda."

That one word filled him with anger. How in hell had Veda been able to consent for her surgery? She had no legal rights to Quinn in any way, shape, or form. It was all in the pre-nuptial agreement he'd had her sign before their marriage.

Juanita motioned for Quil to follow her down the hallway where she walked them to the surgical waiting area.

As soon as he saw Veda, wrath took over him. Despite that she was hunched over, holding her thighs with Becca murmuring in her ear and stroking her hair, *clearly* distraught, Quil couldn't hold in his rage.

"What the fuck have you done?"

Veda's stunned eyes looked up at him, tears streaming down her cheeks. "I—I..."

"Where do you get off thinking that you have *any* claim on my daughter?"

Veda looked down and gulped, her lip quivering.

"If she dies, Veda, so help me *God*." He took a step forward and thrust his finger at her, gritting his teeth.

"Whoa, easy there, big guy," Quil felt his shoulders being gripped from behind as Pax's voice soothed him. "Let's just let off the gas, huh?"

"Don't fucking touch me, Paxton." Quil shrugged out of Paxton's hold only to have him step in front of him and block him.

"Quil," he warned. "You need to back the hell off, dude."

"Get. *Out*. Of. My. Face." Hades was full throttle as he glared at his teammate. Red flames of fury fed his anger and fear and dread of losing his child. "Before I *get* you out of it."

"Veda is your wife and the mother of your children. She would never do anything to endanger Quinn, and you damn well know that. Now, cool your jets before you do something you're gonna regret."

Quil eyed Pax down, finally allowing his words to sink into his furious skull.

He turned and ran his hands roughly from his face into his hair. "Fuck!" he yelled loud enough to stop a train.

He felt as fragile as his hold on reality at that moment as Paxton guided him to a seat, where he bent double and tried to hold in his lunch. God, he was gonna hurl, he was gonna faint, he was gonna *die* if something happened to his child. His sweet Quinn. His little angel with brown curls, the bravery of a lion, and a heart of solid gold. He began to rock and sob as his emotions spewed forth, his ever-guarded control beyond his reach.

He wasn't aware of how long he sat there, pleading, begging, crying, and praying before a voice called. "Mr. and Mrs. Layton?"

Quil shot up, quick as a flash, and braced himself for the worst, his eyes beckoning to the doctor clad in sterile operating gear.

A flicker of a smile nearly had Quil collapsing as the doctor looked from him over at Veda.

"Your quick actions saved your daughter's life, Mrs. Layton."

"Sh—she's gonna pull through? What happened?" Quil grumbled, realizing he hadn't even asked before rounding on his wife. His *wife*.

"Mr. Layton, your daughter had an enlarged spleen. It ruptured after she ate lunch today. She passed out, and your wife quickly called for a code. If you guys had been home, I'm not sure the results would have been as favorable. I guess volunteering has its perks." He tried to lighten the mood as he shrugged over at Quil. "She's in recovery now, and we're gonna move her to a room for observation for several days. Her vitals are stable, and I've started her on a round of antibiotics to lower her risk for infections. Dr. P will be rounding shortly to come check on her."

The doctor waited, seeing if they had any questions before turning to leave the room.

Quil turned upon hearing Rebecca's squeal and pulled Veda to her for a hug. Veda's face crumbled even as she grinned and closed her eyes. Her hand came up to cover her face. The emotion in her reaction was so raw, so genuine, so real that it hit Hades' rock-hard heart, splitting it open like a missile into a mountain. He suddenly realized that he was in love with her, this woman whom he'd misunderstood this entire time. He realized, too, how much she loved his child, how upset she'd been, and that she'd been as scared for Quinn as he had been. He gulped, regretful for all the hell he'd put her through, the things he'd said, the way he'd used her.

He didn't know how it had happened—falling in love—or even that he *could* love again after what Rian had done to him and Quinn. But he knew he planned to love Veda Angeline Layton and love her well. He and Veda were both broken souls who had things to work through, but she was strong and feisty and he admired the hell out of her.

Pax seemed to sense his change in demeanor as he motioned to Becca for them to give Quil and Veda some privacy.

With them out of the room, Veda looked uncertainly over at Quil. Guilt began to eat at him for how angry he'd been with her; he'd known his anger had been misplaced, but the words had been said and they'd been cruel and hurtful. She looked down and appeared to be on the verge of seeking escape when he took a step toward her.

"You... you saved her," Quil stated softly.

"I just reacted, honestly," Veda's voice was barely above a whisper. "One minute she was telling me about how much alike Belle and Jasmine were, the next she was falling to the ground." Veda began to cry again, holding herself in check as best she could as she relayed the story. "I didn't know what to do, except that I knew deep down I was gonna have to do CPR at some point. I'm so glad I didn't have to do that." Her sob shook him to the core, but he needed to hear the whole tale. He waited for her to get to a point where she could continue and she did, despite stammering in the process. "A n-nurse came by and a-asked me what ha-happened. I told her and she a-asked me if Q-Quinn had a medical his-history..."

"You did the right thing, Veda. I'm glad you were here. I'm glad it wasn't me. I would have just been useless... You...you saved our daughter's life."

Veda gasped as she looked up into his eyes. He grinned. Yeah, he'd said it—*our daughter,* for Quinn wasn't just his any longer. Veda was her stepmother, and she'd deserved the title, to be able to tell her as such.

Quillan opened his arms to V and she fell into them, sobbing even harder than she had before. He stroked her dark hair and inhaled her spicy, peachy scent.

"Oh God, Quil, I was so scared we were gonna lose her. I'm sorry. I didn't know what else to do. The doctor said they had to operate, or she was gonna die. I just did the first thing I thought to do."

"Shh, it's ok now, baby girl. She's alright. It's all gonna be alright."

And as he held the woman he loved, he knew somehow that it would be.

VEDA WATCHED QUIL, sitting on Quinn's hospital bed and stroking his daughter's back, and felt her heart melt. She didn't know when in the process she'd fallen in love with him, but somewhere along the way she had, which complicated everything. Love wasn't some knee-jerk reaction to a fight-or-flight response; it was earned, and Quillan Layton hadn't done anything to earn her love. Veda had been certain that love didn't really exist, like a unicorn in a fable, it was only imaginary, thought up by some romantic to make life seem easier than it really was. It was a lie, a falsehood, a way to explain a momentary flux of heightened emotions. But what she felt was deeper, more profound than anything she ever had for a man before. Now a divorce from him would be more difficult, the twin's lives would be harder, Quinn's life would be harder. Dammit!

She tried to reason with her heart. What about him was so freaking lovable in the first place? Certainly not his obvious indifference to the world outside of Quinn and football, his bipolar sexual needs which dominated an appetite larger than the god-like aura surrounding him, his relentless brooding, or his heavy, ever-present baggage.

But there was something incredibly alluring in those caramel eyes; something that called to the inner, damaged woman dwelling inside her, something in the crooked grin he gave her when he was amused, something in the cock of that dark head, that keen intelligence burning through his gaze that said he knew and felt more than he wanted anyone to realize he did. He wasn't a demon, he was a softie who wanted the world to think he was big, bad Hades.

And he wasn't that much different than she was. Two broken-hearted lovers thrust into a dark world simply trying to keep out of the flames of Hell, the flames that licked at their very feet.

She heard Quil sigh as he stood and moved to come sit next to her on the seat that resided in a wall alcove of the room.

"She ok?" Veda asked.

"Alive, thanks to you."

"Stop making me sound like such a hero," Veda pleaded. She wasn't the hero; the doctor was.

"But you are, Persephone."

Oh, and look at that! Now I'm Persephone *again.* Veda thought cynically. *I save his daughter, and suddenly now I'm on his good side once more. Well fuck that, I'm not ok with being loved when it's simply convenient.* Bipolar for sure. That's exactly what Hades was.

She didn't take the bait he was dangling and said, "Quil, I should probably go."

"Go where?" he asked. "Home?"

And where is home exactly? she wanted to ask him, but refrained. She shrugged.

"You know I'm sorry for being so angry with you, right? I was just afraid. I had no right—"

"You had every right to be angry, Quillan. I would've had the same reaction."

He gave her that crooked grin that stilled her heart and soaked her panties, and she had to look away to keep her swooning heart from floating off on some fluffy pink dream cloud.

"Quil, look, I—"

"Veda, I—"

They both chuckled humorlessly as they realized they'd both tried to say something at the same time. Quil touched her arm. "Can I go first?" he asked and she shrugged again.

He pulled a deep breath in and seemed to be mulling his thoughts over before he softly said. "I died at Quinn's age."

"What?" she gasped and held a hand to her chest in shock. "How? Wh—?"

"Our house caught on fire and I was in the back room. My *abuela* couldn't get to me and my father was too overcome with smoke to go back in after me. I was rescued by one of the firemen, but I was clinically dead from smoke inhalation for a full five minutes before I came back to life. Miraculously."

Veda had no words. Holy shit! It was similar to her own story, only she'd been seventeen, not seven. What was it with sevens?

She looked down, her mind overwhelmed with thoughts as she tried to figure out what that meant.

"All I thought about when I was going to lose Quinn was how eerily coincidental yet paradoxical life is. How I had cheated Death at the same age and how worried I was that He'd come to claim her because of me. How I'm the 'god of Death,' and how I couldn't even rescue my own wife from it when she was so damned and determined to seek it out so adamantly. I was overwhelmed, to say the least, and I sincerely apologize for how I treated you."

She gave him a soft smile, forgiving his slights against her for the time being.

"Since you confessed your secret to me, I guess I should tell you that I, too, was clinically dead for five full minutes."

"No, you weren't," he stated incredulously.

Veda nodded. "After the abortion, I went through horrible depression. My nine-year-old sister had died, my baby was ripped from my womb, and my dad had disappeared. I felt like the opposite of Midas; instead of everything I touched turning to gold, it had turned to ash. Sound familiar?" Veda's brow went up, and he gave her another understanding smile. He nudged her knee, waiting for her to go on, so she did. "I decided that I couldn't keep on, that it would be easier to die than to watch my mom and remaining sister go before me. So I drew myself a hot bath, took a razor blade, and cut my wrists—the right way, mind you—and watched the bathtub fill with swirls of my blood until I began to dream. I was surrounded by voices of loved ones, laughs, tears, pain, and happiness. I could see faces I recognized and some I didn't, but I knew that I wasn't meant to stay there. When I awoke, I was being shocked and came to with my mom and sister's faces in view.

They'd called 911 and an ambulance had come. They defibrillated me and got me back."

"Wow, I had no idea." The softness in his voice called to her heart. She shivered when his hand took hers and traced the line in her wrist where one of the scars still lay, raised and paled by time.

"I covered the scar of one with tattoos but left the other, as a reminder."

"Philosophical, much?" Quil winked and Veda gave a little giggle.

"That's what Becca and Pax say about you, you know?"

Quil looked down with a blush. "I still remember stuff too, from my time...beyond."

"Oh?" She was intrigued to say the least, since she had the same cognizance.

"Yeah, a name stuck out to me, I've heard it in my head for so long it's like a prayer or something."

"What's the name?" she asked, a shiver running up her spine in realization.

"Tessa."

Veda gasped, despite that she knew exactly what he would say before he said it.

"What?" Quil's brow drew in confusion.

"I heard that name too... while I was...dead. I also heard the name—"

Quil interrupted with, "Torin?"

Veda's jaw dropped; she was floored and gulped even as Quillan did the same.

"Holy shit, V! I have goosebumps from Hell right now."

"Me too. Quil... How is it that we both have the same names in our heads?"

Quil looked her face over as if seeing her for the first time and gave her a slow smile. "I think you already know the answer to that question."

She shook her head in disbelief as she asked, "Our twins?"

Quil moved his hand to her belly and stroked there, his palm searing her flesh with something more than simple desire. "It has to be. There's no other explanation for it, is there?"

She shook her head again and looked at the face that was leaning into hers in that moment, the lips that were but a breath away.

"I think you *are* home, V, and I don't think there's anywhere else you need to be right now, do you?"

At his question, Veda's eyes closed and she savored the lips touching hers even as she moaned hungrily into them. She dare not disagree.

QUINN WAS able to come home after three-day's time. She was still weak and tired but was healing well and the antibiotics were keeping her infection-free. Much to Quil's dismay, Dr. P, Quinn's hematologist, said she might need to be on continual antibiotics now that she had no spleen—as if Quinn needed any more medications to have to take. He was looking into a new therapy and alternative medications and treatments. When they left the hospital, Quil felt hopeful for the first time in a while.

He didn't want to leave Quinn for any length of time, but Veda reassured him that she would be fine. So, reluctantly, he went back to the complex with his set routine, trying to get his head into the championship game coming on Sunday.

His ankle had healed up and he was ready to play, but Coach Haskins, his offensive coordinator, wasn't having him full out run yet, making sure he saved it for their tougher practices later on in the week. Quil worked out hard at his set time, absorbing himself into his own little bubble. When their first break of the morning came, his teammates gathered around and looked at him as if he were a ticking time bomb.

Brett spoke first, the almighty Zeus, "How's Quinn, man?"

"She's good. Thanks, Brickhouse." Quil gave his QB a grin and slugged at his bare bicep.

"You got our gifts and stuff, right?" It was Linc who asked, concern etched into his big brown eyes.

"Yeah, thanks guys. You didn't have to do that, you know?" Quil was humbled, realizing he'd only been with the organization for little more than six months' time. "We got flowers and balloons all over the house, I'm running out of places to put them."

"I got somewhere you can put 'em," Travis "Ares" Redmond retorted with a grin and Quil laughed.

"Glad she's doing better, man," their big center, Josh Robicheaux, said.

"We were all worried sick, you know?" Pax stated.

Quil had seen more of Pax than the others with Becca coming to support Veda during this time. Hell, he and Quil were sorta like brothers-in-law now. *My brother-in-law! Damn, that's weird*, Quil thought but realized when Pax married Rebecca that's exactly what they would be.

TJ ambled over and slugged at Quil's arm, a smug grin on the big lug's long face. "You know we're always here for you. Whatever you need, right, Hades?"

Quil gave him a grin and looked around at the faces of his teammates—the men who were more like his brothers than his co-workers. They had taken him into their group. They'd celebrated victories together, hung their heads in defeat, bled, sweat, and strived together to get where they were today. They'd titled him, making him their brother, a God of the Gridiron. And Gods of the Gridiron they'd been with an almost perfect regular season record and an outstanding performance. Now they had two games standing between them and the Super Bowl.

"Thanks, guys. Sincerely, I'm glad to be a part of this team and this organization. It's been a long time since I felt like I belonged. I look around and I see that you aren't just my team, you're my family. It means everything." Quil gave them a nod.

They were all quiet, just returning his gesture, before Trav smirked again. "Now don't be going all soft on us, Hades. We need that hard-ass exterior to get us through the next two weekends."

When Quil laughed and stood, Trav pulled him in for a handshake and a half-hug.

"Oh, don't you worry. The Hell I intend to unleash is gonna be brutal."

"I'd expect no less," Brett stated with a wink. "Now let's go practice, god-style."

Their resolve had never been stronger. They were a force to be reckoned with and come Sunday, it was on!

VEDA FROWNED AT QUINN. "Alright, what is it?"

Quinn scowled, crossed her arms over her chest, and looked away from the chicken soup that sat on the tray in front of her.

"Quinn, sweetie, you have to eat something or this medicine is going to make you sick."

"I don't wanna eat."

Veda wasn't used to a pouty little princess. She was used to a vibrant, light-hearted dreamer who never stopped reaching for the clouds.

"Are you hurting?"

Quinn shook her head.

"Ok, is this not what you want to eat? I can make you something else."

Quinn looked down at her Elsa nightgown and her lips started to quiver.

"Quinn, honey, please talk to me. I don't know what you need if you don't tell me."

Big, fat crocodile tears fell from the brown-haired angel's eyes and Veda took her little hand in hers, admiring the flawless light brown skin of Quinn's.

"Baby," Veda cooed and moved the tray aside, pulling Quinn into her arms to comfort. "Are you scared? Honey, everything is fine. That scar is gonna heal and you'll be back to playing like your old self in no time, ok? I promise. It just takes time to heal, so we'll just be watching more TV than usual and coloring and..."

"It isn't that..." Quinn trailed off and looked up into Veda's face, her little round cheeks so sweet and squeezable. "It's... you and Daddy got married, didn't you?"

Uh oh! Veda thought. "Quinn, honey..."

"I heard Tia talking about it. She doesn't think I can understand a lot of Spanish, but I know some words. I know what esposa means and niños, too. She was talking about you and Daddy."

Veda gulped. It should be Quillan telling her the truth, not Veda.

"You're having a baby, aren't you, Veda?"

Veda just looked down.

"Why can't you tell me? Why doesn't Daddy want me to know? Is he trying to replace me?"

"What!" Veda couldn't hide the shock in her tone. "God no, Quinn. Why would you think that, sweetheart?"

"I snooped in your room and saw the little jersey. He thought I was going to die, didn't he?"

Veda's eyes went wide, but Quinn went on before she could respond.

"I know I'm gonna die. I heard the doctors and nurses whispering when they thought I was asleep and the way Daddy looks at me sometimes..."

"Oh, Quinn."

"It's ok. Mommy died and so did my grandmother. I'm not afraid to die."

Veda had no words. What would one tell a chronically-ill child whose life was as fragile as this sweet one's was?

"My sister died too...and my dad," Veda finally said, simply because she could think of nothing else.

Quinn gave her a sad face then said, "I just want Daddy not to be sad when I do die."

"Oh, baby, he's gonna be sad. There's no helping that. We don't enjoy losing our loved ones. It hurts...so very much."

Quinn nodded. "I don't remember my mother. I try, but..."

"It's ok." Veda moved a strand of hair from her eyes.

"Are you my Mommy now?" Quinn wrung her hands in her lap, looking down.

Veda couldn't fight the tears stinging her eyes. "Is that what you want?"

Quinn nodded. "But you and Daddy fight, and I'm afraid you'll leave us."

"Oh, honey," Veda pulled Quinn back in to squeeze her little shoulders and stroke her hair, soothing her doubt. "Adults aren't as smart as you kids are. We do stupid things." Veda pulled Quinn back and gave her a reassuring grin. "Arguing is unnecessary, but we use our brains more than our feelings, so it tends to complicate things. But I can promise you, I'm not leaving you. I'm not going anywhere, ok?"

"Pinkie swear?" Quinn asked and held her pinkie out for Veda to interlock hers.

Veda laughed and wiped at her face. "Pinkie swear."

Quinn gave her that familiar giggle when Veda squeezed her pinkie finger around Quinn's much smaller one.

Great! Veda could kick herself for pinkie swearing to a seven-year-old. She just prayed that Quillan Layton—and her being in love with him—wouldn't be the reason she was forced to break it.

CHAPTER FOURTEEN

Quillan came home late Sunday night after an incredible win. His head and back hurt from the beating he'd taken on the field, and after an ice bath and shower, he'd gotten a deep tissue massage. Now, he looked forward to crashing in his bed.

It had been a close game, hard fought, but ultimately the Gladiators—aka the Gods of the Gridiron—had pulled off another epic victory. Zeus had fired off those thunderbolts he was known for, utilizing Quil and Trav to execute a total of five TDs. Pax and Linc had been on their games too, keeping the offense on their toes. And now they were one game away from the Super Bowl. The thought was surreal.

Quil tried to be quiet as he turned the alarm off and reset it as he entered the house and hung his keys on the hook in the mudroom. He yawned and stretched. It was past midnight.

He felt a pang of disappointment that Quinn and Veda hadn't come to the game tonight, but Quinn was still recovering and shouldn't be jumping about as he knew she would in the box. She'd had surgery just seven days ago.

He moved slowly up the stairs to head to his room, noting that both Veda and Quinn's lights were off in their rooms. As much as he knew they needed rest, he wished he could've celebrated his victory with them.

He'd received a video that he'd played once the speeches were made, the interviews were done, and he'd gotten to check his phone.

It showed a beaming Veda and Quinn, his wife and daughter, cheering, laughing and telling him how proud they were of him. It had truly warmed his heart. This was what he'd always wanted, the perfect family to love and share his accomplishments with him. It seemed too good to be true, and Quil swallowed down his fear. As he'd told Veda, he'd destroyed every woman who'd loved him, and God knew, he didn't deserve either of these amazing females in his life.

He sighed heavily as he opened the door to his bedroom and flipped on the light.

He wasn't prepared for the sight before him.

Veda had nothing on, nada—naked as the day she was born. A long, flowy blonde wig with a crown of lilies covered her hair.

"My, my, who have we here?" Quil murmured, feeling his body tingle.

"Why, your wife of course, *Hades*," Veda cooed, planting a finger in her mouth and sucking it gently, making his dick harden impatiently.

"Mmm, my wife isn't a blonde, last I checked."

Veda gave a little giggle. "My apologies. I always saw Persephone as a blonde." She gave a shrug and walked forward from his king-size mahogany sleigh bed. "Hades had a victorious evening. I thought he might want to celebrate with his queen."

"Mmm, in the worst way, *mi cielo*."

He moved forward, pulling her into his arms as his lips fell to taste hers.

He pulled back as soon as he tasted something on her red lips. It was sweet.

"Mmm, what is that?"

Veda gave another little giggle and opened her mouth. On her tongue lay a seed surrounded by a red capsule. He immediately knew what it was and laughed heartily. "Pomegranate never tasted sweeter, lover." He kissed her again and sucked the seed into his mouth, biting and swallowing it down before he thrust his tongue into her mouth.

His need was fierce and hungry as he loved her tongue with his own, his hands moving over her silky flesh with an urgency he couldn't fight if he tried.

Her hands were pulling his clothes off with haste, and he chuckled as she fumbled with his slacks and freed him, her warm hand moving into his boxers to cup his rock-hard sex.

"Oh, Veda... God, I missed you."

He knew it was true and his heart pounded out a frantic rhythm as his mind soared to a plane where nothing existed but loving this fertility goddess he'd pulled to the Underworld with him.

Soon, they were falling onto the bed, Veda's moans superseding his own as he kneaded her breasts and licked a trail on her neck, sucking with the utmost gentleness as she fisted his cock with an infuriatingly slow, yet mind-blowingly sensual, hand.

"Mmm, Hades, take me back to Tartarus," V stated and pulled him to her by his shaft even as her legs and arms began hugging his hips and neck.

He could have laughed, but he was too wrapped up in the moment—wrapped up in her. This goddess who had him, heart and body and soul, sucked into her bountiful cornucopia.

His hips dipped and he was soon being engulfed in her welcoming, silk-coated heat. A snug heat so deliciously hot, so seductively entrancing, that he wasn't sure he'd ever leave it again.

"Oh God, V... so sweet, so soft. *Vas a ser la muerte de mí, amante.*" His forehead hit hers as he sank into her, their eyes connecting, smiling with a secret only they knew. Their bodies hummed together in perfect synchronization as Quil withdrew and plunged deeper, groaning in blissful agony.

"Oh yes. Speak Spanish to me, my dark god."

"*Dios oscuro*, eh? You're mi *reina brillante*, no?"

"Mmm, yes, I'm gonna come from just your accent alone."

Quil chuckled and angled his hips, his cock stroking her womanhood with slow, unhurried thrusts as his fingertip languidly caressed her embellished bud. "*Ven por mi bebe, ven por mi,*" Quil enunciated seductively.

He kissed her, deeply and with passion, feeling her shudder as she cried her release into his mouth. He grinned and continued to rock into her, plunging and withdrawing as his own pleasure waves began to scorch him hotter and harder, bringing him closer and closer to climax.

Her hands moved over his back and pulled him closer to her. He felt himself falling into the depths, where his lover waited to pull him from the flames, holding him up, away from danger, safe in her angelic arms.

He whimpered as he came inside her, pumping his hips and feeling her sex tighten around him as she found another release of her own. He groaned and spasmed before stilling inside her and cupping her cheek.

"That was one hell of a homecoming, *esposa*."

"Glad you enjoyed yourself, Hades." Veda grinned and kissed his lips.

He savored those sweet rose buds for a moment before pulling back.

"I loved the video of you and Quinny. It made my night."

"She was so happy. I couldn't resist." Veda's smile lit up her beautiful face, making Quil feel such joy.

"How are my other two *niños* tonight?" He looked down at her baby bump and rubbed it softly with his big palm.

"Glad that Daddy's home."

Quil gulped at those words. It jolted something deep inside and his heart melted. He leaned in for another kiss before laying down beside his wife, pulling her into his chest.

Quillan realized things between him and Veda weren't perfect, nor were their sizzling sexual performances enough to sustain a healthy marriage or relationship; but if nights like this could continue, there was hope for a future for them. He longed to say something but knew that words weren't always needed, especially knowing how often their words got them into trouble and how fierce each of them could be with them.

He lay for a time stroking Veda's naked back, listening to her soft breathing and inhaling the spicy peach and citrus fragrance that was his sassy Irish queen.

She was the first to break the silence as she looked up at him. "Quil, you need to talk to Quinn."

He frowned at her drawn brows. "Why? What's up?"

"She's got a lot on her mind. About death and her mother and...us."

"What about us?"

"She knows, Quillan. She overheard Juanita talking and well, she's not deaf, nor is she completely oblivious to your Spanish any longer, so I suggest you be careful what you say when she's in earshot."

Quil sighed. It was sort of a relief that Quinn knew. He didn't know why, but he was glad for it. Although, it wasn't how he'd wanted her to find out, at least now the bandage had been ripped off and they could ease into getting her used to this arrangement.

"She's a smart kid." He shrugged. "I'll talk to her. Don't worry, love." He kissed her temple and pulled her tighter against him, loving how she settled into him, so warm and easily, fitting like a puzzle piece. "Is there something else?" he asked when he sensed tension in her shoulders.

"I was contacted today by *Ink You* magazine. They want to run a story about me—us really—and do a photoshoot of my tattoos."

"That's great, baby girl. I knew you had a future in inspirational speeches after our wedding day. *Eras asombrosa.*"

Veda smiled big. "Thank you, but you're sure you're ok with it? I mean…"

"Of course, Veda, *mi pequeña rebelde*," he pulled her hand to his lips and kissed her knuckles, "so long as it's not too racy or the poses vulgar or anything, and you're comfortable with it, you have my blessing."

She gave a big sigh and stroked at the tattoo residing on his own chest.

They were quiet for a time, enjoying the bliss of sexual union and the stillness of two lovers comfortable in the other's presence. This was one of the few times they'd been in bed together where one—or the both of them—wasn't angry and walking away from the other. It was nice. It felt good and as Veda said, "I could get used to this," Quil thought, *I could too, mi esposa, I could too.*

"So how's life with Quil been lately?" Becca asked with a twinkle in her eye as they ate lunch together that next week. Quinn was in school, Quil and Pax were at practice, and Mam was getting her final round of chemo—praise the Lord—where Walt was hanging out with her today.

She and Becca were dining in an Irish pub downtown, one known for the best shepherd's pie outside of Ireland, and it was—even better than Mam's, if Veda were being honest, but she'd never tell her mother that in a million years. The meat was a combination of venison, beef, and lamb, hand-ground at the restaurant, and simmered with onions in a hearty Guinness gravy with slow-roasted root vegetables and topped with garlic mashed potatoes and sharp cheddar cheese. Veda hadn't been this stuffed in a very long time as she leaned back in her chair, sighed, and patted her full belly.

"If your smile is any indication, I'd say it's pretty good."

Veda shrugged.

"Oh Vey, I know that look."

"Don't."

"What?"

"You know precisely what, you mog!"

Becca giggled. "It looks good on you. It's been a long time since I've seen you this happy and with a man at that."

Veda knew it was true. She hadn't been in love, not giddy like a schoolgirl-type love, since Will. Things had been good between her and Quil; although she wasn't putting a label on it, nor admitting to him her feelings as of yet, she was enjoying how happy they were together. The sex had been incredible, he'd been kind and loving and even thoughtful, and it had all started after they'd told each other about their brush with death and the hereafter.

What were the odds that they'd both died, and for five full minutes, and had had the same exact names in their heads following their near-death experiences? It had to be one in a million. As much as they were different, there were too many similarities that couldn't be ignored. And Veda knew she wouldn't find anyone else who enjoyed her rebel-like nature as much as Quil seemed to, in more ways than one. As dark as Quil could be at times, and broody and solemn and quiet, he was a good man with a good soul and he'd started to open up to her, and not just in the bedroom.

He was philosophical; whether from his own out-of-body encounter or simply due to his curious nature, she wasn't sure. He was smart and giving and loved fiercely. He was protective and confident and sexy as hell, and he was one of the best tight-ends in the league. His love for his children touched her heart, and tonight, he—and the guys and their families—had planned to take them to a medieval dinner show. Veda found herself excited to spend time with her newly-acquired family.

"Well, thanks. I see Paxton has been heeding my warning."

Becca giggled again and nodded. "He's wonderful, sister. I adore him." That goofy grin on her face told Veda all she needed to know, and she reached forward, taking her sister's hands in her own.

"I'm happy for you both, truly I am."

Becca teared up and nodded a thank you.

"Now, what on earth is going on with Mam? Are her and this guy serious or is this some kind of freed from the bonds of death, last fling thing?"

She and Rebecca laughed, and Veda watched her twin's cheeks pinken.

"Right? Every time I call, she's giggling and he's there. He seems nice enough. Maybe since we both have men, she wanted one of her own." Bec shrugged.

"Ach, she must've, eh? I think she had her sights set on him for a while and just never said anything."

"I reckon, sheesh."

"Near death puts things into perspective."

Becca frowned. Veda knew she was remembering the day V had attempted to commit suicide, a month after she'd been forced to have the abortion. She knew that memory wasn't one a person could easily forget.

THE GROUND WAS hard on her back as Veda opened her eyes to see her mother and sister looking her over. Whether she was in the dream world or back in her bleeding body she wasn't sure. She'd been floating, above herself, above town, above the earth, in the clouds. High and weightless, a being of no mass, free to fly, to glide through space and time with ease. And she'd met people, glowing ethereal people with faces she knew, names she recognized, save the two—Torin and Tessa. Who were they and why were the names so embedded there? She saw her sister, Sarah, red hair in curls down her back, bright green eyes smiling into her own, healthy and happy as she'd been before the cancer took her youthful energy and turned her into a thin shell of the once vibrant girl they'd all known and loved.

Veda had come to with a start, shocked to be back where the pain cut her to the core. She was freezing cold as the voices and sounds penetrated the fog of blissful unawareness she'd been surrounded by.

"Wh—?"

"Oh, praise God, you're alive!" her mother's voice called. "Veda, baby, can you hear me?"

Veda's teeth chattered as she attempted to nod, unsure how she could be so alert when she'd felt her life force sucked from her body hours—or it'd felt like hours—ago.

"How could you do it, Veda? Was losing Sarah not punishment enough? Then Pa?" Becca slapped her hard across the face. "Ye selfish bitch."

Veda knew she deserved that; she would have felt the same way if Becca had done it.

"Ma'am, please?" Veda heard the EMT say. "Step back, we need to get her stable."

Stable? She was stable and alive, dammit. She moaned, attempting to say something but fatigue pulled at her eyelids. It was too difficult to ignore, and she found herself succumbing to it even as her sister's voice called to her.

"Don't you dare die on me, Vey. Don't you dare! I need you. Mam needs you. Do you hear me?"

THOSE WORDS HAD BEEN ECHOING inside her brain now for seven long years. The kick she'd needed to get into action once she was taken to the psych ward and forced to come to terms with the volley of sins she'd committed against both the Holy Ghost and herself. The first couple weeks were a fog as she was tested, counseled, and drugged; but knowing how much her sister and mother needed her was what kept her sane, kept her alive, kept her fighting. They did need her. She was the strongest of them and without her, they wouldn't make it. She owed them that much at least, not to leave them. She'd apologized over and over again when she'd gotten home for her hasty and reckless behavior, swearing never to be such again. And she hadn't. She'd not ever touched drugs or let her heart get carried off by another man who would only hurt her in the end. She'd been vigilant, careful, and she'd thrown herself into taking care of the remaining family she had. Now, she saw they both had a fighting spirit within each of them.

She'd not told Becca why she'd done it, not told her about Will's rejection of their child, her father's betrayal, the unforgivable sin she'd committed against her unborn fetus. It wasn't that she hadn't wanted to. They were sisters.

Up until the fated day of the abortion, they'd told one another everything, but Veda knew now that it was because she couldn't stand to see that look on her twin's face ever again—that look of disappointment, shame, and regret. Becca was the saint after all and V the bad girl. How could she possibly explain feelings Becca had never felt before? Veda had been eaten up with guilt following the abortion and suicide attempt, and she hadn't been able to relive her feelings again, not even for the relief of getting that secret off her chest. So she'd bottled it all up instead, setting it aside and letting it fester into a wound of unspent emotion for seven long, hard years.

Becca gave her a sweet, knowing smile now.

Veda returned it, realizing no words were necessary; Becca knew exactly what she was feeling, she really always had.

"I'm glad you're happy, sister. You deserve it. Truly."

"Thanks, Bec."

"But I'm gonna tell Quil the same thing you told Paxton. If he hurts you, he has me to deal with. And I'm not just the quiet little historian anymore."

Veda smirked and arched her brow. "Oh, and who *are* you sister?"

"I'm the Queen of the Sea."

Veda let the chuckle building within out and shook her head. "Do you think that Hades, God of the Underworld, is going to be afraid of you?"

"He should be," Becca crossed her arms over her chest and puckered her lips.

"Oh? Pray tell, why?"

"Because last I checked, water can put out flames."

Veda's brows went up in surprise, and that's when she realized that her sister no longer needed her; Rebecca Christine Ryan, Veda's twin and baby sister by three minutes, could hold her own. It was Paxton who'd better watch out. And with that, they both laughed.

"Daddy, look—there's the queen!" Quinn gasped and pointed to the woman clad in a regal blue gown with gold filigree and embellishments. A gold crown sat atop a head of blonde curly tendrils. The sleeves of her laced up gown draped languidly down her sides, reminding him of the one his Medusa wore on Halloween.

She looked lovely tonight, his *dama serpiente*, clad in a low-cut, fitted turquoise top that made those green eyes of hers pop and a pair of khakis that outlined her exquisite ass.

"Yup, just like my *reinita*." Quil grinned down at his little angel, pulling his eyes from Veda's enticingly plump backside.

To be so little she was solidly built; slender with curves in all the right spots. She was almost past the first trimester of her pregnancy and had a little bump now on her lower abdomen where his babies were nestled. She would absent-mindedly touch it frequently, which made him smile. These past couple weeks had been good, easy, light, and rewarding as they'd begun to explore their love for one another, get to know each other, and simply enjoy each other's company.

The championship game was coming up on Sunday, and the guys had decided to take their families out for a night of fun and entertainment. They were all pumped and looking forward to seeing if they would make it to the Super Bowl. A lot was riding on this game, so instead of having them run more drills, Coach Cavanaugh had given them Friday afternoon off and they'd decided to come out to The Knight's Table, a medieval style dinner show.

They'd been given VIP access—of course—and had free rein to pose with the king and queen, all the knights and horses, and browse the shops and grounds before they were to be sat in their private section away from the crowd.

"Want a picture with the queen?" Veda asked Quinn and looped her arm through Quil's, making his mouth quirk up in a grin even as his blood tingled at her closeness.

Quinn nodded vigorously in response, and Veda gave a sexy laugh that made Quil shiver with desire. He took Quinn's hand and walked her over to the elegant queen; they both gave curtsies in return, getting another grin out of Quil.

They were starting to become a family, the family that Quil had wanted more than anything when he'd asked his college sweetheart to marry him. The family Quil had longed for before cocaine and addiction had destroyed his dreams.

And he'd been blown away that a woman like Veda Angeline Ryan Layton was becoming his dream woman. She'd been so different than him—or he'd thought she was in the beginning. But he'd started to realize how alike they'd been all along; strong, independent, passionate, protective. And what were the odds that they'd both died and come back? And how on earth could one explain how they'd both heard the same names in the beyond? It was fate. Pure and simple.

They were meant to be, Hades and Persephone, the maiden as dark as he was. They fed off one another, couldn't live without each other. He needed her darkness as much as he needed her light, and he was starting to realize how much light she'd brought into his life. Her laugh and love and uniqueness—for she was the most unique person he'd ever known. Her tattoos and piercings were an expression of herself. First done as a symbol of rebellion, now they simply fit her personality. Without them, Veda wouldn't be who she was; her seeking attention was as much a part of her personality as breathing was. She enjoyed the limelight and had sought it by being a cheerleader and a stripper, not because she enjoyed the image it painted upon her, but because that attention had given her a platform, a voice. Now her voice had been heard on podcasts, talkshows, interviews, and the like. Social media was eating her up—and Quil, too—as well as news outlets everywhere. And her magazine photoshoot and feature had come and gone with ease. She had even more confidence now than she'd had before, and tonight, it shined through her inked skin as brightly as the sun. Confidence looked good on Veda Layton.

Quil's eyes weren't the only ones on Veda though; he saw Brooke staring at her from the corner of his eye. His brows drew as Brooke looked up and grinned at him. It might as well have been a challenge as Quillan's blood boiled at the memory of what she'd told him at Thanksgiving. He still hated that Veda had shared a room—if not a bed—with Brooke and her lover. Just thinking about her exposed, naked before them, made him angry and sick to his stomach simultaneously. He wanted to roar and stomp his foot in defiant possession. Veda was *his* and his alone. He would never share her.

Brooke licked her lips and looked back at Veda with a knowing smirk.

He'd never wanted to punch a woman until now.

"You should totally buy a sword," Quil heard Pax joking with TJ, his vengeance interrupted.

"No, an axe or a hammer. He's Hephaestus, after all," Trav said, pointing to a giant axe behind a standing glass case in the corner to Quil's left.

"Daddy!" Quinn's shrill voice got his attention as she came running over with a Polaroid photo in tow. "Look, she let me wear her crown!"

Sure enough, the picture showed Quinn in the oversized gold crown the queen had been wearing. Quil grinned and said, "You look beautiful, *mi corazón.*"

"I wanna buy a costume." Because apparently the one she had on wasn't princess enough.

Quil rolled his eyes but let her lead them into the gift shop where she picked out a wand, crown, and snow globe to go along with a costume.

"Does my *reina* want anything?"

Veda giggled sweetly as she looked up at him. "Your *reina* has everything she could ever want." The sparkle in her eyes made him swoon on the inside, and he realized once again that he'd fallen in love with the beautiful, damaged queen beside him.

"She's gonna have even *more* once we get home." Quil wrapped his arm around her and pulled her into his side, kissing her cheek and getting another giggle out of her.

Once all the acknowledgements were made, pictures were taken, and their merchandise was bought, they were escorted into the arena where they were sat behind the crest of the wolf sigil with the colors of silver and blue. Their knight, clad in shining armor, complete with hauberk and greaves, came riding up atop his stallion. The Wolf Knight, as he was known, greeted them and chatted with Quinn, Lennox, and Lofton—despite his shyness—who were all awed and excited by his presence. He then greeted Trav, Linc, Quil, Brett, Pax, and TJ—and their ladies. He thanked them for coming, congratulated them on their victories thus far, and wished them luck in their ventures. They all asked him questions about his horse, the tournament, and how he felt about his competition.

Once the show began, the pleasure on Quil's daughter's face was contagious as he watched her entranced by every word; the story, the narrator, the beauty of the horses, and allure of the knights pulled her in as if drawn like a bee to a flower. He chanced a glance over at Veda, who grinned back at him then kissed Quinn's cheek in delight.

Had she also been a dreamy little girl seduced by the wonders of the fantasy world? Had she dreamed about a knight coming to rescue her? Only to be disappointed by what fate had seen to give her? First, she'd been had by the manipulative high school jock who'd pulled her heart from her chest and crushed it with an angry fist. Then her father had done what he'd done, then Quil himself— the gloomy god who'd been drawn in by her dark allure, amplified by the glow beneath her alabaster skin—overpowered her, knocked her up, and forced her into marriage. Some knight he'd turned out to be!

The tournament began with a parade of crests, shining armor, and the pounding of hooves as sigils of the wolf, bear, lion, and dragon were revealed. The horses were decked out too in ornamental colors, flags, and feathers. The knights talented their audience with their skills with longswords, dirks, maces, and battle-axes while their servers brought around the feast which consisted of Cornish game hens, vegetables, soup, and salad. During the second half of the show, the knights were horseback and actually jousting. A screen lowered to protect the onlookers from wood shards that splintered across the dirt-laden enclosure.

Adrenaline and excitement overtook them as lance met shield in a well-choreographed collision of medieval proportions. Quil was as impressed by the show as Quinn, feeling like a kid again as he laughed and cheered along with his teammates, the exhilaration infectious.

When it came down to the wolf and dragon knight's battling it out for the heart of the queen, gasps, oohs, and shrieks filled the arena. Quil hadn't seen his daughter, Lennox, or Lofton so amped up and couldn't help but let his own happiness be fueled by theirs; watching them stand in awe of the scene before them was sheer magic in and of itself.

The dragon knight took a hard hit to the helmet and fell to the ground, shield thrown aside, giving the silver and blue knight a clear advantage. In one swift blow with his longsword, the dragon knight was "defeated" and the winner rose in triumph, shedding his helmet, and raising his four-foot steel sword into the air. They all jumped up in applause, congratulating their victor on his impressive win.

Quinn squealed and laughed, a true sight, making Quillan's heart so happy in that moment. He picked her up, pulled her to him and kissed her sweet cheeks in succession.

"We won, Daddy. We won."

He only hoped this would be the same fate as his team, for in three nights they, too, would be on the battlefield striving for victory.

"I LOVE YOU, too. I'll talk to you tomorrow." Veda hugged her sister before they parted ways in the parking lot of the dinner show.

They'd all walked out together with giant smiles on their faces, thoroughly entertained this evening by knights, horses, and epic battle choreography. And their knight, the silver and blue tunic-clad warrior, had won.

Veda smiled and took Quillan's hand as he led them to his Land Rover. A yawning Quinn lounged easily on his shoulder.

There was nothing sexier than her own battle-ready, tall, dark and handsome warrior, save for that warrior with his daughter cradled to him. Nothing. Sexier. Especially to her ovaries, rapidly pumping out pregnancy hormones.

He opened the back door and set Quinn down, her eyelids all droopy.

They'd all stood talking for a good twenty minutes following the dinner show, but the kids had started to grow restless, their little bodies full to the brim with glee. Once their highs had worn off, they'd started to grow sleepy. Twenty minutes might as well be an hour to two toddlers and a seven-year-old, so Val and Linc had bid them all farewell and Quil had been soon to follow suit. Although, if Veda's suspicions were correct, Quil was eager to get his daughter into her bed so he could get his wife into his own.

She grinned over at him as he slid behind the wheel and she buckled her seatbelt.

"What?" he asked with a flirt behind his eyes.

"She was so adorable tonight." Veda looked back at her step-daughter, head now tilted back, surrendered to dreams of knights and medieval romance.

"So were you. I thought I might have competition. Maybe I need a shield and sword."

Veda gave a big laugh, then covered her mouth, afraid to wake Quinn up.

Quil gave a self-satisfied chuckle.

"She had a blast," Veda stated factually.

"I think we *all* did. I know I did." He took her hand and brought it to his lips as he drove the empty streets toward home.

Quil grew quiet as he kept her hand. It wasn't an awkward silence; it was the type of comfortable and content silence one has in the presence of a lover they're precisely that with. Veda looked out at the abandoned streets of downtown through the tinted window of the vehicle. It was close to midnight, and she found herself yawning.

"Are you tired, my love?" Quil asked and moved his hand from hers to her baby bump.

She grinned, not sure whether she loved the fact that he'd called her his *love* or was touching their babies through her shirt more than he had been. "I'm good; not too tired to worship my god tonight." She gave him a wicked grin that promised more as he returned his gaze to the road, and she saw the corner of his mouth lift in happiness.

Soon, they were pulling into the driveway and Quil was parking the car as Veda grabbed up their memorabilia from tonight: cups, pennants, their paper crowns, and a great picture of them with the queen, beaming brightly. Happy Quillan was just as sexy as broody Quillan, and Veda couldn't help but sigh as she looked the picture over with bone-satisfying pleasure at the three of them. Her tummy fluttered and she looked over at the man she loved as he reached in to grab Quinn.

"Mmph," Quinn grunted as Quil pulled her back to his shoulder and hit the garage door opener as Veda unlocked the door.

They were just through it and Veda was silencing the alarm when Quinn cried out, "Mommy?"

The little girl reached for V. Both Quil and Veda gasped in reaction, and V quickly moved to comfort Quinn.

"Shh, it's alright honey. I'm right here." Veda ran a hand through the hair at Quinn's forehead and kissed her temple.

Quinn gave a little sigh of comfort, and Veda's eyes sought Quil's.

Her heart nor her ovaries were prepared for the onslaught as his hungry, caramel brown eyes bore into hers. She gulped as emotions, raw and licking, flowed from him into her and she felt her knees go weak.

The sound of the ice machine pulled them from their gazing, and Veda cleared her throat.

"We should get her up to bed," she said as Quil continued to stare at her, unblinking.

Finally, he came to from his inner thoughts and nodded. He turned and moved up the stairs. Veda followed silently, her mind and heart in a state of shock at her growing fondness for both Quinn and Quillan.

She stood in the doorframe and watched as Quil took off Quinn's shoes, pulled her pants and shirt off, and pulled a gown over her head—all the while his "reinita" as he called her was out like a light. It was amazing how kids could do that, Veda thought. But the little angel was tuckered out and as Quil pulled the sheets to her chin, he said, "Sleep well, *mi corazón*."

When he turned, he seemed surprised that V was there.

"It's gonna be hard with two more," Veda stated, realizing they had their work cut out for them.

Quil's eyes and mouth softened and he separated the distance between them, his big palm cupped her lower abdomen once more. Desire and fulfilment soared through her.

"I guess it's a good thing we have a nanny then, huh?"

The word nanny made her look down. Tia Nita hated her and she told Quil that.

"She's just protective of her family, V. You can understand that concept, *si*?"

"*Si*, but she genuinely hates me, Quil. I don't know that I'm gonna grow on her. She actually glares at me, and I'm pretty sure she's crossed herself in my presence. I'm not convinced she doesn't think I'm a *bruja* and plans to exorcise me. I know I've smelled sage burned in my room before." As much as she was serious, she was joking too and got a laugh out of her lover.

"Veda, you make me laugh. But I promise, she means you no harm. She'll come around. Give her time. I'll talk to her on your behalf."

"I dunno. She probably thinks I've bewitched you. It's pro—"

"You *have*...bewitched me." He cupped her cheek and stroked his thumb across her cheekbone, his eyes flitted over her lips. "I'm under your dark spell, *dama serpiente*."

Veda grinned even as she lowered her eyes. "Well, my father was convinced that I was a *bean sí*, so perhaps I am."

"And do you turn into a hag?" Quil teased, and her eyes shot back to his. He was grinning in amusement. "C'mon. You know that's utterly ridiculous, V. You have the most beautiful soul I've ever seen."

Veda felt her jaw drop, and Quil's thumb pulled it back up to close her mouth.

"I've seen the lovely fairy you had tattooed on your skin. I've traced it and know that's why you have it here," his fingertips moved to her lower back where it sat itching to feel his touch again, "Even if it's to lighten the dark one you think you may represent, but there's no way it's even remotely possible, *mi cielito*."

Veda gulped, feeling heat course through her as his words hit deep inside her heart.

"If you're a *bruja*, then does that make me your *escoba*?" he smirked.

When Veda frowned in confusion, he laughed. "Broom," he answered her unspoken question. She was even further confused, getting another chuckle from the sexy dark god who haunted her fantasies. She'd never heard him laugh so much, and the sound of it warmed her heart.

"Oh," she finally understood, "because I intend to *ride* you?" she answered.

His smile deepened and his hand descended her back and gripped her bottom firmly. "Mmm, *háblame sucia, hermosa*."

Veda had no idea what he'd just said, but as his chest hit hers and his eyes moved over her as if she were already unclothed, she knew it was something sexy. Ah, who was she kidding, *everything* Spanish dripping from his lips was sexy. When his head lowered and he began whispering sweet nothings in that seductive native tongue of his into her ear, his nose teasing her earlobe, she could have melted into a puddle on the floor. She recognized words he'd spoken before: *mala, caliente, fuego,* and *coño,* but he used new and delicious sounding words too that awakened the inner goddess within. She found her fingertips roving over his chiseled chest and moving toward his jeans, fiddling with the button and fly. In two seconds flat, she had him undone and was reaching into his boxers.

"Si, acariciarme, mi amada."

God, why hadn't she had him speak Spanish the entire time they'd made love? It was so sexy; it had her womanhood tingling and her skin humming in desire.

"Mmm," she answered and gripped his hard member in her fist as his lips crashed against hers.

He kissed her like his life depended on it, but before she could explore the lengthy girth that always fascinated her, he was pulling them from Quinn's room and down the hallway.

"You want me, Persephone?"

"Aye, my dark god. I want you so much," she answered and pulled him to her as she fell back onto the bed.

His lips covered hers once more as his hands sought her breasts, squeezing and teasing as her moans echoed in the high, coffered ceiling.

"Only me, *esposa, sólo yo?*"

"Yes, husband, only you." She answered as his hands moved to her pants and he freed them from her hips.

Their need to get each other naked superseded all else and when they were, he moved his hands over her as if touching the holy grail. He kissed her, flipped them over, and settled her astraddle of him as he guided himself inside her, grunting in pleasure as the tip of his cock slid into her slick opening.

"Oh, Hades," Veda whimpered and gasped in both content and awe as his shaft began to feel the void inside her center—the void inside her soul when they weren't joined together.

"My sexy *chica mala*, my sweet goddess, *te quiero*." His voice was strained and full of emotion, his eyes and hands seeking hers, as she rose and lowered herself upon him, loving him with all her might. "Love me. *Sólo yo. Quiéreme*. No one else. Not even Adonis."

The sexy crooked grin of his pushed her closer to the edge even as she answered him with a scoff. "Silly god, you *are* my Adonis."

And as she loved him with her sex and hands and eyes, she hoped he saw that she indeed loved him, every part of him—the good, the bad, the beautiful, the ugly, the fire and the ice, all the dark and the light that made up Quillan Rowtag Layton.

QUILLAN AWOKE to the feel of a hot mouth on his ass cheek and moaned aloud. He could've yelped when that same mouth bit down into the meaty flesh there, but growled in desire instead as his shaft filled with blood, stiffening beneath him. God, he was insatiable for this naughty sex kitten of his and told her so—in Spanish—getting a moan from her as her small hand cupped his scrotum.

"Mmm, like that, Hades?"

Hades liked *anything* she had a mind to do to him, glutton for punishment that he was.

"Flip over."

He did as instructed to see his *chica mala* on her knees, scooting between his now opened legs.

Her hair was all mussed on her head, wavy dark tendrils flowing down her inked shoulders, eyes ablaze and mouth swollen from their love-making last night. How could she have anything left?

But as he let her love his greedy sex with that insanely skilled mouth of hers—and insufferable tongue ring—he started to lose all control. She made him pull his arms over his head, giving her full access without interference as she went to town on him.

The sight of her sucking him down her beautiful throat was almost too much as he whimpered and came close to blowing his load, but just as he was starting to feel himself slipping over the edge, Veda straddled him and impaled herself on his solid cock, making Quil's head fly back in exquisite pleasure.

Veda moved her spine in calculated precision, her bottom bouncing up and down on him with a smirk on her face and challenge in her eyes as he let her dominate him once again. The unbreakable stallion within him fought for control, but curiosity won out and he tumbled, down deep into a fiery pit of torment and pleasure where he cried his release. He sighed as he watched his gorgeous Persephone guide him safely back to Earth, her hands stroking his pecs and abs before she leaned forward to rest on his chest, fitting snugly at his collarbone. He wrapped his arms around her, kissed her sweaty forehead, and sighed again.

"My my, you sure know how to awaken your god, don't you, angel?"

Veda propped her chin on him and looked up into his eyes, a knowing smirk there. "You were too tempting to resist. Like the forbidden fruit. I had to take a bite of that sexy ass."

He chuckled and kissed her plump lips. "I recall that same feeling…on Halloween night." He brushed his nose across hers and fingered the curve of her cheek. "Be careful, *dama serpiente*. Last time you were in the Garden of Eden, you got impregnated."

Veda laughed and kissed him, getting another moan out of him.

God, he wanted to stay in bed with her all day but had to head to practice soon.

She seemed to sense his thoughts and pouted for a moment before propping herself up on her elbows, so sweet and familiar atop him, pulling another smile from his lips.

"You know your name is Irish, right? Quillan."

Quil nodded. "Aye, lass, I did. My mother was Irish." When Veda's brows drew in confusion, he laughed. "My *abuela*, my maternal grandmother, came straight off the boat from Spain. My grandfather, her husband, had Irish roots though, his mother was from Ireland.

"My *abuelos* met at church and had one child, my mother, Victoria. My mother and father met in high school. He would bring her flowers before a game, Easter lilies. It was the closest thing he could find to an Irish flower. She loved her heritage and had always told my grandmother she wanted her son to have a good strong Irish first name." Quil shrugged. "What was Abuela to do when Mother died? Instead of Juan, she named me Quillan."

"Juan?"

"My great *abuelo*'s name. You know Catholics and their traditions." He winked.

"And Rowtag?"

"Well, seeing as my father was Blackfoot, my grandmother wanted to represent that part of me too, with a traditional Siksika name. Only recently did Dad tell her that Rowtag isn't even the Algonquin name for fire." Quil chuckled, amused.

"Fire, huh? Fitting for the God of the Underworld." Veda smirked, and he kissed her beautiful lips because he couldn't resist.

"Right? But Abuela didn't know. She'd simply heard it before in town, so she took it and plugged it in for my middle name, feeling that my mother would've approved. When Dad came home from his time in the woods, he wasn't going to tell her she'd messed up; he didn't have it in him to do so. It was something we laughed about often."

"So, what's the Siksika word for fire?"

"Ishkode."

"Yeah, Rowtag sounds better."

"I thought so too," Quil chuckled and kissed V again.

At her moan, he flipped them over so he was on top and ran his big palm through her hair.

"*Señora*, as much as I want to stay here with you, I have to head to practice." He looked regrettably at his bride, that translucent alabaster skin calling to the primal male in him to explore, mark, and possess every inch of it. Her breasts were full and their pink tips teased him as they hardened beneath his gaze; he could feel his cock stiffening again and groaned in bittersweet agony.

"I guess you'll just have to hurry home then, won't you, husband?" She popped a finger in her mouth and began sucking it, seductively.

"*Madre de Dios*, don't do that, *mujer*, or I'll have to spank you."

"Mmm, that sounds so yummy, *mo grá*."

Ok… Well, maybe he had like five more minutes.

VEDA GRINNED as she looked at the pictures in her email. She sipped the one cup of coffee she granted herself and typed out a response to the project manager, director, and editor who'd organized her photoshoot, thanking them and telling them how much she loved the outcome. Quil might not be thrilled about how much skin was showing, but she was covered—if not as modestly as she wanted to be originally.

Her arm had concealed her breasts and her eyes were downcast, looking down at her growing belly with a maternal smile any viewer would be awed by, her tattoos vibrant against a black backdrop. The article was just as amazing in its power—her voice, front and center, for all to hear.

Veda gave a gasp as she heard the doorbell ring and told Tia she would get it.

V was shocked as she pulled the door open to see Brooke Taylor, looking like a million bucks in a fitted brown dress and gold heels on her doorstep.

"Br-Brooke, what a surprise."

"Hi, I hope I'm not interrupting anything. I just… Can I come in?"

Veda balked and stepped back, swinging the giant mahogany door open.

Veda watched with shock as a befuddled Brooke walked in and blushed. "I'm sorry to barge in like this, but I need to talk to you. Do you—uh—have somewhere private we can speak?"

Brooke looked to Nita, who had her arms folded across her ample bosom, looking like she wanted to light Brooke—and Veda— up in that moment.

"Uh, yes... let's uh, go out to the patio." The patio was enclosed, so it would allow them privacy for a conversation. But it also had glass walls, in the event that Brooke wanted to try any shit Veda would have a witness. "Can I get you anything to drink or—?"

"No, I'm good." Brooke followed Veda out to the glass enclosure overlooking the lake and motioned for her to sit. "Uh, I'll stand but thank you."

Veda didn't sit either, for she couldn't help but wring her hands behind her, anxious for Brooke to tell her why she was there—at Quillan's house—after he'd plainly voiced how he felt about her, multiple times.

Before V could ask, Brooke was stammering. "Look, I know you're probably racking your brain as to why I'm here. I swear, it...I'm not... I..." Brooke sighed and turned her face from Veda's, looking out over the serene lake as a flock of geese flew by.

Veda could see emotion dance over Brooke's lovely features; her hazel eyes, darker than her sisters, with gold flecks, making them appear green with some outfits, brown with others, her high cheekbones and blonde hair, perfect lips with a cupid's bow. Veda had never seen her so serious and couldn't fathom why she suddenly was now.

"I've come to apologize to you, Veda. For how I treated you. For how I manipulated you. For tricking you into feeling like you had to sell your body, well pretty much, for modeling gigs."

Veda's brows literally shot to her forehead. She hadn't been expecting that.

"The truth of the matter is... Since TJ has come into my life, I've been realizing a lot of things about myself: who I really am, why I *am* the way I am. I've done some soul-searching. See, after what happened at Christmas, we had a serious 'come to Jesus'. Well, *he* did. He told me some things about myself that were kinda hard to hear. He laid it out for me, gave me an ear, a shoulder to cry on...and he's been taking me to see a therapist. Turns out, I'm not a cynical bitch so much as I have a mental disorder—well, a couple to be honest. It all stemmed from... Well, something bad that happened to me as a teenager, which I won't bore you with the specifics since my ordeal doesn't even hold a candle to what you've been through. But, needless to say, I've been focusing on righting my wrongs and you were next in the long line of apologies I need to issue."

Veda shivered. Wow, she'd not been expecting this. Not in a million years. She was speechless, so Brooke continued her vent.

"I realized that my behavior toward you was misguided—misdirected would be a better word, actually." Brooke looked down and back up. "Ya see, I've been using sex as my shield for a long time. I didn't even know what I wanted anymore because it was my outlet. I know you can probably relate." As much as Veda had been damaged by both a boyfriend and father who'd not wanted her at a young age, the death of her little sister, an abortion, and an attempted suicide, she'd never used sex as an outlet—well, not like Brooke had—but she nodded all the same. "Thing is, Veda, I don't want you...not sexually. I... I wanted to *be* you. I was jealous of you."

Again, Veda found herself speechless. She'd read Brooke all wrong.

"*Be* me? But why? I'm as fucked up as you are." Veda covered her mouth, apologetically. Pregnancy also tended to break one's filter—not that Veda had had much of one to begin with.

Brooke laughed though, then gave an uncomfortable grin. "You're beautiful, strong, and you're not afraid of anyone or anything."

"You aren't either, Brooke." She remembered all the times Brooke had stood up to TJ. As big and tall as Quil was, TJ outweighed him by a good fifty pounds.

"But I am though. I've realized that I'm afraid of *everything*. I only look tough from the outside. Inside, I'm still that scared little girl who hasn't gotten over the pain." A tear ran down Brooke's cheek as she looked back up. "It's all a lie. A mask."

Veda shook her head, remembering she'd said the very same thing to her sister when Becca had told her how brave she was. She took Brooke's hand in her own. "You're stronger than you know."

Brooke shook her head again. "I'm the weakest one of all of us. You. Val. Sky. Madi. Even Becca. You're all so much stronger than I am."

"Hey, this isn't a competition, Brooke. We're all fierce, independent women, but you know what's strong?" When Brooke looked up in question, Veda answered with, "Admitting that you *aren't* strong, admitting that you have weaknesses... problems, and that you want to fix them."

Brooke gave her a crooked grin and nodded, another tear falling down her tan cheek.

"I'm in love." Brooke laughed when Veda gave her a surprise face. "I know. Me! Of all people. But after seeing you with Quil, I started realizing that I want what all you other broads have, and TJ—God knows why—for some reason loves me, too."

Veda gave her a beaming grin. "Brooke, I'm so happy for you. That's great news."

"Right. It's gotta be one of the scariest things I've ever felt in my life. He wants to get married. Can you see *me* married? Gah!" Brooke shuddered in mock disgust, getting a laugh out of Veda.

"I want to thank you, though, for not running scared of me like everyone else does, for not being thrown off by my aloofness. Most everyone else just ignores me, but you took my challenges and met them. You stood up to me, and I appreciate that."

Veda gave her a crooked grin and a shrug. "I guess I realized what you were trying to do...well, for the most part. But I *did* think you wanted to fuck me. I mean, who doesn't?" Veda winked, jokingly.

"Well, you *are* gorgeous and a true work of art," Brooke smirked and looked her over. "Quil is a lucky man. I wish I were as stunning as you."

"Oh, stop it. You totally are. You're tall and lean and…tan."

"Beauty is in the eye of the beholder," Brooke sang.

It was true. As Brooke pulled Veda in for a hug, V realized how much she admired this woman who'd come to apologize and "right her wrongs." When she pulled back, Brooke leaned down to kiss her, a chaste kiss on the cheek.

"Veda, I want us to be friends. I mean that. I don't want to be your enemy. I know I'm a little rough around the edges, but your strength feeds my own and I need that right now."

"You were never my enemy, Brooke." The word misunderstood came to mind, and Veda thought about how Quil had called them both that word.

Veda smiled as Brooke invited her to come back and model with her, but shook her head kindly.

"Thanks. Right now, I got my own thing going on, but I'll definitely stay in touch."

As she walked Brooke out the door, her words echoed in Veda's head.

"After seeing you with Quil, I started realizing that I want what all you other broads have."

She realized she hadn't yet told Quillan that she loved him.

Tonight. Tonight, she would.

CHAPTER FIFTEEN

The house was quiet when Quil got home from practice. Veda must be at her mother's or the store or something and Tia must be picking Quinn up from dance. Did he really have the house to himself? Wow, that was a change.

He came in, browsing the mail in the basket then moved over to the laptop, logged on, and checked his email. He smiled at the one he saw from Veda with the subject line: Don't freak but I think they're stunning. It was complete with a kissy face emoji. He knew what that meant— he wasn't going to like them.

Damn, he thought as he scrolled down to the first one. His breath caught and his heart flipped over in his chest. They *were* stunning. Absolutely.

His wife was the most beautiful thing he'd ever seen with her radiant, porcelain skin glowing beneath her colorful tattoos, her beautiful face looking down to where his babies slept in her womb. It was breathtaking, utterly. But God, why did she have to be so bare, so naked, so exposed?

Quil took a deep breath in, reining in the jealous god within him. He needed to save it for his game tomorrow night, he knew. This was what she'd wanted, to be a model, and hell, it was better than having her be a stripper like she'd been before. But she was his—dammit, his—and he didn't want anyone else to see this photo. It was too much. Too much skin. He saw red and closed the lid on the laptop, needing to breathe.

But he wouldn't get a chance as Tia Nita came in, frowning as she saw him.

Quinn ran at his legs and reached for him. He picked her up and kissed her flushed little cheeks.

"Quinn, baby, you still gotta take it easy. You weren't dancing hard, were you? You know you just had surgery two weeks ago?" he scolded even as she nodded and giggled.

"I wasn't. Coach wouldn't let me."

Good, he thought, *they fucking listened to me for a change.*

"She had candy," Tia told him.

"Great, now you're gonna be hyper all night."

Quinn giggled. "Where's Veda?"

"I'm not sure... The store, maybe."

He was starting to worry as he checked his phone. Usually she texted him when she left the house. Perhaps her mom had an emergency.

"I'm sure she'll be here shortly. Why don't you go change out of that tutu?"

Quinn moved off to do as he'd asked, and Tia frowned again as she motioned for him to follow her.

"*Que pasó?*" he asked, knowing by the look on her face that something was amiss.

Tia began to tell him about a tall, tan blonde that sounded a lot like Brooke Taylor, coming to the house. *Brooke* had been there? At Quil's? Why? Tia didn't know. But Veda and Brooke had gone out to the patio to have a conversation, a very heavy conversation from the look of it, and they'd hugged and Brooke had kissed her.

Quil's brow arched. What on earth was she talking about?

Quil's mood had darkened by the time he nodded, thanked Tia for the information, and saw her out.

He gulped as he headed upstairs to change into his lounge clothes, grey sweatpants and a Gladiators shirt. Surely Veda and Brooke weren't still doing business together. Surely Veda knew how he felt about Brooke, and surely, she wouldn't dare go behind his back and betray him…would she?

As much as Quillan wanted to believe what he and Veda had was the real deal, he'd been tricked before and a vision clouded his thoughts.

"I LOVE YOU, Rian. I want to marry you. Please say yes."

"Yes, oh yes, Quil. Oh, this is beautiful." Her smiling face looked his over in awe, happiness, and surprise.

He placed the ring on her finger and pulled her into his arms as he kissed her lips.

"I want to get married as soon as possible. I can't wait to make babies with you. Start a family and…"

"One step at a time, big boy," she teased, but he knew she was as eager as he was to start a family as she brushed her nose across his. "Let's tie the knot first, huh?"

"Mmm, yes. You in a white dress…"

She giggled even as he picked her up and spun her around, his heart full and complete as it'd ever been before.

"I'll be the happiest man alive when you're mine."

"And I'll be the happiest bride."

AND SHE HAD BEEN the happy bride. The happy wife. They were the perfect family. He and Rian and their baby girl when she was born. But as time went on and that precious angel they'd created together grew sicker and sicker and no doctor could figure out the problem, Rian had gone into a serious depression. All the signs had been there but he'd ignored them, run from them, buried his doubts in his own grief. When that specialist had finally diagnosed Quinn with a serious medical condition that would eventually be her death before the age of thirty, it was all Quil could do to breathe. He'd been given everything, but it was only temporary. His daughter was very sick and had been her whole life and there wasn't a damn thing he could do but sit back and watch and wait as her disease ate at her until one day, there would be nothing left. But Rian had beaten Quinn to the punch, she'd gone first. Betraying him, betraying her family, with her addiction. An addiction that had slowly destroyed her body... then finally her mind and soul.

Quillan wasn't even sure how she'd gotten that first ounce of cocaine, where she got started, but one day, he'd come home to a screaming Quinn and his wife passed out with powder on her nose. He knew then that his life would never be the same.

The door opened, pulling Quil from his reverie and his gorgeous wife stood there, bags in her hands, with a beaming smile on her face. It cut him to the quick. Was it genuine? Or was that simply a part of the façade she had going?

He shot forward, taking the bags from her arms instinctively. "Where've you been?" The growl at his throat sounded harsher than he intended, so he turned and headed to the kitchen.

"Well, good day to you too, grumpy. I was just about to tell you how hot your cock looks in your sweat pants, but I guess I'll save it. Bipolar Hades," V grumbled under her breath.

He realized he was being irrational but couldn't dampen the anger surging through his veins.

He heard Veda's shoes behind him as she followed. "I thought I'd cook tonight. I went to check on Mam and—"

"We need to talk," Quil set the bags down roughly and turned, sweeping his hand through his hair.

"What's the matter? Is Quinn ok?" she asked and looked around, her face paling.

"She's fine," he ground out. "This isn't about Quinn."

"You hate the pictures, don't you? I knew it. Dammit, Quil, I—"

"It's not about the fucking pictures, Veda!" he shouted and frowned at his tone. He needed to calm the fuck down, but his heart was hammering away in his chest at the thought of Brooke being here in his home, touching his wife, being anywhere near her. "Why in the fuck was Brooke Taylor here?"

Veda sighed heavily and looked down. Great, she didn't want to tell him. She was keeping something from him. Just like Rian had...

"You let her in my house? Knowing how I feel about her conniving ways?"

"What was I supposed to do, Quil? Be rude and slam the door in her face?"

"Doesn't sound too out of the realm of possibilities for the sharp-tongued Medusa," he smarted back, getting a brow arch in return.

"Are you gonna allow me to tell ye, or are you gonna simply draw conclusions?" She planted her hands on her hips in defiance. There was the feisty goddess he knew and loved.

Quil crossed his arms over his chest and waited.

"She came to apologize." When Quil scoffed, V continued, "She's been seeing a psychiatrist and wanted to come clean. She and TJ are getting serious."

"Oh? And you believe her?"

"I had no reason not to."

"Yeah, well, you don't know what she said about you at Thanksgiving or you wouldn't be so quick to trust her."

"You and your damn trust issues need to get a feckin' life." Damn, her Irish accent came out strong when she was angry. "She came in, we went out to the patio to talk, and she was here all of about fifteen minutes."

"Did she kiss you?"

"What?" Veda asked incredulously. "Why would she?"

"That's what Nita said."

"And you believed her?" Veda's voice was becoming shrill as their debate escalated. "You know she *loathes* me, Quil. She made that shit up to make me look bad."

"She wouldn't lie."

"Are you *sure* about that? I'm your feckin' wife. I wouldn't lie either!"

"You have before."

"How dare you! I've *never* lied to you. Omitting the truth and lying are two very different things."

"Coming from the mouth of a former stripper." *Damn, that was low even for you, Quil*, his brain warned.

Veda scoffed and stepped forward, her teeth gritting, lips quivering. "You bastard! Am I going to have that thrown in my face every single fight we have?" When Quil didn't answer, she said, "You know what! I've told you what happened. And if you don't believe me, then I guess I should go. I'm sick to death of always being the bad guy in every situation. I did nothing wrong. I only accepted an apology that was due to me and returned the hug she gave me, so I'll be damned if I stand here and let you take your insecurities out on me. I'm not Rian, Quillan, and I refuse to pay for *her* mistakes."

She grabbed up her purse and turned to leave, only to stop in her tracks as a pouting Quinn looked up at her, clad in her favorite Pocahontas pajamas.

The sight tore deep into Quillan's guilt, and he felt awful for starting the fight in the first place.

"You're leaving?" Quinn asked, her bottom lip quivering.

"Honey, I—"

"You pinkie swore," Quinn accused, a tear falling down her plump little cheek.

"Quinn, I know, but—"

"But *nothing*! A pinkie swear is unbreakable. Teacher said so. You're my mommy now...aren't you, Veda?"

Veda sighed heavily, coming to her knees before his child, but Quil needed to stop this charade before it got any worse than it already was. He'd been wrong to bring Veda here into his home, wrong to trust a woman he'd not known, wrong to think he could ever have that perfect family life he'd always desired because he himself had never had it as a child. "I want her to leave, Quinn."

Quinn's eyes looked up to his. Shock, confusion, accusation, and horror took her features, and his heart broke into a million pieces he'd never be able to put back together, not if he tried for a thousand years. She said nothing as another tear fell and she turned on her heel, silently marching back up the stairs to her room, where she'd come from.

Veda pulled in a shaky breath and rose to her feet, she didn't turn, but Quillan launched forward and grabbed her shoulders, stopping her. He was gonna have the last word, come Hell or high water.

"I was wrong to think that I could trust you. You're far too broken, you and Brooke both, and broken things simply don't work the same way." He wouldn't allow him or his daughter anymore pain. He regretted allowing himself to think he could change Veda, fix her, make her whole. He'd just been kidding himself to think this could work.

"Ha," Veda laughed humorlessly. "News flash, asshole. You're the most broken one of us all. But as broken as *I* am, at least I kept my heart open to love again, not hardened it to the point that when someone falls in love with me, I stay closed off. You're so scared of your past that you can't see what's right in front of you. Open your eyes, Quillan." Her head whipped back to look at him briefly before she jerked out of his hold and walked out the door. He didn't stop her, despite that everything inside him was screaming at him to do so.

Quillan let out the breath he'd been holding as the door slammed behind her, and he felt the silence quickly closing in around him.

He'd tasted the forbidden fruit, indulged in the sweetest, most sinful lust he'd ever had, and it had come with a great cost; the serpent in the Garden of Eden had bitten him back.

QUIL COULDN'T SLEEP the night before the conference championship game. His heart was too heavy, his mind a highway of thoughts, regrets, qualms, and deliberations.

He'd spoken to Juanita again about the interaction she thought she'd seen between Brooke and Veda.

"Are you sure they kissed?" he'd asked.

Tia had shrugged like it hadn't mattered, although it mattered a hell of a lot where Quillan was concerned.

"Tia!" He'd grabbed her shoulders and forced her attention away from the dinner she was cooking to look at him. "Did they or didn't they?"

She'd shrugged again and changed her story. "Perhaps they didn't. It might have just been a kiss on the cheek..."

"Why would you tell me they had if you weren't sure?"

Tia had averted her eyes then.

"Because you wanted me to kick her out?" When she hadn't responded, he'd said, "Jesus, Tia." Quil had huffed out and released her. "She's pregnant with my children for God's sake."

"She's not good for you." Tia's brows had risen.

"How can you say that? Did you not see how happy Quinn and I were?"

Tia had moved back to her task. "We were fine: you, me, and Quinn. It was working out well."

Quil had shaken his head in annoyance. "Well, it won't be just me, you, and Quinn here come five months from now when two more children join the fold."

"And you're sure they're even yours?" she'd smarted and whipped her eyes back to his.

"Wow! I didn't realize how jealous you were of Veda. Why?"

"Not jealous," she'd corrected. "Unconvinced of her."

Tia had never liked Rian either. Although she'd had a damn good reason for that.

"She's not Rian, Juanita. Not every woman is, you have to under-stand that." Maybe he should heed his own words.

"She's bad news. She looks like an inked pincushion."

Quil should've known Tia wouldn't like V's tattoos and piercings, what with her own strong Catholic roots. "That doesn't make her a bad person. She's kind and funny and smart, and she adores Quinn… and I think she's in love with me." He sighed heavily and leaned against the counter, covering his face with his hands.

"Of course she is."

"I'm in love with *her*." When Quil had pulled his hands away from his face, he looked over at Juanita who'd rolled her eyes.

"Of *course* you are."

Quil frowned and looked back at her, confused all to hell and back. "You *knew* this and yet you still fed me a line of bullshit. Why?"

"Seeing how strong your relationship is," she'd smirked and brought the wooden spoon from the bowl she was stirring up to her lips to taste.

Quil's frown had deepened. "You lied to me? On *purpose?*"

"Not lied. Told you what I *thought* I saw. You're the one whose imagination ran with it." She'd looked up at him amused as if she'd just told a huge secret.

"Tia! How could you? She's my wife!"

"Yes, she's your wife. So, don't you think you should start trusting what she tells you instead of someone else?" She'd giggled.

Quil had literally balked. What the hell kind of game was she playing? He and Veda had fought…over nothing. She'd told him the truth and he'd… he'd acted like the biggest asshole in the world. Damn!

When he'd seen the knowing grin on Juanita's face, he'd scoffed again. "You…"

"I told you what I thought I saw and waited for you to defend your wife to me, Quillan. Then I would know what you have is real. I think we both see now that it is." She'd given him a big grin and patted his cheek.

By then, Quil thought it'd be too late for him to go to Veda and tell her how he'd felt. Plus, he was still upset about it and wasn't ready to go running back, tail tucked between his legs, because dammit, he was Hades and Hades didn't do that... or he hadn't... until Persephone.

VEDA, her mam, and Walt sat watching the Conference Championship game. Veda's hair was up in a bun, her sweat pant clad legs were covered in a thick microfleece blanket and her face was free of makeup.

She'd not cried...well, not today at least. She'd cried in the car on the way to her mam's from Quillan's Saturday night, finally giving in to the emotions she bottled up when he told Quinn that he wanted Veda to leave.

The look on Quinn's face had stilled her blood. How could he have told the little girl that? Knowing how Quinn felt about Veda? It had broken Veda's heart in two, and she'd known her tears were as much for little Quinn as they were for herself. Veda also blamed the pregnancy hormones.

She'd been hurt by what he said, by his assumptions, and by the fact that he didn't believe her. Quil had known she didn't care for Brooke that way, and yet he'd let the nanny who hated Veda sway his opinion of her. And that's what had hurt the most. He still didn't trust her.

What was she going to have to do to earn that? Had she not gone with him when he'd taken her from her home, left the job she'd had with Brooke because he'd told her it was over, married him, and saved her sister and Paxton's reputation, come into his home, and loved him and his daughter with all her heart? Where had the disconnect come?

Oh, right, his insecurities! her brain said. He was still convinced every woman was as bad as his first wife, as bad as Eve, or hell, even Lilith, if the truth be told. That they were all out to get him, ruin him, and weren't trustworthy.

No, her brain corrected, *he was scared of ruining* you! That was also true. She remembered him saying that as well. *And yet I'm the fucked-up one?* she thought. Bipolar Hades, she thought for the umpteenth time. Angry, jealous, violent, and insecure god. And yet, he could be so loving and gentle and kind at times. The memory of his love-making, his tenderness, and his words made her heart leap into her throat and as she saw his gorgeous face come onto the TV screen, she pleaded with herself not to cry again.

Her mam and Walt sat quietly as she turned the TV up when the male sportscaster approached Quillan to talk with him before the game.

Her husband looked as sexy as always, dark hair thick and with a slight curl to the right where his natural part and cowlick forced it so, his dark-bearded jaw set, his caramel brown eyes—hiding so much—beneath a set of black, perfectly-shaped brows and gah, his lips...so kissable. Veda swooned even as the reporter stated, "One game away from the Super Bowl, Quillan. How are you feeling tonight about playing against the Seahawks?"

"I'm excited about the game, about my team's capabilities, and mostly the future."

"Your confidence is enviable, as is your record this year. Looks like you've come back strong from your premature retirement. I imagine it feels pretty good to be you tonight." He laughed.

Quil gave a brief half smile before stating, "I'm blown away by our accomplishments this year. I'm blessed, truly. I have an amazing team. I couldn't have done it without them. If you'd have asked me a year ago if I would see myself here, I wouldn't have been able to answer that question. I'm grateful for the opportunity to be back in the sport I love and to have the people I have in my life."

"Speaking of: Congrats are in order. I hear you and your wife are having twins?"

Veda's heart stilled at that question, and she waited with bated breath at Quil's response.

The beaming smile on his face made the tears pop back into her eyes. "We are. We're very excited."

He, of course, didn't mention the fact that he'd asked his wife to leave the house after accusing her of kissing her former coworker, as the reporter continued to ask him football-related questions for another thirty seconds or so before saying, "Alright well, good luck tonight, Quil."

"Oh, luck has nothing to do with it." Quil's gaze grew serious. "It has everything to do with trust, Mike. Without it, you have nothing."

Caramel brown eyes stared into the camera, and Veda literally gasped—was he talking about her? No, he couldn't be.

"Trust yes. Trust in your team and teammates...and uh...Quil?" The reporter looked down and his brows drew on his wrinkled forehead. "Is that a—a pomegranate in your hand?"

Veda covered her mouth as she saw the camera zoom in on a pomegranate in Quil's big hand as he opened his palm.

"It is, indeed."

"New pregame ritual for Hades?" he asked, clearly confused.

"Something like that." Quillan smirked as the camera zoomed out. His eyes burning into the lens didn't fail to convince Veda that time.

The symbolism was for her alone and no one else.

Veda watched as Quillan Layton played yet another stellar game, the Gods of the Gridiron living up to their namesakes as they fought to clench their spot in the Super Bowl. They were unstoppable as the defense held the line, stopped the run and pass. The offense was on fire, and Quil and Travis were practically tied, touchdown for touchdown. The gods of Olympus...and the Underworld were showing the world who they were tonight. If only she could have been there in the box to celebrate with everyone. But she'd chosen not to herself. Becca had begged her to go, but she knew she wasn't in the mood. And she hadn't been. Quil had kicked her out, discarded her, not believed her...and the pain of his mistrust stung every part of her.

Yet tonight, for some reason, he'd been seen with that damn pomegranate that he'd brought with him as some form of apology to her.

The commentators had zoomed in on it multiple times, making funny remarks as to its mystical powers as the Gladiators tore up their game day record.

Quil had the ball again in the third quarter, battling it out as the corner for the Seahawks ran and grabbed for him. He spun away, leaping over a defender before falling hard into the end-zone for yet another TD. Veda couldn't help but cheer for her husband, despite how upset she was with him.

Her mam looked over and smiled big. She'd never really understood the sport but had gotten interested in the recent months since her daughters were now intertwined in the lifestyle. It also helped that Walt was a big Gladiators fan.

Kathleen had been a shoulder for Veda when she'd come home two nights ago in tears. She hadn't been forthcoming about what Quil had said or about his accusations, but her mam had understood a disagreement had occurred and Veda would be home...for a time. She'd not asked and not made any remarks to the contrary, just supported Veda in her plight and said she was there for her. She loved that about her mother, never pushing for information. Veda would tell her when she was ready, but for now she just wanted the Gladiators to win this championship game so that they were Super Bowl bound. They'd fought so hard all season, and tonight it was all on the line.

It didn't look as if they had much to worry about until the fourth quarter when TJ was jerked down hard by a defensive lineman, going down like a boulder and got stepped on. He grabbed his thigh in pain, and Veda gasped. *Oh no!* One of Brett's biggest protectors was injured, and it didn't look good.

TJ was slow to get up, needing help from the other linemen as he hopped on his left foot and was taken to the sidelines.

Great! That's just what we need, she thought as an injury time-out was taken and the offense lined back up for a third down attempt.

Brett was immediately sacked, fumbled the ball, and an interception was made for a pick six.

"Son of a bitch!" Veda swore and slammed her Gladiators pillow down on the couch in anger.

"I should've warned you that me daughter has a mouth like a sailor," Kathleen murmured to Walt, but Veda's eyes were on the screen watching her QB getting off the turf slowly.

Dammit, he better not be injured too, she thought.

The next five minutes of the game were brutal as the offense got their asses handed to them again and the defense couldn't stop the run, letting the Seahawks score again.

Two TDs in minutes, not cool, Veda thought.

But Hades was unfazed as he was in motion behind the line of scrimmage, ready to run when the ball was hiked at second and nine in the fourth quarter.

Zeus threw a thunderbolt across the field, and Veda held her breath as Quil jumped up to catch it. She literally groaned out in pain as Quil was tackled hard by a defender while in mid-air. When he landed, his helmet hit the turf with a jarring blow.

She gasped and stood, holding her belly as she did, her heart hammering a frantic cadence. "Oh my God!"

She held her breath as the defensive player moved off her husband and jumped up and down in victory. Quil continued to lay there, motionless, and Veda's heart sank even as she fell back to the couch, fear creeping into every cell of her body.

"Get up, Quil. Get up!"

But he didn't. Even as his teammates began to run over and Brett motioned for the trainer, kneeling down to touch Quil's chest. No movement, nothing.

The trainer ran over and motioned for the cart. It didn't look good. As the seconds turned into a full minute, V began to shake.

What would she do if Quil didn't get up? Why hadn't she gone to the game? Now she was going to watch as he died right there on the telly? He'd cheated death once before. What if the grim bastard had come to collect? It'd been twenty years…

Please, Quillan, I love you. Please don't die on me!

CHAPTER SIXTEEN

Quil heard his name being called but was only aware of weightlessness, nothingness, as if suspended in air, floating. *I'm dead…again*, he thought.

He opened his eyes to see a beautiful woman with raven black hair, eyes the color of jade, and the brightest smile he'd ever seen. He'd seen that smile before…in the mirror.

"Mom?" he asked in shock.

He was greeted with an even brighter smile and a warm hand cupping his cheek.

"You look so much like your father, Quillan."

Holy shit, he was speaking with the mother he'd never met, for he'd killed her as she'd brought him into this world. Her life had been snuffed out so that he could breathe in his own.

He gulped. She shook her head, as if to say, "Don't think like that."

"Mom?" he asked again. "Am I dead?"

She shook her head again. "No. Just resting. You'll soon return. I can't keep you here, but I wanted to see you."

He frowned, confused. Then he remembered feeling the padded

body strike his with the jolting force of a Mack truck and remembered his head hitting the ground before blacking out.

"I don't have much time, but I want you to do me a favor."

Anything, he thought and knew she could hear his thoughts.

"Take care of your wife, Veda. She needs you, more than you know. Quil, I know life hasn't always been easy for you, but it's time to move on and embrace the blessings you've been given. Let the past go and love again. You'll be greatly rewarded, I promise you. You no longer have to fear losing the women you love."

She kissed his cheek and pulled him into her arms in a warm embrace that washed over his skin and heart, like being enfolded in a soft, heated blanket. It was the hug he'd wanted his entire lifetime from the woman he'd never gotten to be held by. He couldn't stop the tears from flowing down his face as he squeezed her to him, aware of how reluctant he was to let her go. There were so many things he wanted to say, so many apologies to make, so many words unspoken between them, but as she pulled back, her eyes told him she already knew everything on his heart.

Quil sighed, completely content for the first time in a very long time.

VEDA BENT DOUBLE, holding herself together by a thread as she awaited Becca's call.

They'd texted back and forth half the night, Becca updating her on Quil's condition as the news came.

He'd been carted off the field, his neck and chest strapped down. They thought it was a head or neck injury, but no one could verify it because he hadn't awoken.

Veda had gone into panic mode as her phone buzzed with texts from her sister. She'd ran to the toilet and puked up what little food she'd eaten, crying, praying, and swearing before returning back to the game she was no longer interested in.

She'd only kept it on so she could hear of news of Quillan.

The Gladiators had won, but she couldn't bring herself to celebrate the victory. It was bittersweet. They were going to the Super Bowl, but even as Brett had taken the field with Jerry Taylor, the mood had been solemn when he'd accepted the trophy and the confetti fell all around them. The players had spoken of being happy about winning, but every single one of them had said they were praying for their TE.

Hell, they should, he'd gotten them there as much as anyone else had, Veda had thought cynically, but knew her anger and fear was misdirected.

No word came before the news coverage of the game had ended, and the commentators in the studio began recapping the game highlights. Veda's mind was numb to everything that didn't concern her husband, her stomach tightening when Becca had texted her that he'd been taken to the hospital via ambulance.

Of all the times Veda had decided not to go to a game, it had to be when it was so far away—Seattle's record had been one game better than Atlanta's. She'd debated hopping a red-eye out that night, but her mother had advised against it.

She was right, of course. What if Quil awoke to see her there and demanded she leave again? What if he never awoke? What if he awoke, and she wasn't there to see him?

A million thoughts had crossed her mind, but she'd decided to wait and go in the morning. Her mother had volunteered to fly out with her, but Walt stepped in and said he would do it. Veda had given him a soft smile. He was a kind man, and her heart warmed at the fact that her mother had found a good one. She'd called Quil's manager to arrange everything, and he'd promised he would call with any news.

Now, she sat on the couch awaiting said news.

"Baby, you need some sleep."

"I—I can't sleep, Mam. We fought the last time we were together. I can't..."

"Shh, I know, *mo chroí*, I know," her mother cooed and stroked her hair as she sat down beside her. "It's all gonna be ok."

How could she possibly know that?

Becca had stayed in Seattle along with Brooke and TJ. TJ's quad had been bruised, but the trainer had insisted he have an MRI to verify that that was all; he was currently in the same hospital Quil was, in the ER bay for the time being. He planned to be released once the results were back.

Veda let her mam comfort her as she fell into deep contemplation of all that had happened since the night she met Quillan at *RISE*. She closed her eyes, succumbing to the barrage of memories assaulting her and was taken back to that fated night, the night she'd given that luscious man her final first kiss, the kiss that had ended all kisses—the kiss of Death.

QUIL OPENED HIS EYES, rapidly coming to as if from a deep slumber, akin to when one has fallen asleep abruptly and slept far longer than they were meant to.

He was aware that he had missed something, something important, unsure why he couldn't remember what it was.

The sound of beeping, a soft droning noise, and the feel of stiff joints and even stiffer fabric around him forced his eyes down.

He was in a funny-looking gown, a hospital bed and was hooked up to an IV pole.

What the hell? he thought and tried to turn his head. He couldn't move his neck—a brace was around it, he realized—and panic flooded his entire body as he gripped for it. A thought suddenly occurred to him, and he gasped and tried to move his feet.

Oh, thank God, he silently thanked his Creator and sighed heavily as his toes wiggled when he voluntarily told them to.

He turned his head to the left and saw a dark head of hair draped over a slim shoulder. A slender frame was covered by a crimson pant suit and he smiled, feeling love seep into every corner of his soul.

"Veda," he stated, but his voice was far too hoarse and came out as a whisper. He cleared his throat to try again and her head snapped up.

But it wasn't Veda. The disappointment hit him as hard as the force he suddenly remembered that had brought him here.

He blushed, his heart falling as Becca's eyes looked him over.

"Quil! You're awake! Oh, thank God!"

She ran to his side and moved to sit on the bed next to him.

Quil cleared his throat again. "Where's Veda?" he asked dejectedly, aware that Becca probably knew all about the fight he and Veda had had just two days ago, imagining what Bec probably thought about him and the way he'd talked to her sister.

Becca smiled, looking so much like her identical twin at that moment that it took his breath. "She's on her way to the airport to get on a plane."

He didn't deserve to see her, didn't deserve to be in her presence, despite that she was the one person he wanted to see right now, her and his baby girl.

"Quinn?" He asked but knew Tia Nita was taking care of her back home.

"She's good. She doesn't know anything. She didn't finish the game last night, fell asleep."

"Thank God for that," he murmured. She didn't need the fear of losing anyone else. He blamed himself though. He had a lot to apologize to Veda about and would as soon as he saw her again.

He looked up at Becca and gave her a regretful smile. "I don't deserve Veda's forgiveness."

"Why not?" Becca asked and took his hand.

"I've been far meaner to her than I should've been."

"Fight fire with fire, I always say. And Veda is straight fire, as you well know."

"Takes one to know one," Quil mumbled, getting a giggle out of Becca.

"Veda's not afraid to fight, Quil. I think you've seen that, haven't you?"

"She's not afraid of *anything*. Not Hades. Not the Underworld. Nothing."

"Oh, but she is." Becca's brows arched. "She's afraid of losing people. Her loved ones."

So was he. That was the one fear he had, the fear of everyone he loved being taken from him. He always blamed himself for their loss, and it had forced him to try to push her away before he'd gotten too close, forced him to reject his love, her love... but it was too late, he loved her—with every aspect of his being.

"I said some unforgivable things, Becca."

"Obviously, they weren't *too* unforgivable. Your wife is about to fly almost three thousand miles to come see you, so..." Becca smirked again, but instead of getting a smile out of him, he frowned.

"Has it occurred to you that maybe I'm not good for your sister, Becca?" He swallowed down the fear that he and Veda were simply too broken, too dark, too reckless together. Two fires burning together would ignite a conflagration with no end in sight. He would be her downfall, and she'd had enough pain inflicted on her for one lifetime.

"Is that what you think, Quillan?"

He looked away. "Text her and tell her not to come here. Tell her I've been released, and I'm coming home." When Becca gaped down at him in shock, he insisted. "Do it. Right now."

He watched Becca gulp and fish out her phone with shaking hands, texting her sister what he'd just told her to.

In a matter of seconds, the phone was ringing and Becca nodded to him as she stepped over to the window to take the call.

"Veda. Hey! Yes, he's awake...and grumpy as ever." Becca tried to laugh. "He's coming home, so there's no need for you to be here.

Nope, he's fine. I know! Thank God." Becca's eyes sought his. "Yes. I'll have him call you when he lands. Alright. I love you too. Bye."

Becca sighed heavily and placed the phone in the slit of her back pants pocket. The grim-faced Irish lass that approached the bed and crossed her arms over her chest looked far too much like his wife. He gulped as she closed in, pointing a perfectly manicured fingernail at him.

"Now you listen and you listen well, Mr. *Layton* because I'll only say this once. I don't know all what's going on between you and my sister, but you're not to string her along any longer. If you want to be with her then do so, but if it's over, then you feckin' end it. You got me? Veda may be a bit of a rebel, but she's got the biggest heart of anyone I know. I may not look to be as fierce as she is, but she's my blood, and I'll be damned if I allow you to continue to hurt her, husband or no."

With that, she grabbed her purse and turned on her heel out of his hospital room.

QUIL WAS BACK at practice three days later, his team looking at him as if he were a ghost.

I'm Death, remember? he'd wanted to shout because Death was in a horrible mood.

He'd gotten home late on Monday night. He'd been given a clean bill of health with no reason whatsoever to atone for his blackout. No head injury, no concussion, no neck nor spine injury; he was a walking miracle, and he had no fucking idea why he'd been spared once again.

"God isn't done with you," Juanita had cried on his shoulder when he'd gotten home.

God is punishing me, Quil wanted to say, *forcing me to live on in a world as cruel as I am.* He felt like the Devil, an angel who'd been cast out of Heaven—angry, bitter, unworthy of love, reborn into a life of sin and destruction. But he wasn't evil. That much he knew.

So why was he still here on earth when clearly Death had come for him twice before now?

He had unfinished business, of course, with his daughter, his unborn twins, and his wife; but perhaps there was more to it than that. Quil realized once again he was too philosophical, looking for deep meaning in all things. But maybe this was just simply as cut and dry as being a husband and father. And wasn't that enough? Did there need to be anything more than that? It was what he'd always wanted wasn't it? To have a family?

He worked out with his team, avoiding their prying eyes, and ran his drills and routes, Brett not targeting him as much as usual, which really pissed him off.

I'm not a fragile little bird, he wanted to say, but held his tongue as they all headed back into the locker room from the practice field.

Brett came up to him then and patted his shoulder. "You've got a heavy burden on your shoulders, *amigo*." The look in his friend's eyes was full of concern. "I don't know what all your troubles are, Quil. But I know that you were there for me and gave me a much-needed pep talk when I needed it most."

"I'm really not in the mood for a lecture, Zeus," Quil grumbled and turned to pull his gloves off.

"No lecture planned, man. I just wanna ask you one thing, and I'll leave you be."

When Quil turned, Brett crossed his arms over his broad chest. "Do you remember what you told me in my kitchen the first night you and Quinn had dinner with Madi and I?"

Quil thought for a minute. It had been something prolific and philosophic—typical Quil fashion—but he didn't know exactly so he shrugged.

"Your exact words to me were: Don't let your regrets and guilt and pain keep you from the Heaven we're given here on earth.

You've both hurt enough over what happened. Embrace the good that's been left behind."

Quil gulped and looked down.

"Doesn't that apply to you too, brother?"

Quil said nothing as he looked Brett in the eye.

"Hell, Hades, you were unconscious. We thought you were dead. You weren't breathing when I touched you, Quil. They did fucking CPR on you in the tunnel," he whispered and leaned in so that only Hades could hear him. "We all expected another funeral." Brett gulped and looked away, blinking hard before staring hard into Quil's eyes. "Now you're back like nothing's happened. You're a walking miracle. There's a reason you're still here, and I don't think it's just to play the damn Super Bowl."

With that, Brett walked away, leaving Quil to watch his exiting back.

He had to be right. Right? He was Zeus, after all. Quil couldn't have just been brought back for the Super Bowl, but to embrace his life, the love that was left, the woman he wanted in his life more than he'd ever wanted anything.

He was jarred from his inner musings by Brooke squealing as she ran into TJ's opening arms. He'd just left the massage room by the looks of it and he and the trainer were smiling; that was a very good sign. He spun her around and pulled her tighter against him as his lips fell to hers.

"I love you, you big lug," she said as she pulled back and giggled.

The gesture was so unlike Brooke that Hades was taken off guard.

Brooke looked over at Quil after TJ let her down and patted her OL's shoulders, whispering into his ear before heading Quil's way.

"Looks like we have two Lazaruses now," she smirked.

"It would seem so," Quil answered.

"Aw, hell, Hades, don't look so grim." She laughed and slugged at his shoulder.

"I *am* Hades. Grim is my middle name."

"You don't have much to be grim about, dark one. You got a team about to go to the Super Bowl, an angel for a daughter, twins on the way, and a beautiful wife who loves you. Am I missing anything?" Brooke was anything if not sarcastic.

"Nope, I think you named it all." He turned, to appear distracted by his duties.

"Veda told you I came by, I take it." When Quil didn't respond, she went on. "I realize you're jealous…but you don't have any reason to be. I guess she told you that I told her the truth."

Quil turned, she'd piqued his curiosity now.

"I didn't want her, Quil. I wanted to *be* her."

Quil frowned.

"Yeah, I was jealous. I mean, look at her, she's perfect." Veda was far from perfect, but she was gorgeous and feisty and loving and… "She's also perfect for you. You complement each other so well. Who am I to take that from either of you? I just wanted so much what you have together. And," she smiled big, a genuine smile—free of malice —and it took Hades breath, "I've found it now. So, I guess I just want to say that I'm sorry for all the trouble. I was baiting you, but I should've known you and Veda were far too strong for me to shake that foundation."

Her words stilled him. The perch he and Veda were on had always seemed so precarious, fleeting, and fragile, but Brooke had seen far more than he originally had.

She handed him a magazine from her purse and gave him a knowing grin.

"It looks like you might need to read this." Her brow went up, and he looked down to see the *Ink You* magazine in her hands.

He inhaled sharply when he saw the flawless image of Veda on the cover. The picture had been implanted into his mind the day he'd opened his email, but it didn't hold a candle to the finished product before him.

Quillan saw it as if seeing his wife for the first time, her softness, her tenderness, the maternal side of her, a fierce goddess with a heart as big as her attitude. A vision flashed before him, suddenly, of seeing his mother when he'd blacked out three nights ago on the field during the game. The message and words she'd given him flooded in with startling clarity, and he knew where his future lay.

He opened the magazine, flipping to the article of Veda's interview.

As he read her sincere, heartfelt, and endearing words about how Veda felt about him, his daughter, and his unborn babies, his heart melted and realization seized him. He knew in that instant that his love for her was enough, knew she was his—fully and completely—and now he knew what he planned to do with that knowledge.

VEDA HAD DONE her best not to brood, but it wasn't easy. Quil hadn't wanted to see her, hadn't called her upon landing, and here it was, day three since his miraculous recovery and she'd not seen hide nor hair of him.

That was that, then. They were through. As upset as it made her, she was also resigned to the fact that she wasn't going to pine for a man who didn't want her back. She'd done that back in high school, and she'd be damned if she did so again. She wouldn't allow her life to be destroyed by love, even if it felt like it hadn't begun until Quil had come into her life. She refused to be another martyr beholden to it.

She rubbed her belly, where her babies grew, and sighed. No, she had plans that didn't have to include Quillan Layton as anything more than her babies' father. She had done some serious considering and had gotten enrolled to take online classes so she could counsel other women about her own life experiences. It felt good to have a purpose and a plan that didn't include stripping, cheering, or model-ing. She could have the spotlight in a different way that didn't include having to showcase her body.

She sighed again as a ring came to the doorbell of her mother's

...

apartment, turning the tea kettle off and padding barefoot to the door, wondering who on earth could be calling—obviously not her sis or mam, who had keys.

Her heart jumped into her throat when she opened it and saw Quinn standing there, looking eagerly up at her with a pomegranate in her palms.

"Q-Quinn, honey, what are you—?"

"Daddy said to give this to you. That you'd know what it meant."

Veda gulped and squatted down, taking the deep red fruit from the sweetest little girl she'd ever had the pleasure to know. "Oh honey, are you alone?"

"No, Grand Mam is with me." She motioned to Kathleen, who waved to her from the hallway.

"Mam, what are you—?

"Veda, I missed you." Quinn reached for her, and Veda picked her stepdaughter up and held her to her chest. Quinn's arms wrapped around her neck. "Daddy said it's his fault that I haven't gotten to see you. He said things are gonna be different now."

Veda swallowed down the hurt that statement caused. Yes, things would be different.

"Oh, sweetie, that doesn't mean that you and I can't see each other. I love you so much." She squeezed Quinn, trying hard to show her that, if only through osmosis alone.

"I love you, too. Can you come home now?"

"Quinn, I—" But how could she tell Quinn the truth when the desperation in her eyes was so raw? She set her down and motioned to her mam, who held up a finger as if to say, "Wait one minute."

"Quinny, come with Grand Mammy real quick, ok?" Kathleen waved Quinn over, who reluctantly released Veda's hand then to take her step-grandmother's. They walked off down the hallway, leaving Veda to ponder what the hell was going on.

That's when she saw a bountiful bouquet of gorgeous white Easter lilies and her tall, dark, and handsome god walking her way from the opposite end of the hallway.

Her eyes began to roll back in her head and she knew she was about to faint.

As darkness flooded her vision, she was aware of two things: how fast her TE really was and how wonderfully masculine he'd always smelled.

"V. Veda, baby, come back to me, *mi amor*," Hades beckoned to his queen, Persephone, one hand cupping her head, the other resting on her arm. "There you go, open your eyes. There you are."

He wiped the cool cloth back over her face and grinned as her bright green eyes opened. "Way to ruin your flowers and scare your husband back to death." She looked at him dumbfoundedly from the couch he'd laid her on, and he chuckled, his heart light and whole.

"Quil..." she began only to look around as if she wasn't aware of what had just happened. "What are you doing here? I thought..." Quil's brows rose, waiting for her thoughts to clear. "Quinn said things were gonna be different so I thought—"

"Oh, they *are* gonna be different. Very, very different." When Veda looked at him as if he'd lost his mind, he smiled. "And in a good way, *mi corazón*. You see, a man doesn't survive death twice only to come back and take his life for granted. Although, it did take me a couple days to realize what I came so close to losing *and* a few independent women to sway my thinking." He chuckled again.

Veda smiled back at him and cupped his bearded cheek. "Oh, Quil. I was so scared. I—" she gulped and her lip quivered. "I've never been more afraid in my life. I was convinced you were dead."

"Oh, I was. Or at least that's what Brett said, anyway. But here I am. Alive and well and head over heels in love with you, *mi esposa*." He leaned in to kiss her, savoring her lips like he was kissing her for the first time. She was his Heaven on Earth, his Persephone, a light in a world that had once been filled with darkness.

When he pulled back, he frowned in deep regret. "I haven't

always done right by you, Veda Angeline Layton, but that changes today. I love you, I want you, and I want to live the rest of my life proving how much I need you, what you mean to me. Give me that honor, the honor of being your husband, the honor of loving our sweet babies as one big happy family." His palm fell to her rounding belly, taut with the life and promise of their legacy.

"Oh, Quillan. I love you." She pulled him back to her for another kiss, and he chuckled once more before she said, "I promised myself to you already, remember?" She lifted her finger and motioned at her ring. "Despite how fast it all happened, I took those vows seriously...especially after I realized I was in love with you."

He grinned at her and leaned his forehead against hers. "I was so angry, V, so spiteful and hateful and..."

"It's alright. I haven't exactly been without fault either."

"I'm sorry," he pleaded and looked hard into her eyes.

"Me too."

"Give me another chance? I swear I'll never ask you to leave again. I was a fool."

She kissed him in answer, and he sighed before pulling back again to look at her.

"I met my mother," he confessed, and V's brows rose in surprise. "She looks so much like you, Veda. It's as if..." he trailed off then gave her another big smile as her own mouth turned up into one.

"It's so good to see you so happy, Quillan."

"It feels good to have a reason to smile again. You'll be seeing more of them, I promise."

"Good. I could get used to them, that's for sure." She gave him a seductive smile, and he looked her beautiful body over, loving every piercing and tattooed inch of her five-foot two-inch frame.

"Oh, V, I love you, *mi dama serpiente*, with all my heart." When she smiled in return, he said, "I'm going to make love to you now, *mi alma*."

"That's all well and good, Hades, but do keep in mind I tend to like it a little rough too," she teased.

He laughed heartily even as he stretched his body alongside hers and pulled her into his arms. "Oh, I'd expect it no other way, *chica mala*. Now, come lead your god back to Tartarus."

He grabbed the pomegranate and pulled it apart, plucking a seed from its hollow insides. He brought the seed to her lips and groaned in desire as she sucked the sweet capsule into her mouth. She followed suit and did the same, grinning as he licked her fingers then bit into the seed in his mouth. "Mmm," he growled, "Almost as sweet as my Persephone. But nowhere near as spicy."

Veda cackled but soon her laughter turned into moans as Quil began to love her body with his hands and mouth, overcome by a hunger unlike any he'd had before. The god of Death had not lived until he'd been reborn, reborn to love the woman who lived only for him.

EPILOGUE

SUPER BOWL

Quil's heart pounded as he prepared to take the field alongside his brothers, his teammates, his fellow gods. This was it. Everything they'd worked for, everything they'd fought hard for, everything they'd prepared for. The game to end all games. The game to determine the best team in the NFL.

He turned and looked his brothers over, the vibes equal parts excitement and anxiousness.

Even Travis was antsy, bouncing on his tree-trunk like legs. The usually chipper merman, Pax, was more serious than was normal.

Quil arched a brow, grinned, and looked to his captain, the leader, Brett who answered it.

"Guys, lighten up, would ya? It's just a game."

"*What?*" Linc asked in shock and stilled in adjusting his pads.

"Is that a joke?" Josh asked in turn.

Zeus laughed.

"Cap, with all due respect, how can you say that? This is the day we've busted our asses for?" Pax quipped with a scoff.

"We have, indeed. We've fought hard and strong and earned this day with our blood, sweat, and tears. We've proved our worth to the entire nation. Now it's time we just got out there and had some fun. Let's play some football. All in, guys."

"No, wait just a damn minute here," Linc stated with annoyance. "Don't get me wrong, Zeus. I love football and all, but the truth is, I'm gonna fight. I'm gonna kick Bronco ass, and I'm gonna do everything in my power to win this game, fun be damned."

Brett laughed again and patted his brother's back, "Of course, Lazarus. I would expect nothing else. We are gonna fight hard to win...but that doesn't mean we can't have fun doing so." The sparkle in his QB's eyes made Quillan laugh aloud.

"I agree. Let's have fun as we show those horses who holds the reins," he said and elbowed his future brother-in-law.

Pax nodded. "Let's be the gods we're known to be."

They all stepped in and placed their hands in the pile Brett started, giving their chant of, "Gods of the Gridiron."

Their ladies came in then, Madi first, embracing her husband, belly big and round at six months pregnant now. Zeus kissed his Hera; he was all goo when she was in his arms, the stoic QB momentarily softened in her presence.

Quil looked to Val and the twins, who gave loyal Lazarus even more reason to smile. Linc kissed his boys then pulled his wife to him for a searing smooch that stirred even the hardest heart.

The Ram pulled Aphrodite into his arms, and she giggled in glee as he spun her around, his lips covering hers. They would be married in May, and no one was more excited about it than Travis was.

Pax was the next to get his kiss by the sweet and lovely historian who'd stolen his young heart on a blind date. Then finally, Quil who watched his wife saunter over to him, the sight of her never failing to stop him in his tracks. He sighed in contentment as she stopped in front of him, Quinn's hand in hers.

"Daddy! Are you nervous?"

Quil shook his head. "More excited than nervous, *mi cielo*. This is the big day."

"You're gonna do great, husband," Veda cooed and reached for him, just as Quinn did.

Quil picked his daughter up and propped her on his hip as he pulled his wife into his side and covered her mouth with his for a smoldering kiss. She tasted as sweet as always and her body was warm against his own, making his heart beat speed up and his mind soar.

"I love you, *chica mala*," he whispered into her ear so as Quinn couldn't hear him.

She'd scolded him when he'd called Veda that just the other morning at breakfast, saying, "Daddy! Don't call Mommy a bad girl. That's mean."

Veda had snickered under her breath, giving him an arched brow.

Quil hadn't attempted to explain why the fact that Mommy being a "bad girl" wasn't necessarily a *bad* thing. He'd just apologized and said he wouldn't call her that anymore...at least not in Quinn's earshot.

Now, Veda was grinning like she had a big secret, and Quil was already anticipating celebrating post-victory sex with his gorgeous wife.

She licked his earlobe and cooed, "You gonna win for your wife tonight, Hades?"

"Aye Persephone, I intend to do so, if only so that I can reap the spoils of war." He winked and slid his hand down her backside to squeeze the plump flesh there.

"Mmm, you'll reap the benefits either way, *Daddy*, I assure you."

Damn, he might need her to call him Daddy more often and his grin told her that, even as she swatted at him with a laugh.

He kissed her again, kissed his daughter's cheek, and let his girls wish him luck once more before the families were ushered out and they were taking the field to warm-up.

Now to claim victory over the final game of the season and be not only gods, but champions too.

THE FIRST HALF of the game was neck and neck, TD for TD, as the Broncos answered the Gladiators score for score. Travis and Quil worked seamlessly with Brett, layering their attack in sequences of planned moves. Travis would pick up major yardage before the ball was given to Quil to score, then in the following offensive drive, they would switch, Quil would drive the ball down the field before it was handed off to Travis to rush it into the end zone. Quil would be a receiver one play and a blocker in the next; the defense didn't know what to expect. However, at the same time, the Gladiator defense couldn't block the Bronco's run or scores and just when they would stop them, a penalty would be called and they'd sneak a pass or break a tackle. It was an exciting game and a challenge. Everyone was tired and sweating, in more ways than one.

Coach Cavanaugh and Haskins both were encouraging though as they entered the locker room at halftime and a talk was given that was one for the books. Brett talked too, the eloquent, never-shaken QB that had become one of Quil's best friends as well as his teammate. He pepped them all up, telling them that no matter what happened, he was proud of them. They'd fought hard and earned their names, earned the title of gods, and deserved this victory.

"We owe it to ourselves to see what we're capable of. I know we can do it. I know we can!" he said and gave them all a big smile as he ushered them into their team huddle.

The gods emerged from the tunnels with renewal, confidence, and a sense of self. And when the game clock began to tick and they were pounding the turf again, Quil was pumped and ready to win now more than ever.

At fourth and long, he lined up in his spot, behind his QB and to the right, and waited for the snap. When it came, he hauled ass down the field, getting open where he motioned for Zeus to fire his thunderbolt. He watched the pigskin fly, spinning like a missile as it came at him. He shifted back and felt it hit his chest, tucked it into his arm, and ran toward the goal line. He dodged a defender, spun to evade another, and dove for it.

The roar of the crowd was deafening as he rose and looked to the ref whose hands were raised, signaling a TD.

Quil laughed and patted Brett's helmet as he ran at him.

"Way to bring the flames, Hades."

"Hell of an arm, Zeus." Quil clapped Brett's hand and they turned for a funny pose as the flash of cameras in front of them blazed brightly.

It was late in the fourth quarter when the Broncos got the upper hand. Travis fumbled, and the ball was intercepted for a pick six.

The tides had shifted, and Quil held his breath when the extra point was kicked. It was time to break out the big guns now. On the next play, Zeus ran the option, reading the defense as he made to hand the ball to Travis, faked, and pulled the ball back. He started to run, letting the defense go after Ares. Hades came up beside his QB to protect him as Brett hauled ass down the field for a first down.

On the next play, Travis ran the ball for thirty yards, getting in the red zone, and the roar of the crowd and promise of a win was all-encompassing.

With Hades next score and the extra point, they were tied, 24-24, with less than a minute left in the game. The Broncos got the ball and were taking their sweet, precious time as they watched the clock tick slowly down. They had one time out left and, lucky for them, Cavanaugh didn't use it. Quil watched in shock as the QB fumbled, and Pax was reaching for the ball. He was tackled by a number of defenders and there was a tussle.

Quil held his breath as the refs pulled the players away one by one, but it was Pax who shot up with the ball, getting a roar from all the Gladiators—and the fans.

Pax had recovered the fumble; the Gladiators had the ball.

There was forty-eight seconds left, and they had the ball on their own thirty-five-yard line.

Brett was pumped as he pulled his team to the line of scrimmage and set up for a pass play, his eye on Quil. Everything was riding on this. He couldn't make a mistake. At the snap, Quil ran to get mid-field, and Brett threw to Hades on a deep post pattern. He caught the ball on the thirty and was hit, ruled down by contact.

Coach Cavanaugh immediately called for a time-out with twenty-two seconds remaining on the clock. The field goal unit was sent out for a forty-seven-yard field goal attempt.

Quil was exhausted as he watched his kicker line up, Mason Rosas, but held his breath as the snap was called for and the ball was kicked through the uprights with perfection… only to swear in annoyance as he noticed the Broncos had called a time-out in their attempt to ice the kicker.

"Dammit!" Pax swore.

"Calm, Poseidon. He can do it again. No worries," Zeus assured.

Thirty seconds had never seemed so long as Quil again felt his blood pressure rise, awaiting the conclusion of their hard-fought battle.

When Rosas lined up again, the tension could be cut with a knife.

"Come on, Rosas," Linc said and cupped his hands in prayer.

Quil looked on as the ball was snapped, caught by their center, Robicheaux, and laces lined up before kicker Rosas's foot connected with the pigskin and sent it flying.

The sudden roar was powerful as they watched the ball soar through the uprights once more.

Score! 27-24 and eighteen seconds left in the game. Not a lot of time, but it was possible for the other team to score on a Hail Mary; it didn't happen often, but it *did* happen.

Quillan thought he would die before the opposing team took the field. He watched them shuffle for the few yards the defense held them to. The ticking of the clock was tedious before the QB finally had less than nine seconds and sixty yards to go. He hauled back for a Hail Mary and every Gladiator held their breath, praying that Linc and Pax did their part.

The receiver jumped up to catch the ball in the end zone, but

Lincoln jumped higher. The pigskin fell into the cradle of his arms for an interception. He came down on two feet and that was the game—the clock read zero.

"Game over! Super Bowl champs!" Trav chuckled and began slapping his teammates' shoulder pads.

"Holy shit, we did it!" Quil said.

"Yes, we did! Gods of the Gridiron indeed," Brett laughed. "Couldn't have done it without you guys," Brett said to Quil, Trav, Josh, and TJ. He gave them all handshakes and smiles before taking the field and running over to Linc and Paxton.

Quil chuckled as Brett pointed to Linc, "And the Super Bowl game ball goes to."

Lincoln beamed and returned Brett's hug, crocodile tears in Linc's big brown eyes.

Quil felt as if he were unstoppable, *they* were unstoppable, truly Gods of the Gridiron tonight as football champions.

They'd been practically perfect this year and were now reaping the reward as confetti rained down on them and celebration echoed around them.

Quil lost count of the congratulations, the praise, and the pats on his shoulder pads.

Soon, they were standing in the middle of the field, listening to the speeches of Jerry Taylor, Madison McFadden, Coach Cavanaugh, and Brett McFadden surrounded by their loved ones.

When it was Quil's turn to take the podium, he grinned as he looked down at his *reina* and *reinita* smiling up at him.

"I don't know what to say, honestly, aside from thank you. Thank you, Jerry and Madi, Brett, Pax, Linc, TJ, Trav, all my teammates, my coaches, my fans, my wife, my daughter. Thank you for believing in me, for giving me a second chance, for the opportunity to be here tonight. I'm so happy right now, and I simply can't put all my emotions into words. Atlanta, America... Hades loves you!" He roared into the mic with a smile.

He then turned to his wife and kissed her before they moved back to give the next player his turn.

"I always knew you were a champion, Hades," Veda cooed. "I'm so proud of you."

"Thanks, *mi amor*. I'm proud to be your husband, the husband of such a strong and fierce *pequeña rebelde*." Veda gave him a grin, and he kissed her again.

"Daddy?" Quinn asked as she fingered the letters on the ball cap now covering his head, the one deeming him a Super Bowl champ. "Does this mean you're famous?"

He laughed, he'd been practically famous already, but now he would go down for more than being a record-breaking TE. "Sure, Quinny. I guess I am."

"How does it feel?"

He chuckled again. "It feels good, baby." And it did. It felt good to be a champion, a god, a winner. "But you know what, *reinita*? Nothing feels better than being a father and a husband."

And he recalled his words to Pax in the club some four months ago on the same night he'd met Veda for the first time, words that mirrored that.

He looked around the stadium, at all the lights, the crowd, the happiness, at his friends, his brothers, his family—the Gods of the Gridiron. That's what they were now, his family, and nothing mattered more than that. Nothing.

EXTENDED EPILOGUE

NINE MONTHS LATER—THANKSGIVING

"Brett, love, will you grab the turkey out of the oven?" Madi asked as she cradled their son, Xavier, to her breast to nurse.

"Of course, Sunflower. Anything my Hera desires from her king." Brett kissed his wife, then his six-month-old son's cheek.

He moved off toward the double oven as Quil sat at the bar, sipping the beer in front of him and patting the bottom of his own sleeping five-month-old daughter, Tessa.

"Please tell me you made a tofurkey for me?" Pax joked and slugged at Brett's shoulder.

"Listen here, hippy boy, you start eating tofurkey and we can't be friends," Linc said and crossed his arms over his chest, getting a laugh out of Valeria.

"Yeah, what's going on with you, Pax?" Travis asked, propping Lennox on his hip so he could pat Xavier's back. "I think Becca's making you softer than you were, powder puff."

TJ laughed and elbowed his fiancée, Brooke, who gave Pax an eye roll.

"What is it? Pick on Pax day. I thought we were supposed to be thankful for family and stuff."

"Just because we're 'thankful' for you doesn't mean we can't badger you, bro-in-law," Veda said as she pulled the bottle out of Torin's mouth and repositioned him to her shoulder, burping him.

"My sentiments exactly," Quil answered, getting a pout from Pax. "What? It's kinda true. I'm just saying." Quil did his best to shrug with a baby in his arms.

The last nine months had been amazing. First, Travis and Skyla had gotten married. It had been a gorgeous and cool May day, and the weather had cooperated as they partied hard at one of the coolest wedding venues in Atlanta. The wedding had been a decent-sized gathering of about two hundred guests, their closest friends and relatives. Trav and Sky had never been happier. Quil had been humbled to see his friend brought to tears as his bride walked down the aisle to become his. It was a good day, a happy day.

Then Madi and Brett's bundle of joy had shown up a week later. A bouncing baby boy—of a whopping nine pounds and twelve ounces—with his father's brown hair and his mother's blue-green eyes. Xavier was the apple of his parent's eye and clearly nicknamed Hercules for obvious reasons. Pax had joked that he would become a linebacker like he was, of which Brett had told him there'd be no way in hell that was happening.

Almost exactly a month later, Tessa and Torin had made their arrival. Quil had cried when he'd seen them. Beautiful dark brown hair and Veda's green eyes with Quil's dark skin; they were perfect, a little bigger than six pounds each when they'd been born. Quinn had been thrilled to have both a brother and a sister and had made the most darling big sister ever, helping when and where she could to care for them. She was almost eight now and growing like a weed, her condition was well-managed thanks to her routine infusions and alternative medical treatments.

Veda had grown into her role as a counselor for pregnant teens and an inspirational speaker. Her openness to share her story made her approachable, despite that her tattoos and piercings tended to throw some people off. Veda had a big heart beneath that tough outer exterior, and she'd become a great mother to their three children. Their marriage had been as strong and loving as Quil had ever desired it to be, and he adored his family as much as he enjoyed playing football for the championship Gladiators.

They were well on their way to yet another Super Bowl as they'd just won their last game on Sunday and were now 10-2 for the season.

Quinn ran up then with Lofton's hand in hers, wrangling him to a small table where she began instructing him on coloring within the lines. She was so good with Linc's boys, just as she was with her own twin brother and sister. Quil smiled as he watched Lofton following her lead.

Sky and Becca came back in from the patio where Becca had shown her a video of her latest exhibit, one Becca had been hand-selected to help set up at the museum. She would be a curator before too long, of that Quil was sure.

Sky giggled, in on some secret that no one else knew as Becca whispered back and the two women moved to their respective partners.

"What's so funny, Aphrodite?" Trav asked and pulled Sky to the hip Lennox wasn't settled on.

"Oh, nothing," Sky giggled again and caught Becca's eye, who winked at her.

"Something you two wanna share, Amphitrite?" Pax asked and nudged his girlfriend.

"Nope. Girl talk, Poseidon. Nothing that would interest you." Becca's grin said otherwise, but Pax let it go and wrapped his arm around her as he kissed her cheek.

The most shocking relationship definitely had to be Brooke and TJ's. As much as they fit together, they were truly the odd couple, and how they'd gotten together last Halloween—not unlike Quil and Veda—had been both comical and impromptu. Quil had been shocked when they'd stayed together and even more shocked when they'd gotten engaged just last month, on Halloween of all days.

Some things couldn't be explained, and at times, didn't need an explanation; they just worked.

Brett moved from tenting the turkey, to let it rest, to grabbing his big boy from his mother's arms. Big Zeus with a baby was an interesting sight to see, but clearly, Brett loved it as the smile that lit his face mirrored Quillan's own as he looked down at his baby girl. She was so tiny and soft and looked so much like his wife. Tessa Victoria Layton was a Daddy's girl already as she looked sleepily up at her papa. She was milk-drunk as she grinned and sucked the pacifier in her mouth like it was soaked in sugar. He couldn't help but grin in return at his little *princesa*.

Veda moved over to his side then, and he smiled at her as he stroked his son's cheek—Torin Ishkode Layton, they'd named him.

"Hades, you smile too much," she teased.

"It's what I do when I've put the chariot away."

"It suits you, husband, truly." She kissed him to prove her words, and he moaned softly, remembering the love-making that had taken place that morning before the babies had woken them. She'd been as slick and hot as ever, the first push inside that silky snugness almost doing him in.

"Daddy, can I hold baby sis now?" Quinn held out her arms for Tessa. Quil relented, letting her cradle the infant to her chest.

Soon, they were moving into the dining room, and Brett was toasting his guests, his team and his family, grateful to have them in his home and life.

Once they'd eaten a hearty feast and dessert was passed around with coffee and tea, Becca bit into a piece of barmbrack she'd made for the festivities and grimaced when she pulled out a ring, confused as she looked around and finally up to Pax, who grinned at her knowingly.

"I know, you didn't put any trinkets into the barmbrack this time. I did that, because I wanted to do this." Pax pulled his chair back and kneeled, even as Becca shot up from her seat and gasped.

"Oh, Pax." She covered her mouth.

"Becca, my Amphitrite, this last year has been amazing. You've been amazing, and it's time for me to show you just how much you mean to me. I love you and I want you to be mine, forever. Meeting you has changed my life. You're my future, and I want us to make history together. Say you'll marry me, my sweet naia."

Veda snickered even as she pulled her lips in, happy for her twin sister and Paxton.

Quil squeezed her hand under the table as Becca nodded vigorously in answer to Pax's proposal. Pax popped up, grabbed and kissed her, and planted the ring on her finger.

All the table applauded, and Travis snorted in annoyance as Pax frowned over at him.

"What? The Ram have a problem with my proposal? So it wasn't done as fireworks filled the sky, or in front of an audience of millions—so what? Thanksgiving is just as meaningful a holiday as Independence Day is, I'll have you know."

"It isn't that, bro. Calm your fury, *Poseidon*," Ares smarted.

"Classic Ares, starting a fight when he's not the center of attention," Sky snorted and elbowed Travis, pulling at his long beard, the one he hadn't shaved for no-shave November.

"Oh, come now, Aphrodite. We just picked a bad day is all. We'll wait til Christmas."

"Wait til Christmas for what?" Madison asked in humor, giving Sky and Trav a confused look.

"Oh, nothin', just a big announcement is all. Don't wanna steal Pax's thunder. No pun intended, Zeus," Trav answered.

Zeus just shook his head and leaned back in his chair, Xavier snoozing on his shoulder.

"Alright, enough suspense! You gonna tell us the 'big announcement' or seriously make us wait til' Christmas, bro?" Lazarus asked.

"Yeah, don't do that! Spill!" Val insisted.

"Fine."

"No, Trav—"

"Sky's pregnant."

Everyone around the table gasped, laughed, or cheered as they all congratulated the happy couple on their baby to come, toasted them and went around hugging them.

"Guess my baby sis is next, huh?" Veda quipped to a balking Becca.

"Or this one here," TJ said and pointed to Brooke, who simply shrugged.

"You wanna put a bun in the oven, Hephaestus, then you go right ahead." Brooke's brow went up. Clearly, TJ had her wrapped around his finger—or cock. Either way, he had her.

"Well," Veda said as she sipped a cup of tea and leaned into Quillan, patting Torin's bottom as he fussed in her arms. "Looks like the brack didn't lie."

"Never does, I was told," he smirked and brushed his nose lightly across his wife's, getting a moan out of her. "And am I *damn* glad it doesn't."

THE END

AFTERWORD

Thank you *so* much for reading *ILLEGAL FORMATION*.
I hope you enjoyed this heavy and dark, but *happy* ending to my
Gods of the Gridiron series.

If so, please be sure to leave a review.

This book was difficult to write in parts—as you can probably
understand. I hope you come away with two things after reading
this:
First—People aren't always who you think they are. Never judge a
book by its cover.
Second—We all have things that have happened to us, some
incredibly tragic, that we don't share with everyone, so always be
kind to one another.

***

Did you enjoy getting a little glimpse inside *RISE*? Well, Madam Roxie had a short cameo in this book because her own book is coming out next year (March 13, 2021)

Step inside a world of darkness—sin and secrets
RISE: The Prequel Novella to the Sin and Secrets Collection is available NOW.
Grab your copy.

***

(Eden's blurb)

CAGED

At the age of 15, I was plunged into inky darkness so black that all light was extinguished in its wake—into a world of vile sin and unspeakable secrets where the Devil himself was the ringmaster in my own personal three-ring inferno.

But even the Devil has a weakness.

My name is Eden Riser and what follows is the story of my end...or is it my beginning?

SNEAK PEEK AT RISE: THE PREQUEL TO THE SIN AND SECRETS COLLECTION

PROLOGUE

Eden

I unwillingly inhale the acrid sweet scent of cigar smoke as I walk nervously up the stairs, clad in only a thin silk teddy, thong, and stiletto heels. I gulp as the sound of his chair turns and he faces me, that sick satisfied grin on his face forcing me to hold back the little contents in my stomach.

"Dance. Dance for me, my sweet girl." The sound of his rough voice grates out as a smoke ring encircles his head; his suit is perfectly starched, his black hair is slicked back, the poignant stench of his woodsy cologne wafts my way and I want to run to his trash can and hurl.

Instead, I simply nod and move closer, my heart hammering in my chest.

I can hear the faint thumping of the music from the club in the background as I stand in front of him. He grips my curvy hips and moves his eyes over me, lust evident there. It sickens me. He sickens me.

I begin to dance, knowing things won't work out well if I don't do as he asks and he has to prompt me again. Uncle Vince doesn't ask twice.

It isn't long before I'm practically in his lap, of his movements not mine, and his hands are on me, moving familiarly over my womanly body like they've done so many times before.

"It's been a long night. You've had lots of eyes on you," he states as his hand rests on my thigh, he grips it a little more tightly than what's comfortable. "But no hands. Never any hands. Because I'd break them into pieces if they touched what was mine." He smirks and moves his fingertips down my inner thigh. I mentally cringe but try not to let him notice. "Do you know what these men want to do to my sexy little prima donna?"

I nod. But Uncle Vince scowls. He wants a verbal answer.

"They wanna..." I can't say the words. I'm too mortified.

"They wanna fuck you. They wanna claim what's mine...and we just won't have that, will we?" It's okay that I don't answer him this time because his lips are falling on mine and kissing me, with a possession that always makes me recoil. But I don't fight. I never fight. Because fighting is a moot point. He would only inflict more pain and that's something he enjoys far too much; I won't give him the satisfaction.

His hand falls between my legs. I cringe again. I try to relax against the tension in my body but it's hard, so damn hard. Bile rises in my throat, I hold it back but my belly burns like it always does when he puts his hands on me. I feel his slimy tongue invade my mouth and let my mind reach--reach for anything that will take me away from this dismal place I've found myself trapped in. But there is no escape, no escape from his clutches as he pulls me across his lap and begins to grope me.

As he lays me down onto the leather couch next to his desk, the tears begin to fall down my cheeks, spilling forth and filling my eyes. I can't stop them. I always try but there's no way I can stop them. I think deep down Uncle Vince takes a sick kind of satisfaction in my tears.

"Eden, my sweet little pleasure garden, open your eyes and look at me," he says as I hear the sound of his pants unbuckling and his zipper being unzipped.

Fuck him. The bastard. He knows I hate looking at him while he does this, knows I hate him.

I do as he asks--for God forbid I disobey--staring into his black eyes,

eyes that I've grown to despise peering into while he takes me like he owns my body.

He touches my cheek. "So beautiful. Just like your mother."

I WAKE to the sound of my own screaming. Like so many early school mornings. I'm glad my uncle isn't here. He's never *here*—thank God. He's always at the club. Living, breathing, and sleeping the club. He always leaves my body guard, Marco, who at this point has gotten used to my nightmares--and middle-of-the-night screaming--and doesn't come barging in like he used to do in the very beginning. Uncle Vincent is delusional, paranoid, and extremely overprotective of me.

My birth name is Cordelia Adaleden Riser by the way, although I go by Eden. Uncle Vince—my uncle by marriage—forced me to take his surname of Perelli two years ago when he adopted me. I'm seventeen years old. Seventeen...and trapped in a place where I'm completely and utterly miserable in my skin and my life. Trapped with a man who thinks he owns me, body and soul. Trapped in a body that I hate...for I've had curves since I was twelve, curves that he uses to his advantage, curves that I loathe because I feel abnormal because of them.

I lost my parents when I was just fifteen and this depraved man who got custody of me has tortured, beaten, and raped me from the first night I came to live with him. My uncle Vincent was obsessed with my mother, Lydia, whom I'm practically identical to, but ended up marrying my aunt Lauren, my maternal aunt, instead since my mother was happily married to my father. Aunt Lauren died of cancer when I was fourteen, much to my dismay, and not just because I wish she would have lived to be here for me now--she was a wonderful person. Although, if she were here, I would never have been treated this way, I'm sure of it. She would have gotten us out of this hell-hole somehow, for she was a fighter up to the very end.

I get up from my bed and tip-toe to the door. I need some water; my throat burns from screaming.

I open the door and see Marco sitting in his usual chair. He looks up at me as I step gingerly out.

"You ok, Eden?" he asks, concern darkening his big blue eyes.

I simply nod and drop my head. He's bore witness to far too much, seen more of my naked body than I ever anticipated he would, been there to wipe my tears, pick me up off the floor, and bandage my cuts. He's been my rock in the aftermath of my fall from grace. Every. Single. Time.

I love him like a second father...and maybe even more if I'm being completely honest with myself. How could I not though? He's the only man in two years who's shown me any type of compassion. I've even been forced into going to an all-girl school because my psycho uncle wants to make sure no other man lays a hand on me. He trusts Marco though and doesn't know how much this man touches me, both figuratively and literally.

Even now, Marco stands and moves toward me, his giant frame stopping right in front of me. I look up. As big as he is, he wouldn't hurt me for anything in the world. I've seen him beat people to death with his mere fists, but the gentleness he shows me is a stark contrast to that. His knuckle strokes down my cheekbone, and I close my eyes at how calm I become in his presence. How a man of his size can have such a feather-light touch has perplexed me since day one.

"Another nightmare, little dove?" he asks, his tone softening as if he's speaking to a baby instead of a seventeen-year-old girl.

Again, I simply nod. "I want some water."

Marco gives me a crooked smile and I melt a little inside. He's such a teddy bear. "I'll be right back."

I shake my head. "You don't hav--"

"I'll be right back." He winks and moves off.

I watch his big, retreating back, clad in a grey suit. Marco is the intimidator extraordinaire. His hair is jet black and his hands and biceps are inked. He looks as fierce as any tiger I've ever seen and his deep voice could rattle even the strongest spine, but with me, he's practically putty and always has been.

I sit in his chair, the one positioned right outside my door, and look down at the magazine he's been reading. It's a Cosmopolitan. I could almost laugh aloud as I pick it up and begin to read the article he's dog-earred, realizing it's a test he's in the process of taking. "Are you a sex goddess in bed?" I don't know what surprises me more - that Marco is reading a Cosmo or that he's taking a test to evaluate his sexual prowess.

I can only speculate as to the kind of lover he might be. He's one of the biggest men I've ever seen in person, his chest and shoulders broad and thick in his button-down shirt, and he's tall, like six-foot six. He's like the Rock, only not as tan. Despite his size, I imagine his demeanor in the bedroom would be like his placid nature with me - easy, sensual, unhurried...the polar opposite of my uncle. Thinking about sex with any man is revolting now that my uncle has taken my virginity and beaten me into submission, but the thought of sex with Marco, who at thirteen years older than I am, is still younger than my uncle's age of fifty, passes right through my head and embeds there, like a tick feeding on my blood.

When he comes back into the hallway from the kitchen, I smirk as I raise the magazine up and watch his cheeks flush. "I apologize for interrupting your test, *tiger*," I say, mocking the name on the test, for Marco's one of the few people I can truly be myself with.

"I was bored." He shrugs and hands me the glass of ice water he's retrieved.

I sip it greedily, downing half the contents in a matter of seconds. "Thanks," I say, as I wipe the back of my mouth with my hand.

Marco scowls at the cut on my lip my uncle gave me earlier that night when he slapped me for not getting to my knees fast enough, which I immediately realize I've re-opened in my speed to satisfy my thirst. He pulls a handkerchief from his pocket and steps forward, blotting at the corner of my mouth. I hiss as it burns. "Sorry," he grumbles then swears under his breath. "It's not always gonna be this way, Eden. He isn't gonna be around forever, you know?"

"Why do you put up with his shit, Marco?" I ask and eye him.

He appears taken aback, as if I've said the unthinkable. He looks away for long moments then back into my eyes. "You don't understand," he dismisses.

"Enlighten me then."

"Eden, you're too—"

"Don't tell me I'm too fucking young. I've endured and seen more than—"

"Enough!" he yells so loudly that I flinch. He swears again and hangs his head. "I'm sorry, I shouldn't have raised my voice to you, but—I can't possibly explain to you what I owe your uncle. What he's done for me. What he—"

"Enough to let him rape me whenever he pleases and stand by and simply do nothing about it when you're twice his size?" I ask, unearthly calm.

He looks back down at me; his face is so torn it rips into my heart. I tear my eyes from his, knowing I'm out of line with that comment.

"There's nothing I can do. You *do* know that, right?"

How the fuck can he say that? He could kill my uncle with one hand if he wanted to, physically anyway. And he could get me out of here, out of the spotlight, away from the man who keeps me practically home or club-bound, save for going to school. But my uncle has a hold over Marco, something I'll never understand if I try and something I'll never know…apparently. Plus, my uncle is filthy rich, despite that it was accumulated under sketchy circumstances to say the least. Money equals power and power equals untouchable, at least in Marco's eyes. Power only equals hate in my eyes, for my uncle's power over me is all-encompassing, an ocean of plenty and I'm the fish stuck in the fish bowl hidden within a chest at the bottom of that ocean. I'm trapped and drowning and no one can help me, not even the man with the only feasible power to do so.

I look straight ahead, at nothing in particular—certainly not at the creepy picture of me and my uncle that stares back at me, taken outside of our mansion on a crisp Autumn morning, the fake smiles on our faces repulsing me. I begin to sob, despite the many times I've done so in the past, knowing that no amount of tears will change anything nor make my life any easier. To think, just four years ago my life was almost perfect. I had two adoring parents, a dog I loved, was on the cheerleading squad, had a boyfriend, and a group of girls I called friends and now, I'm subjected to physical and sexual torture on an almost daily basis for someone's twisted gratification. That fact is completely crushing. To see how far off base my normal life has now become drives me further into despair and I cover my face as I'm consumed by tears.

Marco scoops me up into his big arms then and I rest against his solid chest, wrapping my arms around his thick neck and burying my nose into his shoulder. I inhale his scent—a sweet reprieve from the sharp woodsy one I'm used to. I sniffle as he lays me down on my bed and protest when he starts to pull away.

"No, please don't leave me," I desperately plead and grab for his shirt.

"Little dove, you know I'm not allowed on your bed."

"He won't know. I won't tell him. You won't tell him. Just until I fall asleep, please?" I beckon to those blue eyes that remind me of a summer sky, back when I was a child and free to enjoy life as I saw fit. "Please, Marco?" I whisper.

He sighs heavily, a man in turmoil, before finally coming back to my side.

The mattress sinks in as his big frame settles onto my large king-size sleigh bed and my tears begin to subside as I let his comforting aura encompass my senses. I'm merely an inch away and look back into his face.

Marco isn't overtly handsome, he doesn't have a baby face. He's not "Brad Pitt handsome" by any means—he's far too rugged. But he has a subtle allure about him that's undeniable. Perhaps it's those eyes that I find myself getting lost in. He touches my face again, and I smile. I'm flirting with a dangerous line by having him so close, I know, but it doesn't stop me from reveling in the solace I take in this moment, so I push the envelope. I brush my nose across his, just a brief touch, a craving for a softness I never get from my uncle.

He visibly shivers. I look into his eyes. There's a hunger there I'm familiar with but it's different too. His eyes reflect desire, a desire my uncle's black eyes never have. Vince's eyes mirror possession, dominance, and punishment—there's none of that here in Marco's. I separate the distance between us and tilt my head up, my lips falling to his in the briefest kiss. A "thank you" for the tenderness he's shown me over the years. A gesture of warmth in this cold world we both have been plunged into.

The lips against mine are soft—nothing like what I'm used to—supple and unhurried. They pucker, kissing me back, but not with the urgent fierceness I've come to know and hate. I pull away, surprised by this newness and frown, confused, into Marco's face.

He gives me a crooked grin in return and responds with, "Eden, my little dove, you shouldn't kiss me like that."

I don't need to ask why; I know the answer. I nod and ease back to my pillow, laying my dark hair across it as Marco's big palm cups my cheek once more. His thumb begins to stroke my cheekbone—easy and soft, like a butterfly kiss—and I close my eyes, my mind at ease.

He murmurs sweet nothings to me as slumber begins to take me, "Sleep well, you're safe tonight." I'm fading into sweet abyss with my dark knight, logic and worry and fear evaporating from me, when I think I hear Marco's soft voice whisper in my ear, "One day, and soon, he won't ever be able to hurt you again, my little dove."

**GET YOUR COPY OF RISE HERE—
AVAILABLE NOW**

ALSO BY SHANNA SWENSON

~THE ABUNDANCE SERIES~

Abundance

Return to Abundance

Escape from Abundance

Stars over Abundance

Abundance Legacy

Starlight Valley: The prequel to Abundance (FREE ebook)

~THE GODS OF THE GRIDIRON SERIES~

PERSONAL FOUL: Prequel novella

UNSPORTSMANLIKE CONDUCT

FALSE START

PASS INTERFERENCE

ILLEGAL FORMATION

~THE SIN AND SECRETS COLLECTION~

RISE: A Prequel Novella (Sin and Secrets)

(Released November 13, 2020)

Marked by Sin (Sin and Secrets: Book 4)

(Coming March 13, 2021)

~Aurora Rose Reynold's HEA WORLD~

Until Kingston

(Coming 2021)

LEARN MORE AT WWW.SHANNASWENSON.COM

ABOUT SHANNA SWENSON

Shanna Swenson is a cardiac sonographer by day and a weaver of various fictional tales by night.

She's been an avid reader all her life and began writing at the age of fourteen. She finally published her first novel, *Abundance*, after it sat patiently on her laptop for well over fifteen years and she hasn't stopped writing since.

Shanna fits her zodiac sign of Cancer with a capital C and enjoys life's simplest things—sunsets, rain, and coffee—to name a few.

When Shanna's not supporting her fellow indies with her face buried in a book or writing her next novel/novella, she enjoys action and horror movies, pro football, hiking, working out, and traveling with her own "knight in shining armor".

You can find her on the following social media platforms.

Her website is www.shannaswenson.com

- facebook.com/shannaswen
- twitter.com/shanna_swenson
- instagram.com/shannaswen_author
- goodreads.com/Shannaswen
- amazon.com/author/shannaswenson
- pinterest.com/shannaswen
- bookbub.com/profile/shanna-swenson